WHEN SOMEBODY LOVES YOU

Also by June Tate

Riches Of The Heart
No One Promised Me Tomorrow
For The Love Of A Soldier
Better Days
Nothing Is Forever
For Love Or Money
Every Time You Say Goodbye
To Be A Lady

WHEN SOMEBODY LOVES YOU

June Tate

headline

First published in 2006
by HEADLINE PUBLISHING GROUP

1

Cataloguing in Publication Data is
available from the British Library

0 7553 2965 1 (ISBN-10)
978 0 7553 2965 6 (ISBN-13)

Typeset in Sabon by Palimpsest Book Production Limited
Grangemouth, Stirlingshire

Printed and bound in Great Britain by
Clays Ltd, St Ives plc

HEADLINE PUBLISHING GROUP
A division of Hodder Headline
338 Euston Road
London NW1 3BH
www.headline.co.uk
www.hodderheadline.com

With love to my darling cousin Pamela and her husband Bryan, remembering the great time we spent together in British Columbia, and the memorable drive through the awesome Canadian Rockies.

As always, love and thanks to my two wonderful girls, Beverley and Maxine. They are my *raison d'être*.

CHAPTER ONE

May 1936

It was chilly in the early morning air as Elsa Carter started setting out the fruit and veg stall in Kingsland Market, one of many in the area designated by the council for the market traders. It was a large open space, filled with lines of stalls selling all manner of things. At twenty-two, Elsa had worked in the market for two years, preferring the open air to the seclusion of a shop.

'Bloody chilly, love, ain't it?' remarked Ruby, whose stall of kitchen utensils was situated next to Elsa's.

'I'll warm the pair of you if you like!'

They both turned and looked at the big, powerful man passing, carrying a couple of crates of carrots.

'If you're not careful, Bert, you'll give yourself a hernia,' Elsa retorted, 'then you'll be no good to anyone!'

He chuckled. 'My missus says I'm useless anyway so I ain't got nothing much to lose.'

The women laughed, then returned to their preparations. There was always a feeling of camaraderie about these early mornings before the public arrived to shop. It was a hard life, out in all weathers, fighting the elements when the rain and wind swept through the market, sending tarpaulins flying and scattering the empty crates which had been stowed beneath the stalls for removal at the end of the day. Yet in clement weather it was a colourful place, buzzing with people and repartee from the stallholders, urging their customers to buy the goods on display.

1

'How's that young man of yours?' enquired Ruby.

'Fine, thanks. Bored with covering local events. He's got this burning ambition to work in Fleet Street.'

Peter Adams, Elsa's boyfriend, was a reporter on the *Southern Daily Echo*, and was anxious to move up the ladder. Fleet Street was his eventual goal.

'He'll make it one day,' said Ruby. 'He's a smart lad. That article he wrote about that councillor caught with his hand in the till was brilliant.'

A smile of pride spread across Elsa's features. 'Yes, he was commended by his boss for that. It's just that he gets frustrated.'

'Show me a man who has a shred of patience,' said Ruby. 'If any man was to get pregnant, the baby would be born at four months. They wouldn't be able to wait!'

'Oh, Ruby! What a thought.'

The older woman grinned. 'If they was to have a period, can you imagine the fuss? My husband is dying if he gets a bloody cold! Me, last month I worked with a raging temperature all day and when I got home my husband had no sympathy. "When is my dinner going to be ready?" was all he was interested in.'

'What did you say to him?'

'Not a lot. I told him to piss off, I was going to bed.'

Elsa smiled to herself as she finished the stall. She stood in front of it and eyed the fruit and veg with great concentration. She took a pride in her display and her boss, who had a green-grocer's shop in another part of town, apart from keeping her supplied with goods was content to leave her alone to run the stall, knowing she was good at her job.

An hour later, the public started to trickle in and another day of business began. Elsa had her regulars who kept her on her toes, such as Danny, the flamboyant pianist at the local pub who used to tell her off if her make-up wasn't right.

'Got up in a rush this morning, darling? Didn't bother with the old mascara, naughty girl. God, I would die to have eyelashes as long as yours. It isn't fair!'

Her favourites were two elderly sisters, both widowed and sharing a house. They did nothing bit disagree.

'Why are you buying cabbage, our Edith?'

'To have with the mince I'm going to cook.'

'You know I hate cabbage. It makes me fart all night,' said sister Madge. 'Buy parsnips instead.' There then ensued a long diatribe – and they ended up buying both.

Elsa kept a keen eye out for those who were light-fingered. If you weren't careful the odd orange would be slipped into a bag whilst she was serving, but she had a sixth sense about such people and few ever got away with it. But when she saw children eyeing her fruit with longing eyes, she would often give them some bruised examples which she'd had to remove from display.

'You're too soft-hearted,' Ruby would call over when she saw what was happening.

'That kid looked as if he was half starved,' she would say.

'Probably is,' agreed Ruby.

They were both aware that many people around them were living in poverty, sometimes because the man of the house was spending his meagre wage at the pub, instead of providing for his family. Sadly, it was the norm in the poorer areas.

As Elsa rearranged the stock, she thought about her own father.

George Carter was a white-collar worker. He worked as a clerk for the council, a job that held a certain cachet among their neighbours, whose husbands mostly worked in the docks. He was normally a decent father and husband, until he took a drink, when his character seemed to metamorphose. He became violent and unpredictable, taking out his temper on Margaret, his long-suffering wife. The morning after, he would be full of apologies, promising it would never happen again . . . but it always did.

During the good times Elsa always prayed that her father, whom she did love, would overcome his weakness, then when again he failed she would feel let down and angry. She would plead with her mother. 'Why do you put up with it? Leave him!'

Margaret would look at her and say, 'Don't be silly! He's a good provider, and, most of the time, a good husband. How would I live if I left him?'

'We could get a flat together. You could get a job, and I'll help with extra money from my wages.' Putting her arms round her mother she said, 'I can't bear it when he hits you. You deserve better.'

A customer arrived, taking such thoughts from her mind.

As the day progressed, a relatively new trader to the market, calling out his wares, caught Elsa's attention. Unlike her and others, he had a large van parked with the back open. Inside it was piled high with all manner of articles. On a long table in front of the van, goods of varying description were spread out.

Clive Forbes was an attractive young man with laughing brown eyes, a wide smile and masculinity oozing from every pore as he stood on the tailboard of the vehicle. His van was always surrounded by women, young and old, lapping up the flattery he dished out whilst he persuaded them to part with their cash.

'Now, darling,' he said to one young woman, 'I have some lovely cushions here. I can just imagine you, laid back against them waiting for your husband to come home. My God, but he's a lucky man. If you were my wife, I wouldn't let you out of the house in case some man ran off with you when my back was turned!'

The girl blushed, but she stepped forward and bought two cushions.

At that moment he looked up and saw Elsa watching him. He smiled broadly and winked.

She turned away. She didn't like Clive Forbes. He had tried to flirt with her several times, but whenever he approached she made sure there was plenty of space between them. She sensed that underneath his friendly exterior there was another character, one that was far more unpleasant, and certainly not someone she wanted to get to know.

At the end of the day, Elsa piled her goods on a cart and, making several trips, packed them away in a small lock-up garage nearby, before she eventually made her way home. She would have time for a meal before she met Peter, who was taking her to the cinema. She loved the cinema. Here she could go and forget her worries about her mother and father. It was a means of escape, and when things were really bad she would go on her own. There in the dark, there was a certain security and comfort and she would lose herself for a few precious hours.

She was looking forward to seeing Peter too. They had been courting for almost a year now, but as far as marriage was concerned they had decided to wait until he managed to find work with a national newspaper and earn more money.

She loved Peter and was looking forward to being Mrs Adams, yet at the same time she was worried about leaving her mother alone to cope with her father. His drunken outbreaks were not a regular thing, thankfully, but it was like sitting on the edge of a volcano waiting for it to erupt. Then, when it did, the fall out was horrendous.

As Elsa let herself into the house, the aroma of cooking filled the air. 'That smells good, Mum.'

'Lancashire hotpot,' said Margaret. 'One of your favourites!'

Kissing her mother on the cheek, Elsa said, 'It is when the cook is as good as you, Mum.'

'Ah, flattery will get you anything,' Margaret quipped.

'That's what that Clive Forbes thinks anyway,' said Elsa with a sardonic tone to her voice. She had already told her mother about the new trader's advances towards her.

'You don't like him, do you?'

'No, I don't. He's a smarmy devil, yet the women, young and old, all seem to fall for it. Honestly, you should hear him.'

'Ah well, love, some of those poor women only hear flattery from him and seldom from their husbands.'

'Starved of affection, is that what you're saying?'

'Something like that,' said Margaret as she returned to the kitchen.

Sitting down, Elsa kicked off her shoes and massaged her feet. My poor mother is starved of affection, that I do know, she thought. When he was sober, her father was the perfect gentleman, but she couldn't ever remember him showing any tenderness towards his wife. Not like her Peter, thank God! Peter always gave her a cuddle and a kiss and told her how nice she looked. She supposed that had something to do with his being a reporter. Anyone who wrote like that must have some emotion to be able to do so, with feeling. And she well remembered that when a small child had drowned and he'd had to cover the story, Peter had been moved almost to tears when he told her about it.

'I was there when they pulled her little body from the water,' he said, in a choked voice. 'Her poor mother was distraught. She'd turned her back for only a moment and the child had fallen in the river.' He took a deep breath in an effort to control his tears. 'I'll never forget it as long as I live.'

Elsa had put her arms round him and held him tight. She was looking forward to seeing him tonight.

'I'll just pop upstairs to wash and change,' she called to her mother. 'I'll be about twenty minutes.'

When she came back to the living room, her father was sitting reading the paper.

'Hello, Elsa. Had a busy day?' he enquired.

'Just the usual,' she said as she sat at the table. 'Peter and I are going to see *Mutiny on the Bounty* this evening.'

'Should be a good film,' he remarked. 'Charles Laughton is a fine actor. It won an Oscar for the best picture if I remember rightly. I prefer cowboy films myself.'

As the three of them sat round the table eating, Elsa couldn't help wishing that this ideal family scene could last for ever, but in her heart she knew that it would be ruined when her father went on another bender. She felt helpless. Her mother was adamant about not leaving. She wondered why abused women stayed with their men. Yet today she could see perhaps why. Her mother would weigh up the times when things were calm and convince herself that George wasn't so bad, and Elsa was forced to admit that he certainly wasn't as bad as some of the men in her neighbourhood who beat their wives every Saturday night after a skinful of alcohol. She would *never* put up with it!

Elsa met Peter outside the local Odeon cinema where they queued for seats in the circle.

Putting his arm round her he asked, 'How are you, love?'

'Bit tired but fine. What have you been up to, then?'

'There was a warehouse fire in the docks, so that was a bit of excitement, but luckily no one was hurt. They think it was caused by someone throwing a lit cigarette away. By the way, Gerry, my mate at work, wondered if we would like to join him and his girl for a jaunt round the pier on Sunday. What do you think?'

7

'That'd be nice. It's ages since we've been down there – but only if we look at the penny slot machines!'

'You only want to look at the naughty pictures on What the Butler Saw!' he laughed.

'How did you guess?'

They settled in their seats and watched the newsreels and were thrilled to see pictures of the tumultuous send-off as the *Queen Mary* sailed for New York on her maiden voyage.

'I would love to be a passenger on her,' Elsa whispered.

'All you need is thirty-five pounds,' he said.

'By the time I've saved that, the fares will have gone up,' she replied.

They watched as Benito Mussolini stood on a balcony in Italy, declaring that the country was a fascist empire. He was a short ugly bald-headed man who waved his arms around as he spoke. The news moved on to show rioting between Jews and Arabs in Palestine. Eleven people had died and fifty had been injured.

'I don't know what the world's coming to,' Peter muttered, more to himself than to Elsa.

The next item was more interesting to her than to Peter. There was a new fashion craze. The smart set were having their ears pierced! The Duchess of Kent and the Duchess of Gloucester, who were trendsetters, had both had it done, and it appeared that Queen Mary had had hers pierced as a little girl, by her maid.

'Don't know that I fancy that!' Elsa declared. Then they settled back to watch the film. She gave a smile of contentment as Peter put his arm round her shoulders. No, she certainly wasn't starved of affection!

They walked back through the park. The May evening was balmy and they sat down on a seat as they neared the exit. Peter took her into his warm embrace.

'Good film, that . . . and of course you know it was based on fact, don't you?'

'Yes, I read about it.'

'There are still families on Pitcairn Island who came from some of the *Bounty* crew.'

She laughed. 'I bet none of them were as good-looking as Clark Gable!'

'Mmm. Fancy him, do you?'

'He could put his feet under my table any time!' she declared with a broad grin.

'Listen, my girl. The only man with his feet under your table is me, and don't you forget it!' He tilted her chin and kissed her soundly. 'I bet Clark Gable doesn't kiss any better than that.'

Breathless from his eagerness, she said, 'I wouldn't think so for a minute.'

He stroked her cheek. 'If only we could afford to get married now, then I could show you what a real man is like.'

With eyes shining mischievously, she said, 'I can hardly wait.'

'Well, you don't have to, you know.'

'Peter Adams! Whatever next? You wouldn't like me if I was fast and loose!'

He laughed heartily. 'You're quite wrong, Elsa darling. Men love fast and loose women, but they don't usually marry them. They want their wives to be virgins.'

'Well I don't know, if that doesn't take the cake! That is typical of a man. They want it all their own way.'

He was highly amused. 'And most women want their husbands to have had some experience before they take their bride to the marriage bed.'

'Whoever told you that?'

'I'm a reporter, darling. I know all about human nature, I deal with it every day.'

'You've been listening to too many tall tales in the pub, that's what. Men always stretch the truth when they've had a few beers!'

Kissing the tip of her nose, he said, 'You are wonderful, you know that?'

'I do know. That's why you want to marry me. Now come on, it's time to go home.'

And off they went, arms round each other. Content to be together.

CHAPTER TWO

The next morning Clive Forbes was rearranging the goods he had stacked in his lock-up garage when a small van pulled up outside. Looking up, his expression changed to one of anger as the driver climbed out and walked towards him.

'A bit bloody late, aren't you?' he stormed. 'I expected you last night. I wasted two hours hanging around for nothing!'

'Sorry, Clive,' the driver apologised. 'The Old Bill was about and I couldn't take the chance.' He opened the back of the van and waited for Forbes to inspect the goods inside.

'How hot are these things then? I don't want to get clobbered for your stupidity.'

'You won't get no bother over this stuff; it came down from the north. Local bobbies won't be looking for it, you can be sure. It's small potatoes to them.'

The market trader inspected boxes filled with china and sets of saucepans. In another box were curtains in different colours and lengths. The last one contained a selection of children's clothes ranging in size from babies to four years old.

As he went through the goods, his bad mood faded and he smiled to himself. This was a good load, one that would make him plenty of money if he got it all at the right price.

The two men started to haggle. Clive remained cool and calculating, but the bringer of his bounty became enraged at the money he was being offered.

'You are havin' a laugh, aren't you? It wouldn't be worth my while to sell all this to you for the price you're offering . . . and frankly I think it's a bloody insult!' He started to close the van doors.

'All right, keep your hair on!' Clive rubbed his chin and pretended to give the deal some thought, then offered the price he'd been prepared to pay at the beginning.

After a moment's hesitation, the driver asked for five pounds more.

Shaking his head, Forbes said, 'Sorry, that's just a bit too rich for me,' and started to walk away.

'All right then, but I am being railroaded here! Don't think I'll be bringing any more stuff to you – you're a bloody bandit!'

They exchanged money for the goods, and Clive started transferring the boxes into the interior of the building, knowing that the next time the other man had articles to move in a hurry he would return. As he walked back to the van for the last box, he caught sight of a woman's cocktail watch in a velvet case. Picking it up, he eyed it carefully.

'I'll take this as well,' he said.

'Not at your bleeding prices you won't.'

'What do you want for it?'

Much to his surprise, the seller was given the money he asked for without a quibble, which made him think he should have put up the price.

As if reading his mind, the market trader said, 'I wouldn't have paid a penny more!'

When he'd finished stacking the new goods for sale, he took out the watch and studied it. It had a dainty face surrounded by marcasite and the strap was made of the same stone; very feminine, he thought. He had a mind to tempt young Elsa Carter with it. She fascinated him. It was probably her aloofness that got to him, apart from those green eyes and long lashes. It was also the way she looked at him with deep suspicion. Not that she'd any reason to do so. He always bought carefully, knowing that although most of his stock wasn't exactly kosher, it was never hot enough to cause him problems. So what was it she saw, as she gazed in his direction? It was unfathomable to him. He didn't normally have trouble getting women: indeed, sometimes his charm attracted women he wasn't at all interested in, and on occasion it could be a problem until he brutally told them to get lost. But Elsa was a different kettle of fish, which only made her the more attractive. When she hadn't responded to his advances his masculine pride had been dented and he vowed to get through to her one way or another.

The following Sunday was a fine day and Elsa dressed herself in a floral frock in readiness for her jaunt with Peter and his friends. She liked wandering around the pier, with its sideshows, penny slot machines and small cafés. When it was warm enough, she and Peter would sit on deckchairs and gaze out across Southampton Water. But today would be their first time there this year. Hearing a knock on the front door, Elsa ran downstairs to meet her young man.

It was pleasant walking along the road. Being a Sunday it was quiet and as they walked past the dock gates Elsa couldn't help but compare the peaceful scene today with the usual cacophony experienced on a weekday, with trains trundling across the road from the terminus to various goods yards and the stream of workmen pouring in through the gates to fulfil their daily employment. She loved the atmosphere of such days. There was always a buzz of excitement. Ocean liners would blast forth through their funnels, as if telling all and sundry that they either had just docked or were about to sail for foreign and interesting shores. However, today was for strolling, contemplating, and relaxation.

Gerry and his girlfriend Jean were waiting as they approached the pier. Peter paid their penny entrance and they started to stroll along the wooden slats, through which one could peer down below at the swirling water and the flotsam, which seemed to wind itself around the struts, holding the whole place together.

They stood for a while, looking over the side, watching the small fish darting about just under the water, before moving along. They looked in the window of a small shop selling souvenirs. There were picture postcards of the *Queen Mary* and other liners. Cards of different views of the town. Comic cards showing fat ladies in various bathing costumes, usually on a beach, with saucy repartee.

'You'd be hard pressed to find any sand round here,' Elsa proclaimed sarcastically. All the nearby beaches were covered in pebbles which were very uncomfortable.

'They've got lovely sandy beaches at Highcliffe and Bournemouth,' Jean said.

'I know,' Elsa acknowledged, 'but it's making the journey. I'll make do with the stones at Netley; it's so much nearer.'

'Oh, look,' Jean said, 'a fortune-teller!'

There was a small booth, outside which stood a placard. 'Cassandra. Foreteller of the Future,' it read. 'Readings, two shillings.'

'I'd love to have a go. What about you, Elsa?'

'No, I don't think so. I don't believe in it.'

'Oh, come on. I'll go if you will. Please!'

'Go on,' urged Gerry. 'Every time we come here Jean wants to have her fortune told and she never does and I hear about it for weeks after. Do it as a step towards my keeping my sanity.'

Looking at the excitement shining in the other girl's eyes, Elsa reluctantly agreed.

'I don't want mine done,' she said, 'but I'll come in with you if you like, to give you moral support.'

Jean was delighted and stepped inside, followed by a reluctant Elsa. They sat opposite the woman in the gypsy scarf, and the old crone grabbed Jean's hands.

'Hold the crystal, my dear. Make a wish,' she was told, 'and we'll see if it will come true.

'I see you with a young man,' the woman droned. 'But this is not the man you will marry. He is not to be trusted. He has an eye for the ladies.'

Jean looked devastated.

'He is just playing with you. You take care, my dear, he'll let you down badly. You work in an office. Beware of jealousy from another.' There was a look of sheer malevolence on the woman's countenance. She carried on. 'It will be a long time before you find any real happiness.'

Jean burst into tears at this point and ran from the booth.

She's just out to make trouble, thought Elsa. She is full of bitterness and this comes out in her so-called readings. Well, I'm not having it. She suddenly stood up, to the woman's surprise.

'Why are you spreading despair and misery among those who come in here? Don't you know that is a wicked thing to do?'

'How dare you say such a thing to me, missy? I have been doing this for years.'

'And how many lives have you tried to ruin?'

'Get out! Get out of here and don't you ever come back!'

Calmly Elsa replied, 'I can assure you I would never dream of it.'

'You be very careful, young lady. You don't know what I saw in the crystal. I can tell you it wasn't pleasant.'

'As the only thing you could see was your own reflection, I can imagine it *wasn't* pleasant!' She turned on her heel and walked out. Once outside she took Jean by the arm and led her away, telling others who were waiting, 'That woman is a charlatan, and I don't want to see you waste your money on her. She's a wicked woman, and believe me, she wouldn't tell you things you'd hope to hear.'

Gerry put his arm round his weeping girlfriend. 'Leave it, love,' he said. 'It's all kidology anyway. No one can see into the future. Come on, I'll buy you an ice cream.'

'What was all that about?' asked Peter as he took Elsa's arm.

She just shook her head and walked on, and he said nothing more. They all sat in deckchairs eating ice cream, then moved on to a shooting gallery, where the boys tried to outdo each other. The atmosphere once again was a happy one and when they all went into a café for some lunch the incident was forgotten.

Inside the fortune-teller's booth, however, Fanny Braxton, known as Cassandra, was still fuming about the young woman who had called her bluff. And what really irked her was that the girl had spoken the truth. She didn't have the gift of second sight, although she sometimes told people a little of what they wanted to hear before putting in the knife and destroying their hopes with dire prophecies. It gave her pleasure to see the doubt and uncertainty on their faces.

Fanny was a bitter and twisted woman, who had never recovered after the man she loved proposed to her sister. She called her sister a traitor, accused her of stealing her man, and wouldn't believe that he'd never show any interest in herself.

'It was all in your imagination!' her sister had cried. 'Never once did he ask you out, it was always me that he liked.'

'You never gave me a chance, flaunting yourself at him like you did. He'd have come to me in time.'

'Never! If you really want to know, he used to laugh about the cow-eyed look you gave him whenever he was around.'

The thought that the man she desired had laughed at her had been the last straw, and frustration and anger grew into malevolence and bitterness. After that, she would try to destroy any happiness that showed as her clients sat down at her table. Today when that young girl had told her the truth, it had only fanned the flames of hate she was nurturing in her soul. The young women who visited her later that day paid for it, and many of them left her booth in tears. Nevertheless, it was an easy way to make money, and Fanny Braxton was a greedy woman.

On Monday morning in the market, business was brisk with housewives stocking up with vegetables after the weekend. During a lull when Elsa was replacing stock from her display, she was interested to see Clive in deep conversation with Jed Sharpe, a tattoo artist who had a small place in Oxford Street.

Jed was an unusual character. He was handsome, tall and lean with smooth dark hair worn in a ponytail. In his left ear he wore a gold earring, and his bare arms were decorated with ornate specimens of his work. Elsa wondered if he did them himself. She looked at his long tapering fingers. On one hand he wore a heavy gold ring. He was a pleasant enough character and Elsa wondered just what he had to do with Clive. They seemed to be having a minor argument and eventually Jed left with an angry expression, jabbing his finger towards Clive as if threatening him. Forbes was looking furious and he kicked out at a packing case before he spotted Elsa watching him. He stopped and grinned across at her, but his eyes were still shining with anger. Elsa turned away.

As she did so, she saw a stooped figure walking in her direction. Even without her gypsy scarf, Elsa recognised the fortune-teller and hoped she wouldn't be stopping at her stall. The woman cast a baleful glace at her but to Elsa's relief she walked on. However, the small hairs on the back of her neck seemed to stand up and Elsa felt that the old crone was trouble. But how? And why? Shaking her head, Elsa returned to her work, as another customer required her attention.

Fanny Braxton was livid when she recognised the girl who had caused her to lose customers the previous day. As she hurried away from the market she swore to get even with her in some way – and soon.

Jed Sharpe strode away from the market, still fuming. He'd wanted to thump the slimy trader. But he'd warned him forcibly against dabbling with his sister's affections. Anne was young and impressionable and he knew that she was susceptible to the flattery of the good-looking Forbes. And now she had a crush on the man, which he encouraged whenever she shopped in the market. Nothing Jed could say to her about Clive Forbes made any difference. At seventeen she was stubborn and resented any interference from her older brother.

'He's no good!' Jed had told her. 'If you're not careful, you'll find yourself in a situation you can't handle.'

'Like what?' she had demanded.

'If he asks you out you are not to go. He's a man who uses women; he won't behave like a gentleman, that I'm sure of! Besides, I think he's dishonest. I bet you any money you like that half of the stuff he sells fell off the back of a lorry.'

She had stormed off in a huff.

CHAPTER THREE

It was midday and George Carter was not in a good mood. His boss had taken him to task over a mistake he'd made, copying some figures for the council treasury.

'Good heavens, Carter, this could have really put the cat among the pigeons. You made it look as if this department had over-spent its budget! My head would have been on the block if I hadn't had Jenkins check your figures.'

That he'd made an error was bad enough but the fact that Jenkins, whom George suspected of being after his job, had been the one to see his mistake was very hard to swallow.

'Just be more careful next time,' his boss said as he slapped George's pay packet down and strode out of the office.

George glanced across at Jenkins, who was preparing to leave for the weekend, and caught the satisfied smirk on his face, which only infuriated him more. He put away the papers on his desk, then rose from his seat and walked out of the office, his wage packet in his pocket.

Across the road from the Civic Centre, George sat in the rose garden and lit a cigarette to try to calm down, but the more he thought about the slimy Jenkins, the angrier he got. He knew that he himself was a good worker who had had a decent repu-tation within his department until Jenkins had arrived the month before. Ever since then the man had tried to undermine him whenever possible. Young upstart!

Carter put out his cigarette and made his way home.

Still in a foul mood, he entered his house and immediately started to find fault with everything his wife did.

'This tea tastes as if it's been stewed for ages.'

'But I just made it when you came in,' protested Margaret.

'Then you didn't boil the water properly.'

She made no comment, recognising the belligerent note in his voice. She started to tremble and dropped a metal spoon with which she was stirring the homemade soup.

'Oh, for goodness' sake!' he snapped. 'I've never known a woman as clumsy as you.'

And when she put his lunch before him a while later, he poked at the food on his plate and demanded, 'What sort of muck is this to serve to a man who works hard to provide for his family?'

'It's shepherd's pie. Your favourite,' she murmured.

He sent the plate and its contents across the room. 'I'm going out for a decent meal,' he said.

As the front door slammed, Margaret burst into tears, knowing that he would return with a few drinks under his belt and she would be the one to suffer. She began to scrape up the mess from the walls and the carpet, tears streaming down her face.

It was in this state that Elsa found her when she returned from the market at the end of the day. Taking a look round, she knew immediately what had happened.

'Where is he?'

'He said he was going out to get a decent meal. He'll go and get drunk, I know.'

'But the pubs closed hours ago.'

'He's probably gone to the working men's club,' Margaret said.

'I've had enough of this!' said Elsa. 'He's not going to come back here to this house and beat you again.'

'You go out, love,' pleaded her mother.

'Indeed I won't. It's time he knew that we are not going to put up with his bullying. Come on, you and I will go out and have something to eat. What's good for the goose is good for the gander.'

'We can't do that! He'll go mad if he comes home and I'm not here.'

Elsa took her mother by the shoulders. 'Enough is enough. It's time someone stood up to him. If you aren't strong enough to stop him, I am.'

'You have tried before, Elsa, and you only got the worst of his tongue.'

This was true. Many a time, Elsa had stood between her parents, protecting her mother from further blows, and suffered verbal abuse from her father for her efforts.

'A tongue-lashing doesn't hurt, Mum. He has never dared to lay a finger on me, but he will not lay a finger on you again while I'm here.'

'No, but when I go to bed, I'll be for it,' cried her mother pitifully.

'We'll bunk in together,' said Elsa. 'And if he gets out of hand, we'll go round to Peter's.'

'Oh, no! I couldn't let Mr and Mrs Adams know my business.'

'Good heavens, Mum, it's not your fault.'

But her mother's pride forbade such a thing. 'I won't go. I couldn't live with the shame.'

'All right, we'll sit it out here. After all, he'll eventually fall asleep, he always does. And tomorrow we'll look for a flat to live in together.'

'But what about you and Peter when you get married?'

Elsa gave a wry smile. 'God knows when that will be. It's too far away to worry about. Now wash your face and put on your coat.'

Reluctantly, Margaret did so, but said stubbornly, 'Leaving isn't what I want to do.'

*   *   *

It was a few hours later that George Carter staggered in through the front room. 'Margaret!' he yelled. There was no response. He looked in the kitchen, then, standing at the foot of the stairs, he called, 'Margaret, come down at once. Do you hear?'

The house was unusually quiet, he realised. The wireless was switched off and the back door locked. He heaved himself up the stairs with the aid of the banister and searched both bedrooms. They were empty, which infuriated him. Where the bloody hell was she? Margaret was always here when he came home.

Once back in the living room, he stood in front of the mantelpiece, staring at himself in the mirror. Gone was the carefully turned out gentleman. Instead his hair was messed up, his tie awry. His face was bloated and red from too much beer, his mouth a tight angry line. He looked at the dainty china figurines, which Margaret loved so much. With a mighty swipe he cleared them, sending them scattering into pieces on to the lino-covered floor. He then hurled two of the dining room chairs across the room, breaking a pot plant in the process. Picking up a brass ornament, he threw it at the mirror over the fireplace, smashing it. Then he flung himself into a fire-side chair and fell asleep.

An hour later, that was how Margaret and Elsa found him. Sound asleep, snoring, his mouth open, saliva visible at the side of it.

Margaret, seeing the broken china and glass on the floor and the chaos that reigned, looked devastated.

Elsa looked at the pathetic creature before her. This was her father. She was filled with disgust. Taking her mother by the hand, she said, 'Come on, we'll go to bed in my room.'

'What will he do when he wakes?' Margaret whispered.

'If he's got any sense, he'll go to bed. He won't dare come into my room.'

'I wouldn't bank on it,' said her mother.

'I'll put a chair under the door handle. You go on up and I'll bring us a cup of hot milk each.'

'For God's sake don't wake him,' Margaret pleaded.

'Old Nick himself couldn't wake him at the moment,' she answered.

In the early hours of the morning, Elsa woke to hear her father coming up the stairs. She glanced across at her mother who thankfully was asleep. She heard him enter his own room, then the bathroom. She watched and held her breath as the handle of her door was turned quietly, but the chair kept him at bay and he didn't try to force it. Elsa let out a sigh of relief, and went back to sleep.

The following morning, Elsa told her mother to stay in bed, and she would get the breakfast. As Margaret started to protest, Elsa said, 'I want a word with Dad and it's better you are out of the way.' She was quite prepared to tell her father that she and her mother would be leaving, but as Margaret was so reluctant to go she would have to find another way to solve the problem. One thing was for certain – she couldn't stand by and do nothing any longer. She was going to put a stop to her mother's suffering once and for all.

When George Carter walked downstairs it was to find his daughter waiting. Beside his breakfast plate were the broken pieces of her mother's precious figurines. He looked up at Elsa.

'You will leave my mother some money for the things that you broke,' she said, 'and the mirror will have to be replaced too.'

'This is none of your business,' he snapped.

'Indeed it is, and let me tell you another thing: last night will be the last time you come home in that state.' As he opened his mouth to berate her, she continued, 'If you do it again, I'll make sure that everyone at your work place knows you are a drunk and a wife-beater!'

'You wouldn't dare!'

'Try me! All these airs and graces you put on may fool others, but perhaps they need to know what sort of man you really are.'

He looked horrified.

'In future you will treat my mother, your wife, with the respect she deserves. I have waited too long for you to change. I have listened to Mum, who despite the way you treat her when you've had too much to drink still defends you to me. Well, you've pushed my loyalty too far. Now I am doing what I should have done ages ago.'

Looking at the defiant young woman before him, George knew without a doubt that his daughter meant every word.

'I don't mean to—' he started.

'That's enough, Dad, save it; I've heard it all before. One more wrong move on your part, and believe me I'll be round to your office like a shot. I'm sure your boss wouldn't employ a man like that!'

'And how would we live if you did such a thing?'

'It wouldn't be your worry. We'll both move out, and you can take care of yourself. Now I suggest you eat your breakfast while I take a cup of tea up to Mum.'

'Where is she?'

'In my bedroom. Perhaps it would be better if you moved into my room and then Mum and I can share the big bedroom.'

'Now, that's going too far!'

She leaned towards him. 'No, Dad. You went too far last night rampaging around the place, breaking things. God knows what would have happened had Mum been at home. She has put up with your shenanigans far too long and so have I. It stops now.' She poured a cup of tea. As she walked towards the stairs she turned and said, 'I'll get Mum to change the sheets today.'

Margaret Carter had been listening to the conversation from

24

behind the half-closed door, her hand over her mouth. What audacity her Elsa had! And to her amazement, George seemed to have taken it all without argument. She knew that she had been a fool to put up with his ways for so long, but when you were married and had children you had to make do. It was the way of married couples. If everyone knew what went on behind the closed doors of all the houses in the street, there would be many surprises. People didn't wash their dirty laundry in public, it just wasn't done.

'Drink this, Mum,' said Elsa. 'I'll wait until Dad goes to work before I leave.'

'You'll be very late,' said Margaret.

'Once won't make much difference,' Elsa assured her. 'I'm a dab hand now at setting out the display and some of the baskets of fruit are already made up, so don't you worry.' Putting the cup down on the side, she went back to the living room.

'What happened to you this morning, my girl?' asked Ruby when eventually Elsa arrived at the market. 'Sleep in, did you?'

'I'm afraid so.' Elsa thought it was a good enough reason and it stopped further questions.

'That's not like you,' Ruby remarked. 'I was getting worried in case you were sick or something.'

'Oh, that's kind of you, Ruby, but as you can see I'm fine.' She was still seething with anger that once again her father had reverted to type. Seeing the mess on the walls where he'd thrown his food had just been too much. He had destroyed her mother's dignity for the last time. She suddenly wished Peter were here. He was always so supportive when things were bad. Elsa proceeded to get her stall ready. As she did so, she watched two uniformed constables strolling around. This wasn't an unusual occurrence as the local police did this on occasion. But she noticed that Clive very quickly hid some of his stock at the back of his van.

As they approached his pitch, he smiled broadly at them and said, 'Good morning, officers. Nice day for it. Can I interest you in a gift for the missus? Got some nice frilly nighties here.' He held up a pink lace-trimmed one by the shoulder straps.

The coppers both declined and walked on.

Elsa, who had been listening, shook her head. That man had the cheek of old Nick.

Clive caught her gaze and walked over to her. 'This would look good on you, or should I say you would look ravishing in it?'

'Either way I'm not in the least bit interested,' she said.

'Now you do surprise me, lovely Elsa. You are so very feminine, I was sure you would like pretty things.'

'I do, but not when they fall off the back of a lorry!'

He feigned indignation. 'What aspersions are you casting in my direction, madam?'

She gave him a defiant look. 'I saw you put some of your stuff out of the way when you saw the law approaching. Why would you do such a thing if it was kosher?'

'Oh my, but what a suspicious mind you do have! I was merely tidying my stock, that's all.'

'Of course you were,' she answered, and bent down to lift a basket of fruit on to the display.

Clive walked back to his pitch with a frown. That girl was too observant for her own good; he would have to be more careful in future. As he titivated the goods on display on the table in front of him, Jed Sharpe's sister Anne came along and stopped in front of him.

'Hello, Clive.' She simpered.

He smiled at her and said, 'Well just look at you. I'm surprised you're not in films, you're so pretty. And where are you off to?'

'Just wandering round, looking at the shops. I thought I might go to the pictures tonight but my girlfriend isn't well.'

'No work today?'

'I rang them this morning to tell them I was ill,' she said and lowered her gaze. 'I wanted to come and see you.'

'Now that's very naughty,' he scolded. 'If your brother finds out he won't half give you what for.'

'Jed doesn't run my life!' she protested.

'No, but he looks after you. How is your mother?'

He knew that Anne's mother was in hospital suffering from TB and her father was away at sea most of the time, which was why her older brother took care of her.

'She's all right, as well as she can be.'

And while she's away, the mice will play, thought Clive. He gazed at the girl before him. She might well pretend to be sweet and innocent but he, knowing women so well, had already seen the look in her eye. She was a young predatory female, determined to enjoy life, and Jed was going to have his hands full.

'I'm not doing anything this evening,' he ventured. 'I like a good film myself. How about I take you to see one?'

Her attitude immediately changed. Her eyes shone with a look of triumph. 'That would be great. Where shall we meet?'

'I'll pick you up in front of the bus station at seven o'clock. All right?'

'I'll be there,' she said with a broad grin.

'Your brother wouldn't like it if he knew,' he said.

'Who's going to tell him? I certainly won't.' She leaned forward provocatively. 'Will you?'

'As far as I'm concerned it's none of his business.'

'Precisely!'

He watched her walk away, swinging her handbag like a child. He would have a good time this evening, that was certain. She was so very ready to be taught the ways of a woman and he was a master at it. He would enjoy every moment.

CHAPTER FOUR

Margaret Carter was making bread. As she kneaded the dough, she prodded, pulled and then thumped it with great vigour.

'There, you bastard, take that!'

It was unlike her to swear, but she was angry with herself. Angry that it took her daughter's courage to sort out her husband when she should have been the one to stand her ground – a long time ago. She stretched her aching arms. I need a cup of tea and a cigarette, she thought, and opening a cupboard she removed an earthenware jar. From the depths of it, she took out a packet of ten Woodbines and a box of matches, plus four fingers cut from a pair of leather gloves. George didn't hold with women smoking, and so when he was at work she would go into the garden, pull on the finger coverings to avoid any nicotine stains, and puff away to her heart's content. It was the one thing that would calm her shattered nerves. Today, she poured a cup of tea from the pot simmering on the hob and sat in a chair. Lighting the cigarette, she drew deeply on it and slowly blew out the smoke, marvelling at her own boldness.

She thought back to the time when, as a young bride, she'd been so proud to be married to such a gentleman. Indeed for the first year she had been really happy. George took her out to the cinema once a week; at weekends in the summer they would pack a picnic, catch a bus to the New Forest and spend a day there. It was true that her husband was a rather reticent man, never showing any outward signs of affection, apart from calling her 'dear', but she put that down to his good manners. He would always commend her cooking and say how much he'd enjoyed his meal, and she had been content with that.

However, when she was three months pregnant, he'd been late home one evening and, to her horror, had arrived smelling of alcohol, was unsteady on his feet and had verbally abused her. When she had answered back in her own defence, he'd hit her so hard across the face she'd seen stars as she staggered across the room. In the morning, he'd apologised, profusely, saying it would never happen again. Believing him, she forgave him, but he did it twice more during her pregnancy. Terrified of losing her unborn child, she tried hard not to displease him. Then Elsa was born – and with a baby, what choice did she have? This morning, however, when she heard Elsa standing up to her father, she decided that she would change too. She would be a doormat no longer. After all, she did deserve better, as Elsa had said, and better she was going to get!

It was changing the sheets that had done it. In the past, she'd been frightened when she went to bed, wondering if George would wake from his drunken stupor and beat her again. She no longer wanted his sexual advances, but had been too scared to refuse him. Now she wouldn't have to worry about that either.

Lifting her cup, she said, 'Cheers! To Margaret Carter . . . reborn!'

Later that day, George Carter walked into his house thinking that at least he would only have Margaret to cope with until Elsa had finished work. He was sure he could talk her round; after all, he'd always had the upper hand with her.

'Hello, dear,' he said quietly as he hung up his coat.

'Hello, George,' she said with a firmness he'd not heard before.

'Look, about last night—' he began.

'I don't want to hear another word! Elsa was right, enough is enough and you might as well get used to the idea that things have changed. Your supper is in the oven, so help yourself. I'm going next door to have a cup of tea with Mrs Pilmore. Goodbye.'

He was speechless. He looked around. The table was laid for one with a teapot waiting to be filled from the kettle on the stove, a cup and saucer ready and a small jug of milk. A loaf of bread stood on the bread board with a cloth over it to keep it fresh.

What is going on? he wondered. He had honestly thought as he walked home that things would return to normal. He walked upstairs and looked in the small bedroom usually occupied by Elsa and was surprised to see his hairbrush set carefully laid out on top of the chest of drawers. He opened the top drawer and found his underwear neatly folded, and in the wardrobe *his* clothes were hanging. He then went into the bedroom he normally shared with his wife and saw that Elsa had moved her stuff in there. He was livid. He honestly hadn't believed she'd go this far. He stomped off downstairs and took his food from the oven, already plated, and put it on the table. He certainly wasn't going to put up with this!

Margaret stood outside the front door, shaking from head to foot. Despite her determination to be strong, she had been inwardly quaking as she spoke to the husband who had ruled the house with a rod of iron. She fished into her pocket and took out a cigarette and, with trembling fingers, lit it. She puffed on it, filling her lungs with nicotine, and felt herself beginning to unwind. Eventually throwing away the stub end, she walked to the house next door and lifted the knocker.

Anne Sharpe was primping and preening in front of her bedroom mirror. Tonight she had a date with Clive Forbes. She was very excited. Clive was so sophisticated, unlike her brother Jed. She had seen Clive dressed smartly in a suit, out with some friends, and thought he looked really handsome. When he smiled at her, her heart pounded and her legs seemed to turn to water. He was a real man, unlike the boys who were always trying to chat her up. What did they know about life? Whereas Clive looked as if he had lived it to the full. She wondered how it would feel to be held in his arms and kissed. She crossed her arms in front of her, closed her eyes and let her imagination do the rest. Well, this evening she would find out! She felt sure that he would demand it in return for spending time with her . . . but would he want more? The very thought of the danger of this likelihood thrilled her and scared her at the same time. He must be really inter-ested, or he wouldn't have asked her out. She picked up a cardigan and made her way downstairs.

'Where do you think you're off to?' asked her brother.

'I'm going round to my friend Ursula's house, and then we're going to the cinema.' It was only half a lie, she told herself.

'Come straight home afterwards,' he told her.

Anne didn't answer, but let herself out of the house. If only you knew, she thought, and, laughing, she walked down the road.

Forbes didn't look forward to the prospect of spending the evening with Anne with the same enthusiasm. Indeed, he was beginning to regret making the offer. Stupid kid! Always hanging around him, but at least she wasn't jailbait. She wanted to be with him so much it was almost an embarrassment. Well, he would show her what it was like to be out with a real man. It would either frighten her off or make her more eager; in either case, she was easy meat and probably still a virgin. To take her cherry would be a change from his usual conquests, many of them married, frustrated women looking for affection and good sex, and he was just the one to fulfil their needs. After all a man needed his oats, and with married women there were no ties. Marriage was definitely not for him; well, not for a long time anyway. He supposed later he would appreciate a home and a wife to look after his needs. Now he had a flat in Henstead Road in the Polygon area, which he rented as he couldn't afford to buy a place there.

The Polygon area was a somewhat more salubrious area than Kingsland Market where he worked. He liked that. It was as if he were living two lives. Here his neighbours were middle class, as opposed to the working class crowd who shopped in the market, looking for a bargain. When he came home and changed into a decent suit, he felt middle class also.

His parents had a two-up two-down house in the Chapel district. There children ran around the streets barefoot, their clothes ragged, their noses dripping and their hands grimed with the dirt of playing, happy enough with their poor existence, not knowing anything different. He had grown up in such a place but had seen how the other half lived and he wanted to do the same. Well, he was halfway there. Maybe he did earn a living in the market, but the money he earned there would take him up in the world. He was bright; he would think of another occupation, when he had enough money, although at the moment he had no particular business in mind. When he had enough dosh, then he would decide.

With a sigh, he let himself out of the door and made his way towards the bus station and Anne Sharpe.

Anne, who had arrived early, was pacing up and down, fearful that Clive wouldn't show up. Had she been foolish, she wondered, pestering him? If he didn't show up, she would be humiliated, but such was her longing for the man that she decided to wait. With relief, she saw him sauntering towards her. Primping her hair, she struck what she hoped was a provocative pose: hand on hip, legs well placed, and her bust thrust out.

My God! thought Forbes as he saw her. She looks like a prostitute waiting for a punter!

When he reached her side, he pushed her arm off her hip and said, 'Don't stand like that, for goodness' sake. Some one will ask how much you charge!'

Tears brimmed in her eyes, which filled with shame at his words. She wasn't common! She had her best dress on. He had no right to say such things, but she was too embarrassed to argue.

Seeing her reaction, Clive thought, For God's sake, don't bloody well burst into tears or I'm off. He took her arm gently.

'Come along, little Anne; let's go to the Odeon. Robert Donat is in *The 39 Steps*. It's a mystery and I'm told it's very good.'

He bought tickets for the front circle, but led her along the back row, which caused her heart to flutter. This was where the couples sat who wanted to kiss and cuddle. As they settled, the lights of the cinema were lowered, and they sat watching the newsreels.

The young girl felt a thrill as her escort placed an arm round her shoulders, and she snuggled into him. He turned her head towards him, leaned forward and kissed her. His kisses were gentle and persuasive at first, but as she responded they became demanding until she could hardly breathe. He stopped abruptly as the secondary feature film began and concentrated on the screen.

The film was a Western with Gary Cooper playing a cowboy taking a wagon train through Indian territory. It was an exciting story and Anne was so engrossed in it that she was startled when Clive softly placed his hand on her breast and started to caress it. She looked quickly at the people sitting on the other side of her, but they were watching the screen, as was Clive she was astonished to see. She didn't know what to do, so did nothing. He slipped his hand inside the neck of her dress, and her bra. As he moulded the soft flesh with his hand, she felt nervous, yet excited. She placed her hand over his to try to hide what was happening, but as his fingers stroked her nipple she closed her eyes. Oh my God, what was this feeling? She felt hot; her body seemed to be behaving strangely. Deep inside her she felt the throes of passion spreading through her. Was this what love did to you? At seventeen, she'd never experienced such wanton feelings.

As the film came to an end, Clive removed his hand and when the lights went up he asked casually, 'Do you want an ice cream?'

Unable to speak, she nodded.

As she watched him stand in the queue in front of the attendant carrying the tray of ice creams, held by a strap round her neck, she wondered what would happen during the main feature. When he returned, he asked if she'd enjoyed the film.

She smiled and said, 'Very much, thank you.'

The lights dimmed once again, and Anne waited to see what would happen. Nothing did. Clive was absorbed in the film, listening to every word as the plot thickened and the tension grew.

At first Anne was disappointed, but eventually she too began to watch the screen, until it came to an end and they stood for the National Anthem. Once outside the cinema, Clive really wanted a beer, but knowing the girl was only seventeen, too young to be served alcohol, he decided to take her home, via the park, where he would try his luck. Then he would still have time for a pint before the pubs closed.

It was getting dusk as they walked towards Anne's home through Hoglands Park. Clive led her over to a wooden bench which was partially hidden by the hanging branches of a tree. As soon as they sat down, he took her into his arms and kissed her, his hand groping for her breast.

'You are a very tasty bit of work, young lady,' he whispered in her ear.

'Do you really think so?'

'Mmm.' He slipped the tip of his tongue into her mouth. She

was so surprised, she began to pull back, but he held her head, and continued the slow invasion of her senses. As he felt her excitement mounting, he felt for her skirt and pushed up the hem of it, his fingers gently stroking her slim hips, until his hand went between her thighs. His thumb caressed her womanhood slowly until she moaned as she reclined in his arms.

He continued to kiss her – at least that way she couldn't call out, he thought – as he found his way inside her knickers, slipping his fingers inside the wet and warm delight which he sought so eagerly.

Foosteps and voices could be heard coming nearer, and Clive, cursing to himself, straightened Anne's dress. Taking out a cigarette, he lit it, and looked at his watch. 'Well, best walk you home,' he said.

The girl was stunned, confused and frustrated. The man who had taken such liberties with her body was no longer interested, but she, unused to the longing unleashed in her hormones, was unsatisfied and dismayed. Wasn't he interested in her any more? Was it all about a grope in the park and nothing else?

Seeing the sudden anger in her eyes as they stood under a lamppost, Clive realised that he'd handled the situation badly.

'Sorry, darling, but what else could I do? We didn't want anyone looking on while we made love, did we?' He tipped her chin up and kissed her briefly.

'Will I see you again?' She hated herself for asking but couldn't help it.

'You bet we will. Now do you want me to take you to your door or leave you at the end of the street?'

Thinking that her brother would go crazy if he knew she'd lied and even worse had been out with Clive Forbes, she knew that she had better be careful.

'I'll be fine if you take me to Orchard Lane. I can soon get home from there.'

Excellent, thought Forbes. I can pop into the Alma Inn for a drink.

At the corner of Orchard Lane, he pecked Anne on the cheek. 'You take care now.'

He walked into the pub and ordered a pint of bitter. As he sat and enjoyed the beer, he thought it had been quite a productive evening. Whenever he wanted he could pluck that little darling. But where and when? There was no hurry, he thought with a broad grin. She would keep.

CHAPTER FIVE

Margaret Carter stayed in her neighbour's house making conversation for as long as she could, not wanting to face her husband again until Elsa came home, when she knew she would have strong support, but finally Mrs Pilmore stood up.

'Well, Margaret, I must get on,' she said.

'Of course. I'm sorry to have taken up so much of your time,' said Margaret, embarrassed at having overstayed her welcome.

'It was a lovely surprise to see you on the doorstep. We must do it again soon. The morning would be better, though, when the old man has gone to work.'

'You must come in to me,' Margaret said hastily.

Once outside, she thought, It's no good, I'll have to face the music, but I must stick to my guns, or I'll let Elsa down.

George Carter was sitting in an armchair by the fire when his wife walked into the living room. 'You took long enough!' he grumbled.

Margaret ignored him and started to clear the dirty plates from the table, taking them into the kitchen to start the washing up. Suddenly hearing her husband's voice behind her made her jump and she dropped a plate, which shattered as it hit the stone floor.

'For goodness' sake, woman! You are so clumsy.'

'You shouldn't creep up behind me like that,' she said boldly.

'Margaret, this nonsense has got to stop,' he said.

'It's not my fault I dropped the plate. You made me jump out of my skin.'

'No, I don't mean that. This changing of bedrooms. It isn't right. You are my wife, after all.'

She turned and looked at him, her eyes blazing. 'That doesn't give you the right to rape me!'

He paled, but as the memories of years of abuse flooded her mind resentment and anger boiled up inside her – and Margaret found her courage. 'Many a night when you were drunk, you forced yourself on me. You treated me like a whore. What would your daughter think of you if she knew that, eh?'

He was visibly shaken. 'You wouldn't tell her, would you?'

'Not unless you make me. I am prepared to clean and cook for you, do your washing and ironing, as a good wife should, but I will no longer share a bed with you . . . and if you come home once more in a drunken stupor, I'll walk out!'

'I don't know what's got into you,' he cried.

'I have decided to reclaim my self-respect, George. You have all but destroyed me over the years: well, I deserve better. I am no longer the doormat you wipe your feet all over. I am a person in my own right, not just Elsa's mother or your wife. I am Margaret Carter. Woman!'

He looked at her with amazement. 'Have you been drinking?'

She laughed at him. 'How like a man! When things get difficult, they go running to the bottle. Well, I've just found mine.'

At that moment, Elsa walked in the back door. As she entered the kitchen, she looked from one to the other. 'Is everything all right?' she asked her mother.

'Just fine,' Margaret answered. 'Your father and I have just been having a conversation about the new house rules.'

Glaring at the pair of them, George stomped back into the living room, picked up his newspaper and sat down. He rustled the pages angrily, but he said nothing.

With a slow smile Margaret said, 'What would you like to eat?'

Elsa peeped round the door at her father, then hugged her mother. 'Egg and chips will do nicely, thanks. I'll just run upstairs and change out of these dirty clothes.'

When she was alone in the bedroom, she wondered just what had occurred between her parents. But whatever it was, for once her mother seemed to have held her own. The next few days would be interesting and she wondered just how long her father would put up with the new regime. Time would tell, but for the moment things were quiet, if not without a certain tension, but that was to be expected.

The two women sat together eating their supper, trying to make conversation, which wasn't easy with George sitting there, indignation oozing from every pore, but they made a brave effort, and escaped to the kitchen afterwards to wash up.

'I don't think I can stand this much longer,' whispered Margaret.

'You have to stick it out,' Elsa retorted, 'or we'll be back to the bad old days. I've brought some magazines home; we'll sit on the settee and read them.'

They heard George switch on the wireless to listen to the news.

'Come on,' said Elsa.

They did as they planned until Elsa said, 'I have to be up early in the morning, so I'm off to bed.'

Not wanting to be left alone with an irate husband, Margaret said, 'I'm tired too. I can do with an early night.'

They rose to their feet.

'Goodnight, Dad. See you in the morning.'

He just glared at his daughter.

Margaret walked to the stairs and said nothing.

Once they were in the bedroom, Margaret said quietly, 'He won't put up with this for long. I know him.'

'We'll just have to wait and see, won't we? The main thing, Mum, is to act as if things are normal. When he comes down in the morning, give him his breakfast as you always do, and in the evening chat to him normally. For goodness' sake don't give him the silent treatment; it will make matters worse.' Turning back the covers, she grinned at her mother. 'And don't snore!'

'I'll have you know, young lady, I never snore. It's your father you hear, not me!'

The market was busy the next morning and Elsa was kept on the move. She could hear Clive calling his punters to try his bargains, and as usual there was a crowd of women listening to his spiel, and buying his goods. She had to admit he was good at his job.

Eventually, around lunchtime, there was a welcome lull, and as Elsa began to replace the goods that had been sold from her display she noticed a young, well-dressed man talking to Forbes. He was different from the usual customer in the market and she was curious. She wondered if he was English. Somehow she thought not. He carried himself with a certain dignity and he had a distinctive style of his own. His shoes looked expensive, as did the rest of his apparel.

Jean-Paul Devereux had been watching Clive Forbes for most of the morning and had been impressed by his salesmanship, his expertise, his charisma, and his way with the females. When there was a lull, he introduced himself. Holding out his hand, he said, 'Jean-Paul Devereux, from Paris. I like your style.'

Looking at the wearing apparel of the man standing before him, Clive said, 'I like yours too! You didn't buy that gear in England, that's for sure. I like good clothes myself.'

'Do you earn enough on your stall to buy the things you really like?' the Frenchman asked.

'I do all right. I dress well, and live fairly well. I'm not saying I couldn't do with more. Why? What's it to you?'

'I could perhaps use a man like you. Why don't we meet later and discuss it over a drink?'

Only hesitating for a moment, Forbes agreed. Why not? It wouldn't cost him anything to listen. 'Yeah, all right. Where?'

'I am staying at the Star Hotel. Meet me in the residents' lounge at seven thirty.'

'Fine,' said Clive. 'Well, what do you think of the market then?'

'It's good, and busy.' Glancing across at Elsa he said, 'Some traders are better-looking than others.'

'You can forget about her. I'm sure under that skirt she's wearing a fucking chastity belt.'

Jean-Paul burst out laughing. 'I'm assuming you have tried to find out?'

'Didn't get near enough for even a sniff,' admitted the trader.

'I'll see you later,' said the Frenchman and he strolled over to Elsa's stall. 'Good morning, mademoiselle. I would like to buy some fruit, please.'

Charmed by his good manners and perfect English with its attractive accent, Elsa asked, 'What would you like?'

'A selection, I think. Two apples, a couple of bananas, and an orange will do nicely, thank you. I am staying in a hotel and I like to have fruit fresh in my room.'

'Are you visiting?' she asked, her curiosity aroused.

'Yes. I am here just for a few days on business. Southampton is a nice town, and, if you will forgive my boldness, as I look at you I now know what they mean by an English rose. You are a perfect bloom.'

Elsa felt the colour rush to her cheeks as she packed the fruit in brown paper bags. 'Thank you,' she said.

Taking his fruit, Jean-Paul paid for them and smiled at Elsa. 'I hope we meet again before I leave,' he said, and walked away.

Intrigued by the stranger, she watched him walk through the market, wondering if he would turn round and look at her, but he didn't and she found she was disappointed. Then she chided herself for her indulgence. What was she thinking of? It was just such a change to meet someone like him, here of all places. What would such a man have to do with Clive Forbes, she wondered. She glanced over to his pitch and saw him watching her. She looked away.

The trader was wondering just what the foreigner had said to Elsa to make her blush. She didn't seem angry about it so he supposed it was a compliment. Whenever he'd tried that tack, she'd knocked him back. As he was pondering over this, he saw young Peter Adams, Elsa's boyfriend, approaching. What a shame he hadn't been there a moment earlier. He'd have had something to say about the smooth stranger, Clive was sure.

'Peter! What on earth are you doing here?' Elsa asked.

'That's not much of a greeting I must say. Throwing yourself in my arms I could accept,' he teased.

'What, here in the market? What would people think?'

'As if I cared. I've been down doing some reporting in the docks over some poor sailor who fell from the gangway last night and crushed a leg, so I thought I would call and see the woman of my dreams.'

'That's the second compliment I've had today.'

'Oh? And who has been playing up to you, might I ask?'

'A Frenchman, no less.'

'A sailor?'

'Oh no. He was well dressed, said he was here for a few days on business. He said I was a perfect bloom, as in English rose.'

'You be careful, my girl. All these Frenchies think they are good lovers, but most of the married ones have mistresses. Besides, they eat frogs' legs and snails, very unsavoury. How could you like a man who did that?'

'I didn't enquire into his eating habits,' she said, chuckling with amusement.

'And don't you go looking into his other habits either! I must go, darling. Do you want to go out for a quiet drink this evening?'

Not wanting to leave her mother in the house with her father yet, as things were, she said, 'I need to wash my hair, but come round if you like and I'll make you a cup of tea.'

'In that case I'll give it a miss, as I want to write up a story I'm working on. I'll pop by sometime tomorrow and see you, if I can.' He leaned forward and kissed her cheek, then with a wave he was off.

As he walked he pondered over Elsa's remarks about the Frenchman and, being curious by nature and profession, was intrigued. As it was a seaport town there were always strangers wandering around, and he was constantly on the lookout for a good story.

It was pure chance that Peter was in the bar of the Star Hotel later that evening. He had been trying to interview the barman, as he had heard the injured sailor had visited the bar before his accident and he wanted to find out if the man had been inebriated. He stayed to have a glass of beer. Standing at the bar, he looked in the mirror and saw, in the reflection, Clive Forbes walk in and make his way to the residents' lounge. After a short while, he passed by and glanced in. Forbes was in deep conversation with a stranger. Lingering behind a tall potted plant, he tried to hear their conversation, but he was too far away. He was able to hear enough to know the stranger was a foreigner and wondered if he was Elsa's Frenchman. What on earth would he have to do with the market trader, he wondered.

Clive Forbes was wondering the same thing as the Frenchman made small talk whilst waiting for their drinks to be served. Clive sat back and waited.

Eventually Jean-Paul got down to business.

'I am buying and selling too,' he said, 'in Paris. I have a shop not far from the Eiffel Tower.'

'What sort of thing do you sell?' the market trader asked, his curiosity roused even further.

'Antiques, furniture and fittings mainly, and bric-a-brac, but good quality and expensive stuff.'

With a frown, Clive said, 'I don't understand. Why do you want to talk to me? I don't sell that kind of stuff. Mine is all cheap and cheerful, the kind of thing that my punters can afford.'

'I deal in various other things too,' ventured the stranger.

Forbes was no fool. If this chap was dealing legally, he wouldn't be talking to him.

'Go on.'

'I am, as you English say, branching out, and I need someone who can hold certain items for me or another person to collect at a later date.'

'Why don't you do it yourself?'

'It isn't always convenient.'

'But you don't know me from Adam. I could run off with the loot and disappear.'

Jean-Paul just laughed. 'I have watched you, and I'm certain that much of what you sell isn't legal, so you know how to be careful. Besides, if you did decide to help me you would be well paid. I chose you because you have the charm and savvy to talk your way out of things, if necessary. Nevertheless, I have to warn you that it would be very dangerous to cross me, and my associates.'

'How much would you pay me?'

'Five per cent of the gross on each delivery.'

'You are joking, aren't you?'

'No, I'm very serious.'

Clive sipped his beer and leaning forward said, 'No deal. This stuff is obviously hot and yet you want me to chance my arm for a crummy five per cent. Ten per cent or you can get knotted!'

Jean-Paul looked disappointed. 'I will have to talk to my associates. I am not at all sure they will agree.'

Forbes just shrugged. 'Please yourself.' He wasn't going to get into such a deal with heavy stuff for a stranger unless he was going to be well rewarded. He drank his beer, rose from his seat, shook hands with the Frenchman and said, 'Let me know.' And he left.

Meantime, Peter had approached the reception desk.

'Can I help you, sir?' the receptionist asked.

Pointing out the stranger Peter asked, 'Can you tell me if that is Mr Jenkins? I was supposed to meet a Jenkins here, but we have never met.'

'Good gracious, no,' said the girl, 'that is Mr Devereux from Paris.'

'Thank you, my dear,' he said, smiling. 'You have just stopped me making a fool of myself,' and he walked out of the hotel. As he made his way home, he felt a flutter of excitement. Although he hadn't been able to hear their conversation he had a nose for a good story and he was sure that something dodgy was going on here. He would try to find out more about this mysterious man. The very fact that he was talking to Forbes was enough to whet his appetite. Whistling, he made his way home.

CHAPTER SIX

Fanny Braxton shut the booth on the pier for the day. Business had been slow and she was feeling depressed. She walked slowly along Oxford Street, looking in the shop windows until she came to Jed Sharpe's tattoo parlour. His grandmother had been in the same class as Fanny at school, and she sighed, thinking back to her childhood when she was happy. She felt suddenly alone and bereft.

Jed came to the shop door with a client who was leaving. He recognised Fanny and asked, 'What's up? You look as if you have lost a pound and found a penny.'

'I was thinking about your grandmother,' she said.

Jed, who had been fond of his relation and could see the sadness on the woman's face, said, 'Come in. I'm about to make a brew.'

Although she'd known Jed all his life, Fanny had never been into his premises before. The interior was small. The walls were decorated with pictures of various tattoos on offer to his clients. There was a table with a chair on either side and a free-standing light which Jed used to illuminate the delicate detail of his work.

'Sit down, Fanny,' he said and went to the small back room which housed his kettle and teacups.

As she waited, she studied the pictures of snakes, hearts, anchors and naked ladies. There was one splendid picture of a colourful dragon which she particularly liked.

Jed came back carrying two mugs of steaming tea. He handed one to her.

'Cheers,' he said. 'I miss the old girl too.' His grandmother had died two years previously. 'She was a character was Gran. She had a tattoo, you know.'

'She did?' Fanny was really surprised.

Grinning, Jed said, 'Yes, she insisted I give her one on her arm for her fiftieth birthday. It was a heart with the name Fred on it.'

'But her husband's name was Charlie!'

He chuckled, 'I know. But he'd gone by then, so I figure she felt free to do it.'

'But who was Fred?'

Shrugging, he said, 'I never found out. She refused to tell me, but she had a twinkle in her eye when I'd finished it.'

'Crafty cow! I never knew about a Fred.'

'But by then you and she weren't friends, were you?'

Fanny looked down into the murky depths of her tea and said, 'No. We fell out years ago.'

'It was when your sister married, wasn't it?'

Fanny remembered clearly. Ada, Jed's grandmother, had told Fanny a few home truths when Fanny had been screaming oaths about her sister's stealing her man.

'For Christ's sake, Fanny, give over will you!' Ada had said. That bloke never fancied you. He fell for your sister the moment he set eyes on her. When are you going to admit that you are just an obsessive fool?' And so the row had escalated until Fanny had told her she never wanted to see her again. She had never forgiven Ada, and they hadn't spoken since. Now it was too late.

'Yes,' she said. 'We had an almighty row.'

'Shame. Life's too short to carry a grudge.'

Fanny remained silent for a while, contemplating his remark, but the hate festering in her heart was still there. 'How's your young sister?'

'Growing up too fast,' he admitted. 'I try to take care of her whilst Mum's in hospital, and of course Dad isn't home long enough to control her.'

'Well just watch she doesn't fall foul of some bloke who will break her heart, that's all!'

Sipping his tea, Jed thought how pitiful the woman in front of him was. She had wasted her adult years through bitterness and jealousy, and look at her now. A lonely old woman without a friend in the world – and living a lie. He knew that she had no special gift, which in itself wouldn't be a sin if she used her position for good, bringing happiness to those who chose to visit her, but she did the opposite and he thought that *was* a sin.

'How's business?' he asked.

'Slow. That's why I closed up.'

'Ever thought of spreading a bit of good cheer instead, to your clients? It would help keep your business going.'

'What do you mean?' she asked, puffed up with indignation.

'Come on, Fanny, I've heard how you cause mischief between couples. It seems to give you pleasure. It's not right.'

Her mouth narrowed into a tight line. 'Don't you dare to tell me how to run my business, young man. I was working before you were even thought of.'

He knew he was wasting his time. 'Please yourself.'

Fanny rose to her feet. 'That's exactly what I intend to do. You're just like your grandmother. You both interfere.'

He lit a cigarette. 'If you were a bit more like my gran, Fanny, you would be a much better person!'

She stormed out, cursing him.

It was Anne Sharpe's half day. She left Woolworth's by the staff door and headed for the market – and Clive Forbes. Ever since he'd taken her to the pictures, she hadn't been able to get him out of her mind.

Once she arrived, she stood at the back of the crowd and

watched him selling garish figurines to the women in front of him, but she wasn't listening to his spiel, just thinking of how he had held her, caressed her and kissed her, until she became aware that he was flirting with a young woman.

'Bet you know just where you would place this lovely statue,' he said, holding up a figure of a Spanish dancer.

Looking slightly perplexed, she said, 'I'm not at all sure that I do.'

'Invite me round, darling. I'll find the right place.'

There were a few giggles from the others at his double entendre. The woman blushed.

Jealousy coursed through young Anne and she stepped forward into the crowd, pushing her way to the front, where she glared at him.

Clive ignored her and held the other woman with his gaze, smiling at her, an invitation in the expression in his eyes.

'Well, darling, what do you say?'

'I think you are being very cheeky! My husband wouldn't like what you just said to me.'

'Well I won't tell him . . . will you?' And he laughed.

'Oh, you!' she said. 'How much?'

'Because you are so pretty, five bob. I'm giving it away because I like you,' and he wrapped the figurine up and handed it to her.

She passed him the money, smiled, and left.

'So, ladies, are you going to let that young woman be the only one with good taste? These lovely ladies,' he said, pointing to the half dozen he had left, 'will only be seen in the houses belonging to those ladies who know a bit of class when they see it!'

There was a rush to buy the others.

Clive then turned his attention to the baby clothes he had in a box. Holding up a matinee coat he said to another woman, 'How about this for your baby, darling?'

'I haven't got any babies.'

He looked askance. 'You haven't? If I were your husband you would have a baby every year. I do have a lunch break soon if you would like me to help you out.'

'You cheeky bugger! My kids are four and five years old and that's enough of a family for me, thanks.'

The crowd laughed, and he just grinned at her. 'Just my luck,' he said and moved on to another item.

It was lunchtime and the crowd thinned. Anne walked over to him and said, 'What do you think you're doing flirting with all those women?'

'I'm selling my goods, that's what I'm doing.'

'Well I didn't like it!'

'And exactly what does it have to do with you, girlie?'

The coldness of his tone shook young Anne. For all her brashness, she was a seventeen-year-old girl, unworldly and vulnerable, and now she was embarrassed and didn't know what to say.

'It made me feel jealous!' she admitted.

Clive stared at her. 'Now you listen to me, darling, I'm not one of those stupid lads that moon around you with their tongues hanging out, and just because I took you out to the pictures one evening doesn't give you the right to be jealous. Understand?'

She nodded.

'It was a mistake, I can see that,' he added. 'You are far too young for a man like me.'

'No I'm not!' She was horrified at his words. She wanted to go out with him again and now it seemed her wishes were to be dashed. 'I'm sorry. I won't be so stupid again, honestly.'

Forbes heard the anguish in her voice, then looked at her rounded bust, remembering how the soft flesh had felt in his hand. It would be a pity to throw away such a chance of deflowering her. She was so up for it, stupid bitch, and he would be getting his own back on bloody Jed Sharpe with his holier than thou attitude, coming round and telling him how to live his life. Instead of that he should be explaining the facts of life to his sister.

'All right then,' he said, 'but just remember I am my own man. You never tell me what to do.'

'I won't, I promise . . . does that mean you'll take me out again?'

Christ! Doesn't this kid ever give up? he asked himself. He looked at her, thinking she deserved everything she got.

'I might and I might not, I'll think about it. Now away you go, I've got work to do and I don't want you hanging around.' He turned away and started sorting goods inside the back of his van.

Anne had no choice but to leave.

Elsa had been watching the interchange between them and it worried her. She knew young Anne was at home without her mother or her father, so there was no parental control. Her brother probably did his best, but it wasn't the same. It was apparent to anyone watching that the girl was smitten with the market trader, and that did not bode well. Elsa was convinced the man had no scruples, but she didn't see what she could do about it. She was sure that anything she said to Anne would make no difference at all. It was a dilemma.

She watched the girl walk away and sauntered over to Forbes's pitch.

'She's a bit young for you, isn't she? she said.

His eyes glistened and the corners of his mouth twitched with amusement. 'You making me an invitation, Elsa darling?'

'You should be so lucky,' she retorted. 'Anne Sharpe is a vulnerable young girl. Leave her alone!'

Walking round the front of his display, Clive stood facing Elsa. 'What are we now, Mother Superior? Trying to save souls, are we?'

'I am trying to save a young girl from getting into trouble.'

He crossed his arms and leaned against his display, grinning broadly.

'And what makes you so sure she'll be in any trouble, might I ask?'

Elsa was getting angry. 'Don't play games with me; you know very well what I mean. She's got a schoolgirl crush on you and I don't want you taking advantage of it.'

'I'll make a deal with you, Elsa. You come out with me and I'll leave the little virgin alone.'

'I wouldn't go out with you if you were the last man on earth!' she declared.

'If I was the last man, you would have no choice.'

'A woman always has a choice and you would never be mine under any circumstances.'

Enjoying the situation enormously, he laughed at her. 'Then you have made my choice for me. I'll have the little virgin.' He walked away leaving Elsa fuming.

At the end of the day, Elsa started to pack her goods away and Clive, having done his, strolled over.

'Let me give you a hand lifting those heavy baskets,' he offered.

'No thanks, I can manage perfectly well.'

Ignoring her, he lifted two of the baskets full of fruit and put them on the cart she used to transport them to the nearby garage, which was used to store her leftover goods overnight before they were replenished with fresh stock in the morning. When it was full he wheeled it over to the storage place and pushed it inside, unloaded it and returned it empty for reloading.

'This is too heavy for a woman,' he remarked. 'What is your boss thinking of?'

'He knows I can manage,' she told him.

He stood staring at her, then in a quiet voice said, 'You wouldn't need to manage if you had my help. I would be only too pleased to assist you.'

Meeting his gaze she said with heavy sarcasm, 'How kind of you. But what would be the price for such assistance, I wonder?'

With a look of exasperation he said, 'What is it with you? Every time I try to be nice to you, you throw it back in my face! What have I ever done to make you dislike me so much?'

'Whatever makes you think I take enough interest in you, Mr Forbes, to form any opinion at all?'

With a slow smile spreading across his features he said, 'Oh, now don't tell fibs! You watch me far too closely not to be interested. I've seen you when I've been selling, looking in my direction.'

'Listening to the rubbish you tell the women who stand around, maybe. I am always amazed that so many of them are so gullible as to be taken in by you.'

He laughed loudly. 'It's called salesmanship and I'm bloody good at it.'

'Well, I have to say, it certainly seems to work.' She couldn't take that away from him.

'There you are, you see, you can be charitable when you want to. Are you sure you don't want to save young Anne Sharpe from a fate worse than death?'

Elsa longed to swipe the smile from his face. The arrogance of the man! But she retaliated. 'You could take some lessons on gentlemanly behaviour from the Frenchman who was at your stall the other day. Now he did have style.'

The smile disappeared. 'You be very careful not to be taken in by him and his smoothness. Not everyone is what they seem.'

Putting the last of her goods on the cart, Elsa lifted it by the handles and as she moved off said, 'Maybe you're right, but I know who I would rather listen to. Goodnight.'

Clive fumed to himself. Again he had failed to get round Elsa, but he wouldn't give up on her just yet. He gave a sly grin. How surprised the little darling would be if she knew that the Frenchman was not averse to selling stolen goods! That fact gave him a certain satisfaction. Miss Goody Two Shoes would get her come-uppance one day, but he hoped he'd have managed to break down her barriers first.

CHAPTER SEVEN

Jean-Paul Devereux was in the storage room behind his antique shop in Paris, carefully wrapping two valuable Russian icons he intended to take to England with him on his next visit. This would be a legitimate sale to a private collector he knew in London, but he also had a few small packages he would need to deposit with Clive Forbes for a few days until he found a buyer.

He decided to use Southampton as his base whilst he pursued his business. It was within easy reach of the capital and it would enable him to keep an eye on Forbes . . . and he wasn't averse to seeing more of the pretty female market trader who had taken his eye the last time he was in the town.

Leaving his manager in charge, he wandered along to a nearby café and sat drinking coffee, enjoying the passing cavalcade of people. Tonight he was taking Giselle, a young model, to the Pigalle, where they would take in a show at the Folies Bergères, and later to dine. After that they would return to his apartment and he would make leisurely love to her. It would be a satisfactory evening. He found himself fantasising about doing the same with the English girl in the market. Would she be an ardent lover? She appeared to be a little shy, but a man never knew what untold talents simmered under such an exterior.

Elsa, unaware of her secret admirer, had other things on her mind. The situation at home between her parents was a worry to her. Her father had been behaving himself as far as his drinking was concerned, but he was deeply resentful of the new house rules and he was becoming difficult. He would constantly complain about everything when he was alone with Margaret, trying to wear her down.

'My shirts aren't starched enough. This food isn't hot enough. The windows need cleaning – you would think there was a heavy fog outside!'

Margaret was weary of it all, and of trying to be a strong woman, for years of bullying had made her a nervous wreck. However, she fought to maintain the small amount of freedom she had won. She found it easier to ignore his jibes than to retaliate verbally. But in her own way she managed to take her own revenge. She starched the shirts until her husband almost cut his neck on his collars, and served his food so hot that he burnt his tongue. Once, out of sheer frustration, she starched a pair of his underpants and chortled to herself in the kitchen as he let out a yell as he tried to put them on.

George eventually got the message, and reverted to sulking around the house. It made the atmosphere a little uncomfortable, but both Margaret and Elsa decided they could live with it, although Elsa wondered just how long it would be before the man reached the end of his tether.

She confided her worries to Peter one Saturday evening when they had gone dancing.

'I can't see him continuing to live with the new rules much longer without blowing a gasket.'

'Has he been drinking since?' Peter asked, knowing the family history.

'No, he hasn't.'

Putting an arm round her, he gave her a hug. 'Stop putting yourself through the wringer, darling, worrying about what might happen. That way leads to madness and a nervous breakdown.'

He kissed her forehead. 'Come on, let's dance, and you forget about the old devil for a while.'

It wasn't difficult. Peter was a good dancer, he also kept her amused with funny stories about the jobs he was sent on, and their outcomes.

'You wouldn't believe it but I went to interview this old dear who rang the office and swore there was someone in her house. She said that she could hear this person talking. It turned out to be her son's bird he's brought home from abroad – some kind of parrot. He'd forgotten to tell his mother it could talk! When she realised, she was so angry she looked at the bird and said, "You old bugger, you scared me half to death!" The bird looked at her, fluffed up his wings and said clearly, "You old bugger!" It was hilarious.'

'What did she do?'

'Well, she could see the funny side of it, but she was worried to death because the vicar was due to call that afternoon.'

Laughing, Elsa asked, 'What happened?'

'I told her to cover the cage with a cloth. I hope it worked.'

'It would be more fun if it didn't.'

'Naughty, naughty,' he admonished, but he laughed too.

As they sat out during the next dance he asked, 'Have you seen that Frenchman again?'

Surprised, Elsa said, 'No. Why do you ask?'

'I happened to be in the bar of the Star Hotel later that evening after you told me about him, and Clive Forbes was there, talking to a foreign man. I thought it was a bit strange.'

'How do you know the man was French?'

'Because I asked at the reception desk. It must be your Frenchman. If he turns up again, let me know, will you?'

'Whatever for?'

'I wish I could tell you, but there is something fishy going on between them, of that I'm sure. There might be a story in it.'

Elsa remembered Forbes telling her not to be taken in by the Frenchman and now she wondered if there was a reason for such a remark, but she didn't tell Peter. She would wait and see if he ever came back. He was so charming she hoped that her fiancé was wrong in his assumption, but Peter was very shrewd at smelling out a story, which made him the excellent reporter that he was.

The band played the last waltz and they traversed the floor before collecting their coats and walking home.

'Come in for a cup of coffee before you go home,' she suggested.

As they walked round to the back door, Peter pulled her into his arms and kissed her. 'Any chance that we'll have the settee to ourselves?' he asked.

'We'll have to see,' she said.

George Carter was sitting by the fire reading when they entered.

'Hello, Mr Carter. How are you?' asked Peter.

'Fine, thanks, and you?'

'Not bad.'

'I see the Hindenburg crossed the Atlantic in forty-six hours.' He folded his paper. 'You wouldn't get me up in it, I can tell you that!'

'It's all progress, you know. I think I'd like to go. It would be a great experience.'

'The new Spitfire, now that's another story. That I wouldn't mind. But I don't like the news about the Spanish civil war,' he remarked. 'War has a habit of spreading, mark my words.' He folded his paper. 'I'm off to bed. Goodnight, young fellow, Elsa.'

'Goodnight,' she called from the kitchen.

Peter walked into the kitchen and put his arms round her waist. 'The old boy seemed quite affable,' he remarked.

'Put me down, you idiot, I'll drop the coffee cups. Yes, well, it's good when someone else comes into the house and talks to him. It lifts the atmosphere.'

Taking a cup from her, he said, 'At least we can be alone for a while.'

But Elsa had been thinking over Peter's remarks about Clive and the Frenchman. 'You know, I'm sure that man Forbes is selling dodgy stuff.'

Peter was instantly intrigued. 'What makes you say that?'

'The other day when the Old Bill was walking around, he looked very shifty and he dived into the back of his van. I'm sure he was trying to hide something.'

'Perhaps you'd keep your eyes open and then you can tell me if anything else happens.'

'He might get the wrong idea about me if he thinks I'm watching him,' she said.

Laughing, he said, 'Then be discreet. We don't want to warn him off if he is dodgy, do we?'

Elsa wasn't at all sure she wanted to be involved in any way, but thinking about young Anne Sharpe made her agree. She wouldn't like the girl to get herself mixed up with anything unsavoury.

The girl in question wouldn't have been put off had she been warned, such was her desperation to see Clive Forbes again. Indeed, the hint of danger would probably have given her an added thrill. But she was frustrated that Forbes had been so cavalier in his attitude to their next meeting. She desperately wanted to visit the market to see him, but decided to wait until her half day. So she was surprised to see him enter the store where she worked, just before closing time.

Sauntering over to the jewellery counter where Anne stood staring at him, he said, 'Hello, how are you?'

'What are you doing here? Why aren't you working?'

'I closed early. I have to drive out to Chandlers Ford this evening and I need some company. Want to come along?'

Anne was delighted.

'Will I have time to go home and change?'

'I'll drop you off and wait in the pub . . . but don't take long.'

He had done a deal and needed to pick up his goods. He thought it an excellent opportunity to deflower the eager little virgin!

Clive sat reading the *Daily Mail* whilst he drank his pint of beer. He tutted over more pictures of Edward VIII and Mrs Simpson. He couldn't see what the man saw in her. To him she looked more male than female; smartly dressed, of course, but as far as he was concerned that was it. He could see why *she* was keen. The woman wanted to be the next queen of England. Well, he couldn't see that happening. An American and a divorcée . . . not in a million years!

He looked up as Anne poked her head round the door. He drank the remains of his beer, got up and walked outside. Climbing into the driving seat of his Austin, he opened the other door from inside. 'Get in,' he said.

'You might have held the door open for me before you got in,' Anne complained.

'If you are looking for a gent, my dear, find someone else,' he said, turning on the ignition.

Clive didn't make conversation as they drove up the Avenue and out of the town, but Anne didn't mind. It wasn't every day she was able to ride in a car. She sat back with satisfaction and looked at the passing scenery.

How green and fresh everything looked. The bluebells and cowslips in the hedgerows had died back and now the wild daisies and poppies were blooming. She loved the countryside and wished that her family lived there instead of the busy streets of the seaport town.

Stopping outside a second-hand furniture and bric-a-brac shop,

Clive took some boxes out of the boot of the car and knocked on the door. The man who opened it helped take the boxes inside and closed the door behind them.

It was about twenty minutes before Forbes emerged, smiling. Getting into the car, he said, 'Right, let's go to a pub and have a drink and some sandwiches. I know one where we can sit outside.'

Anne tried not to show her disappointment. She had hoped at least he would take her out for a meal, but she smiled and said, 'That'll be lovely.'

To her surprise she enjoyed herself. With such a willing audience, Clive started to tell her his plans for the future, how he would certainly move up in the world and retire young – when he'd made his fortune.

To the young and inexperienced girl it was enthralling, and she considered herself fortunate to be out with such a man. As dusk fell, they walked back to the car.

'Have you ever been to the old Roman road?' he asked.

Thinking it was another pub, she said she hadn't. She was therefore very surprised when Clive drove the car off the road and down a narrow track surrounded by trees. Eventually, he stopped the engine.

'Is this the place?' she asked.

'It certainly is,' Clive answered, and switched off the headlights.

Anne felt her heart pounding. Deep within the trees, it seemed very much darker and somewhat eerie. There was no one nearby and for one moment she felt both scared and excited. Here she was, alone in a car with the man she was besotted with . . . but what would he do now? In the cinema, he'd caressed her breast; in the park he'd put his hand up her skirt . . . but here . . .

Clive didn't waste much time. He was here for a purpose. Taking Anne into his arms he kissed her passionately, whilst at the same time he unbuttoned the front of her blouse and slipped it off. Then he unfastened her bra, releasing the pert breasts, which he devoured with his mouth. He undid her skirt and slipped it down to her knees, his eager hands then doing the same with her underwear. Both were discarded to the floor of the car.

By now there was no retreat for the young girl, and she wouldn't have wanted it if there had been, such was her own frenzy. Her hormones ran riot and she kissed him fervently, and as his fingers explored the most intimate parts of her she writhed and groaned, her breathing heavy.

Clive stopped his expert invasion of her body and reached into the back of the car for a rug. Then he dragged her out of the car and laid out the rug on a bare patch of ground, where he pushed her on to her back, removing his trousers with a flourish.

As he lowered himself on top of her he said, 'You are really going to enjoy this.'

Anne Sharpe lay naked, spent, sore and confused. In her inexperienced mind, she had often imagined having sex, but her imagery was far from the reality. There had been expertise, but no tenderness, no affection – no words of love. She had been manipulated and tuned – like a car engine, she thought – until her responses had been more primeval than anything else . . . and there had been passion from both of them, but nothing more.

Clive pulled on his trousers and shirt, lit a cigarette and looked at the naked girl on the rug, then at his watch. 'Get dressed,' he said abruptly. He went to the car, picked up Anne's discarded clothes and threw them at her.

Tears of anger trickled down her cheeks. She felt used. When she was dressed, she paused as she went past him to the passenger door.

'You bastard!' she said, staring him in the face.

He laughed. 'I told you, if you want a gent, you're with the wrong man!' When she was seated he climbed into the driver's side, turned on the ignition and the headlights and backed out of the old Roman road. But as he drove back to Southampton, he glanced across at the girl beside him and saw the tears trickling down her cheeks. Somehow it disturbed him. He'd done what he set out to do and had satisfied his own sexual needs, but she wasn't a bad kid, he mused. He reached across and patted her knee.

'Come on, darling, it wasn't that bad. How would you like to come out for a meal at the weekend?'

Anne looked at him as she angrily brushed her wet cheeks with the back of her hand, and asked herself why she liked this man so much. When he smiled at her as he was doing now, her heart flipped and she knew she couldn't refuse him anything, but she had her pride.

'If I'm not busy,' she snapped.

Clive burst out laughing. He liked a girl with spirit. 'I'll have to wait and see then, won't I?'

As they drove on, Anne smiled softly to herself. She felt she had recovered some of her dignity.

CHAPTER EIGHT

A week later, Elsa was bending down behind her stall, sorting out a box of fruit, when she heard a voice.

'Is there anybody serving here today?'

When she stood up she was surprised to see the Frenchman standing smiling at her. '*Bonjour*,' he said.

'Oh, hello. You took me by surprise. Can I help you?'

'I am here on business for a few days. I hate to eat alone and I wondered if you would have dinner with me tonight?'

Elsa was completely taken aback by the unexpected and sudden invitation, and hesitated.

The Frenchman, seeing her dismay, said, 'Please, don't think me too forward, but I know no one here. You could tell me a bit about the town. It would help me enormously as I hope to come here often, and I do need to know about the place. I may even be able to start a business myself, who knows?'

Having recovered her equilibrium, Elsa thought it would be a perfect opportunity to learn more about the man, maybe to find out about his dealings with Forbes. Peter would be pleased with her if she could, so she gracefully accepted.

'Thank you, that would be lovely.'

'I don't know any of the restaurants, but if you will come to my hotel at seven o'clock this evening, I can find out about one at the reception. Will that suit you?'

'Yes, that'll be fine.'

'*Bon*. I'll see you then. I am staying at the Star Hotel.'

She watched him walk over to Clive Forbes's pitch where they had a brief conversation before he left the market, waving to her as he walked away. She glanced at Forbes and caught him watching her. She was annoyed when she felt her cheeks flush, and hurriedly turned away.

On her way home she rang the office of the *Southern Daily Echo* to tell her fiancé about her dinner date, but he had already left, so she continued on her way home to wash and change, wondering what sort of evening was ahead of her.

Jean-Paul was waiting in the foyer of the hotel when she arrived.

'Would you like to have an aperitif in the bar?' he asked.

'That would be nice.'

They sat drinking sherry and the Frenchman said, 'You look lovely, *chérie*.'

Elsa smoothed the skirt of her pale green dress and shook her lustrous hair, pleased with the compliment. 'Thank you. How long will you be here in Southampton?' she asked.

He shrugged his shoulders and said, 'I have no idea. I have to go to London on business some time this week, but I want to walk around the town centre, get a feel for the place, maybe see if my kind of business would do well here.'

'What business are you in?'

'I sell antiques. I think it would be unique to bring a touch of France over here. What do you think?'

'I know nothing of the antiques trade, but a touch of France sounds intriguing, I must say.'

'Would you say there is big money in the town?'

'There has been a recession, as I'm sure you know – you have probably read about the men from Jarrow. There is a lot of un-employment, but the wealthy always seem to have money!'

He smiled at the note of disparagement in her voice. 'I know. It never seems fair, does it?'

She had to smile. 'There will always be the haves and the have nots. That's life.'

'And what about you, Elsa? Where do you belong?'

Laughing, she said, 'I manage.'

'But what are your hopes for the future?'

She sat contemplating her answer. 'Marriage, children, I suppose.'

He looked appalled. 'Is that all?'

'What do you mean?'

'Well, look at you! You have such potential. A lovely-looking woman, good at business – I've watched you on your stall and frankly I think you are wasted there.'

'Wasted? Why wasted? I do a good job,' she said defensively.

'Don't misunderstand me, you are excellent at what you do . . . so why are you not in business for yourself? You never make money working for another person.'

'I couldn't possibly afford to open my own business.'

'Have you never heard of bank loans?'

She gazed at the attractive man before her. She looked at his expensive clothes, his beautifully clean hands and neat nails, and thought he had probably never had to scrape a living in his life. And somehow it angered her.

'You have no idea how hard life can be for people who have little money. To get a loan from the bank you have to have some kind of collateral. I have none and no hope of any. You have no idea of my situation, so how can you sit there and criticise me?'

'Please, I am not criticising, believe me. I just think you have so much talent and it is wasted.' He leaned forward and said, 'Don't be cross with me, lovely Elsa, please.'

She said, 'I'm not, but you are a stranger to this country and I can't expect you to understand the structure of our society and the limitations it brings.'

'Of course you are right, but we have the same problems in our country, you know. We had bad strikes, but the new government has changed that for the moment. Not all the French are wealthy, you know. We have our poor peasants who have very little yet sometimes I believe they are happier for it.' He emptied his glass and said, 'The receptionist suggested the Tivoli restaurant is very good, so shall I call a taxi to take us there?'

'Why don't we walk?' she suggested. 'Then you can see some of the shops in the town. It isn't that far from here.'

And so they left the Star Hotel and walked up the High Street to the Bargate, which was the remains of a medieval building, straddling the road.

'This used to be the entrance to the town years ago,' she explained as they passed by. 'And of course we are a major seaport. It was from Southampton that the Titanic sailed on its fateful voyage.'

'Such a tragedy,' he said.

They stopped to look at the variety bill outside the Palace Theatre.

'We have another theatre too,' she explained. 'The Grand puts on plays from London, so you see we are very civilised!'

'Now you are teasing me.' He laughed.

They arrived at the Tivoli restaurant and the head waiter led them to a table.

Elsa was impressed by the savoir-faire of the Frenchman when he ordered from the menu and then the wine list. But then she had not expected any less from this sophisticated man who was intriguing her more the more she saw of him.

'Tell me about Paris,' she said.

As they ate, Jean-Paul painted a vivid picture of the city he loved, telling her of the Louvre, Sacré Coeur, Notre Dame, and other places she had but read about, and she was fascinated.

'You should come to Paris and see for yourself,' he suggested.

'If that were only possible,' she said.

Leaning forward, he said, 'Elsa, everything is possible if you want it enough!'

She tried to hide a smile. 'Is there anything you have really wanted that has been unattainable?'

'A beautiful woman, sometimes.'

She had to laugh as it was said with such sincerity. 'Ah well, it doesn't always do to have everything you want in life.'

He chuckled and said, 'You are probably right.'

After the meal, they caught a tramcar back to the Star Hotel where they sat in the lounge and drank coffee and brandy.

'Thank you so much for a very pleasant evening, Elsa. I don't know when I've enjoyed myself more.'

She looked at him and said, 'Oh, Jean-Paul, you are everything I've heard about Frenchmen – you are so full of charm.'

He raised a quizzical eyebrow and asked, 'What do you mean?'

'The French are known for, let me see . . . the stylish women, the charming men. Then, remembering what Peter had said, she suddenly asked, 'Do you eat snails?'

Jean-Paul's laughter echoed as he said, '*Escargots* . . . of course! And oysters. Have you never tried them?'

Shaking her head, she said, 'No, never. What about frogs' legs?'

'They are hardly worth the trouble.' Then, looking at her with some amusement, he said, 'You should try all these things yourself.'

'The nearest I've ever got to such things is a stall that sells whelks, winkles and jellied eel.'

'Now that is really living!'

'Now *you* are teasing *me*!'

Catching hold of her hand, he kissed the back of it and said, 'Elsa, you are delightful. Will you come out with me again before I return to France?'

'Yes,' she said, and this time there was no hesitation.

He rose to his feet. 'Come, I will call a taxi to take you home.'

'There is no need,' she said, 'I can walk.'

'Indeed you will not. I would take you myself, but I have to meet someone.'

He waited with her at the reception desk until the taxi arrived, and when Elsa gave the driver the address, Jean-Paul paid him before he left.

Tilting her chin, the Frenchman kissed her softly. 'I look forward to our next meeting. *Au revoir, chérie.*'

As she was driven home, she felt a little guilty about Jean-Paul's kiss. Peter definitely would have disapproved, had he known, but she dismissed it as harmless. Then she wondered who her escort would be meeting at this time of night.

Had she but glanced out of the back window of the taxi as it drove away, she would have seen Clive Forbes walk into the hotel entrance.

The two men sat in a quiet corner of the residents' lounge, where they couldn't be overheard.

'I'm a little surprised to see you again,' said Clive.

'Why? I said I'd be back.'

Shrugging, Forbes remarked, 'Yeah, well, I take everything with a pinch of salt until proved; it's safer that way. So . . . what do you want?'

'I want you to look after two small boxes for me until someone can pick them up.'

'And what's in it for me?' The market trader stared at his companion. 'I want to be paid well. Did you talk to your associates?'

'Yes, and we decided we will pay you eight per cent at first. If you are satisfactory we will pay you ten. Take it or leave it, my friend.'

Clive knew from the tone and demeanour of Jean-Paul he wasn't to be moved on this point, and therefore to argue would be useless.

'How much this time?'

'One hundred pounds.'

'Make it one hundred and twenty and you've got a deal.' Clive had been bartering all his life, and tonight was no different as far as he was concerned, but the Frenchman thought differently.

'That's not how it works. We offer you a price, you accept or decline. It makes life very simple.'

'How long do you need me to hold the goods . . . and what are they, by the way?'

'Maybe a week, maybe less, and you don't need to know what the goods are, just hold them in a safe place until someone contacts you.'

'You're asking a lot.'

'I'm paying a lot!' snapped Jean-Paul.

Forbes thought for a moment and then said, 'All right. Do you have the stuff here?'

'Yes. I'll bring them to you in the market tomorrow, with the cash.' Standing, he said, 'I'm off to bed now, I have a lot to do tomorrow.' He shook hands with Clive. 'We may do a lot of business together, which will be lucrative to us both, but I must warn you, don't try to get clever, my friend. It would be very dangerous.'

'You be clever and make sure you keep me happy moneywise and then there would be no need for any trouble, would there?'

'We understand each other, good. I'll see you tomorrow.'

'And no doubt you'll be seeing the market virgin?'

Laughing, Jean-Paul said, 'We dined together this evening. She is utterly charming.'

As Clive left the hotel, he was livid. That smooth bastard had taken Elsa out! He had tried so hard to get beneath that haughty veneer and got nowhere for his trouble and some bloody frog with his smooth chat had made it without effort. He was not a happy man. And he wouldn't be beaten by him. He too would get round the girl, just to prove that he could.

CHAPTER NINE

'You did what?' Peter was walking Elsa home from the market the following evening when she told him about her date with the Frenchman.

'I thought it an excellent opportunity to find out about him, and maybe the connection with Clive Forbes.'

He was furious. 'I only said to keep an eye open, Elsa. I certainly don't agree with you having dinner with him.'

'Whyever not?'

'I can't believe you need to ask! Who knows what that could lead to, him being French and all.'

Elsa started laughing. 'Are you saying he might make me his mistress? That sounds exciting!'

'I am being deadly serious. Besides, if he has anything to do with Forbes, it's bound to be dodgy. You have no idea what sort of man he is. He could be some big criminal for all you know.'

'No, I can't imagine that,' she said.

'There you are, he's worked his bloody charm on you already.'

'There's no need to swear!'

'You are certainly not to see him again. I won't permit it!' His cheeks were crimson with outrage.

But Elsa was a fiercely independent woman. 'What do you mean . . . you won't permit it! How dare you tell me what I can and can't do? You are not my husband, and even if you were, I am not to be ordered about. I saw what it did to my mother and believe me I certainly won't let that happen to me.'

'All right, keep your hair on! Blimey, there's no need to go off at the deep end Elsa. I am only looking out for your safety and welfare.'

'I can manage that for myself, thank you.'

'Now be reasonable, darling,' he coaxed. 'How would you feel if I had to wine and dine some beautiful woman to get a story?'

'That's different.'

'Not really. Just be careful, that's all. I love you, you goose, that's why I'm worried.'

She capitulated. 'All right, it may have been unwise, but I could perhaps pick up some useful information for you. After all, he was the perfect gentleman.'

Not wanting to anger her again, he said, 'I'd rather you didn't.'

'He told me he might be opening a business in the town,' she said, trying to justify her actions.

'What sort of business?'

'Antiques. He said he'd like to bring a touch of France over here.'

'That's what I'm afraid of,' Peter muttered.

Ignoring him, Elsa pressed on. 'Clive Forbes doesn't deal in antiques, so perhaps there is no particular connection.' She really wanted to believe it.

'No, sorry, darling, but there you are wrong. Their meeting was not one of friends; they were definitely cooking up something. It was a very earnest conversation. I know what I saw,' he persisted.

They stopped off at a small café and ordered fish and chips for their supper. There they caught up with each other's family news, both deliberately ignoring the name of the stranger who had momentarily come between them.

Elsa and Peter were not the only ones who were at cross purposes that evening. Jed Sharpe was having an almighty row with his young sister Anne.

73

'Don't you dare to lie to me, you sneaky little cow! You were seen out with Clive Forbes the other evening, coming out of that new restaurant in Above Bar.'

Standing defiantly she blazed back at him. 'What if I was? He took me out for a meal, treated me, which is more than you ever do. No one bothers if I'm alive or dead in this house!'

'That's hardly fair and you know it,' Jed snapped. 'Dear God, I do my best, what with visiting Mum, seeing there is enough food in the house, trying to keep it clean. It wouldn't do you any harm to pull your weight.'

'What do you mean?'

'Let's face it, Anne: it would break your arm if you were to pick up a bloody duster. It's all you can manage to do your own washing and ironing.'

Her guilt only made her more angry. 'I wash your stuff as well. It's not my fault Mum's in hospital.'

He tried a different tack. 'Look, I know things are not that good, and I am aware that you are only seventeen, but in life we have to make do with what hand we are dealt. Just think, it's far worse for our mother. She's the one who is really in trouble.'

Tears brimmed in Anne's eyes. 'I know . . . I'm so frightened that she'll die – like Auntie Florrie.' Looking up at her brother, she asked, her voice filled with anguish, 'If that happened what would we do?'

Jed took her into his arms and held her as she cried into his shoulder. Poor kid, she was such a feisty girl that he forgot how vulnerable she was, that she might have her own fears. Being a practical sort, he had already prepared himself mentally, should he have to face the demise of his mother, but to a teenager it must be a terrifying thought.

'Now then, no one has said that Mum is going to pop her clogs for a long while.' He handed her a handkerchief and said,

'Mop your eyes, there's a good girl, and don't get mad at me when I try to look after you.'

Sniffing, Anne said, 'I'm sorry, but Clive is just being friendly.'

'He's far too old for you, love. A man like that wants far more than holding hands in the cinema. I wouldn't want to see you end up in trouble, that's all.'

Bloody hell, thought Anne as she wiped her face, if he only knew how far she'd gone with the market trader, he'd half kill her and then sort out her lover! Clive had taken her out to dinner the other night, which had thrilled her, then later, in the back of the car, he'd made love to her and this time he'd been kinder to her. Feeling starved of love as she was, to her it meant everything, and in a funny way it gave her a sense of pride. She was not just a teenager now, but a woman . . . she couldn't say that to Jed, though.

'You can't expect me to stay at home all the time!'

More than a little exasperated, he said, 'Of course not, but go around with your friends, boys and girls your own age. Surely they go dancing and to the pictures?'

'Yes, they go to the Guildhall every Saturday evening.'

'There you are then. Enjoy yourself, I'm saying, but with your own age group.'

'Spotty-faced oiks, you mean . . . and don't think they are all angels. Most of them have got the arms of an octopus.'

Jed hid a smile, remembering his own teenage years. 'Yes, but you can handle them, Anne. Clive Forbes is a different kettle of fish and if you were honest you'd agree.'

'Well at least he's all man,' she quipped.

'What's that supposed to mean?' Jed asked, immediately suspicious.

'Oh, for goodness' sake, I say that about Errol Flynn and Gary Cooper. Now if Clive was like George Raft, then you might have something to worry about!'

'Clive hasn't the sophistication to be the gangster type that George Raft plays,' her brother said, 'and don't try to change the subject. If I hear you have been out with Forbes again, I'll beat the hell out of him and you too, mark my words! Now get off to bed or you'll be late getting up in the morning.'

As his sister stomped up the stairs, Jed ran his fingers through his hair in desperation. If only his father was at home to take control. The burden of being the head of the house could be really heavy at times.

Bob Sharpe had been a merchant seaman all his life, and when his wife had been diagnosed with TB he'd spoken to his son.

'Look, Jed, to stay at home would drive me crazy. At least being away I can provide good money for my family, and you're an adult now. I can safely leave you to be the man of the house whilst I'm at sea.'

He had kept his word and the family had never had to scrimp and scrape as others had. Whenever he came home, he was laden with gifts, like Father Christmas, which was exciting for all, but it was Jed who really *was* the head of the household, the one who had to make the important decisions, take responsibility. A fact that he was made to understand only too well when he and Anne visited their mother the following Sunday.

The tubercular ward at the Isolation Hospital was separated into single rooms with the front wall of glass, with French windows which opened to the elements when required, so that the patients, although in bed, were able to fill their lungs with good clean air. There was a round window between rooms where Chrissie Sharpe said patients stared at one another, like fish in a bowl.

Her condition had made her less than robust, but Jed was shaken to see how rapidly she was deteriorating.

'Hello, Mum. You're looking ravishing!' he teased as he showed her a basket of fruit that Elsa had made up for him.

Handing over a bunch of flowers, Anne kissed her mother. 'This is such a beautiful view,' she said as she looked over the sweeping lawns and large fir trees.

With a wan smile Chrissie said, 'It is, right enough, but given the chance I would sooner be boiling a pile of dirty clothes in my own scullery.'

'It'll be some time before we let you do that,' said Jed, 'even when you do come home. You will need to build your strength. Never mind, Anne will take care of you.'

Chrissie chuckled softly. 'Well things must have changed a great deal then. Domesticity was never our Anne's way of life.'

'We manage between us,' her daughter said, hoping her brother wouldn't let her down.

'She manages just fine,' he said.

One of the nurses entered the room and quietly said, 'Mr Sharpe, could you spare a minute? The doctor would like a word.'

Jed felt as if an iron-clad fist had taken hold of his heart as he stood up. 'Won't be long, Mum.'

'Sit down, Mr Sharpe,' said the doctor when Jed entered his office. 'You have no doubt noticed how your mother's condition has deteriorated?'

Jed nodded. 'I was shocked when I saw her today. It's only been a week since I was last here, but the change is very noticeable.'

'There is no easy way to say this, but your mother doesn't have much longer, I'm afraid, and I want you to prepare yourself and your young sister for the inevitable. We will of course keep her as comfortable as possible.'

'How long?' Jed could scarcely bring himself to ask.

'Three weeks, a month at the most.'

Burying his head in his hands, he murmured, 'Sweet Jesus!'

'I understand that your father is away at sea?'

'Yes, he's working on a cruise-liner sailing round the world.'

'Any chance of getting him home in time?'

Shaking his head, Jed said, 'No. He's about due to dock in Australia.'

'That's tough on you, my boy,' the doctor said.

'I'm used to it by now, but I do wish the old man was around at this moment.'

The doctor nodded. 'I'm sure you do. There's nothing else I can say, except that I am sorry. Go back to your mother now. The tea trolley should be round in a minute. If there is anything you need to know, just ask. My nursing staff are here to help in any way we can.'

'Just don't let her suffer!'

'I give you my word.' He stood up and shook hands with Jed, and patted him sympathetically on the shoulder.

Jed walked out of the building and took out a cigarette. He had to try to get his head round the dire news. How was he going to break it to Anne? Did his mother know? He had forgotten to ask the doctor. He paced up and down as he smoked, but still he couldn't take it all in. Eventually he ground the stub beneath his feet and walked back into the hospital.

'You're just about in time,' said Chrissie. 'I can hear the trolley down the corridor. It'll be a few minutes before they get here. Give our Anne some money to go to the shop and buy me some of those custard cream biscuits. I really fancy one.'

Once Anne had departed, Chrissie patted the bed. 'Come and sit here, son.' When Jed had done so, she took his hand and said, 'The doctor gave you the news, did he?'

He looked at his mother, amazed at her calmness. 'You know, then?'

'I've known for quite a while, even before I was told.' She stroked his cheek. 'You forget, I watched Auntie Florrie die. I know the signs.'

Tears welled in his eyes. 'Oh, Mum.'

'Now you listen to me. You'll have to arrange everything, as your dad will be away. In the top drawer of the chest of drawers in my bedroom, you'll find a Co-op book. I've been paying in for my funeral.'

'You what?'

'I just had a feeling, and your dad was earning good money, so it seemed only sensible. I don't want anything fancy, but I would like the hymn "There is a green hill far away". It's my favourite. I know it should be sung at Easter, but never mind.'

'You've given this a great deal of thought, haven't you?'

'Well, love, lying here for months on end, there doesn't seem much else to think about.'

'You could think about getting better!'

'Oh, I did that in the beginning, bless your heart. I didn't bloody well want to die, our Jed . . . but in the end, I had to face up to it.'

'You are an extraordinary woman,' he said in a choked voice.

'No, just practical. When you're married to a seafarer, you have to be. Now you'll have to watch over our Anne. Try to keep her on the straight and narrow.'

'What do you mean?'

'She has big ideas, always had, but under all that she's just a lost little girl.'

The conversation stopped there as Anne arrived at the same time as the tea trolley, and they sat drinking and chatting with Chrissie until visiting time was over.

On the bus ride home, Jed was mentally searching for the words that would help him to break the news to his sister once they were inside their own house, and he was finding it very difficult.

He made some sandwiches and a cup of tea, thinking it best to wait until Anne had eaten because once he had given her the bad news she wouldn't feel much like it.

After the meal, Jed took a deep breath and said, 'You know the doctor called me out today?'

'Yes,' she said, gulping the last of her tea and pouring another cup.

'I'm afraid he didn't give me good news about Mum.'

She stopped pouring and asked anxiously, 'What did he have to say?'

'I expect you noticed as I did that she didn't look so well.'

Anne almost dropped the teapot, and with widening eyes she repeated her question. 'What did he say?'

'He said that she was deteriorating and that she didn't have much longer in this world.'

The colour drained from her face. 'Are you telling me that Mum is going to die?'

He couldn't speak but just nodded.

'Did he say how long?'

'A month at the most.'

The scream of anguish that came from his sister was like the cry of an injured animal. She stood up, knocking her chair backwards, and swept the cups and saucers from the table, sobbing, 'No, no, no!'

Jed stood and tried to take her into his arms to comfort her, but she punched and pummelled him until he had to force her arms down by her sides. Then he held her in an iron grip and tried to calm her, as she sobbed as if her heart would break.

It was some time before Anne quietened and Jed released his hold. Taking a handkerchief from his pocket he wiped his own eyes, for they had cried together, releasing their shared grief.

'What are we going to do after?' she wailed. 'Who will look after me?'

'I will, of course. Haven't I always done so?'

'Does Mum know?'

'Yes. We talked about it when you went for the biscuits.'

'Talked about it . . . talked about it? How could you both do that? How could she talk about dying?'

'Our mother is a wonderfully practical woman; she's had to be all these years with Dad away. She was the one who brought us up really, if we're honest.'

'He should be here. Can't we get him home?'

Shaking his head, Jed said, 'No, love. He's on the other side of the world. But don't you worry, Anne. As long as I'm alive, I'll take care of you.'

'But what if you get married? What then?'

Despite their sadness, he smiled. 'I haven't got anyone in mind, but even if I had, there will be a home for you wherever I live, so stop worrying.' He rose from the chair and began to pick up the pieces of broken crockery. 'Why don't you go to bed?' he said. 'Bathe your face in cold water first, because it's all swollen.'

She kissed him unexpectedly on the cheek. 'You are a good brother.' And she fled towards the stairs.

Jed heaved a huge sigh as he put the broken pieces in the dustbin. Now he was really worried. Anne's reaction had been so drastic it had taken him by surprise, and he knew that he was going to have to handle her very carefully during the next few weeks if he wanted her to be able to cope with the loss of their mother. If only their father were here!

He had to be strong for his mother and his sister, but right this minute he needed someone to be strong for him, to help him hold it all together. Never had he felt so alone.

CHAPTER TEN

Over a shared pot of tea and some toast the next morning, Jed glanced at the pale face of his sister and asked, 'Do you feel like going to work? I can make a phone call to tell them you're not well.'

She shook her head. 'I couldn't sit in an empty house all day thinking. I'll be better off keeping busy.'

But when she left the house her mind was in a haze, and she wandered aimlessly towards the park where she sat, alone on a bench. Here she gazed at the birds pecking around, looking for food, and was vaguely aware of pedestrians passing by, but her mind remained blank. She tried to face the fact that soon she would be without a mother. It had been a long time since Chrissie had been at home leading a normal life and it seemed to Anne that she had been in the hospital for ever, but at least she could go and visit her, hold her hand. The thought of not being able to do this was more than she could bear, the feeling of pain she felt at the thought indescribable.

Like a zombie, she rose from the seat and walked towards Kingsland market, entering the area without looking left or right until she stood before Clive Forbes's pitch.

It was a little early for business. Clive emerged from the interior of his van and saw the young girl standing before him. He was about to berate her for bothering him when something about her demeanour stopped him. He slowly climbed down from his vehicle and walked round the front of his display until he stood and looked at her.

'Anne, what's wrong?' he asked, because clearly something was.

She looked up at him. Her eyes seemed to be expressionless. 'My mother is dying,' she said in a flat voice.

'Oh my God!' he murmured to himself. The last thing he needed was a distraught girl hanging around; it would put off the punters. Putting an arm round her he led her to the front of his van and sat her in the seat. Searching around, he found the vacuum flask he had filled with tea, and unscrewed the top. He poured some into a cup, then added two spoonfuls of sugar. Handing it to her, he said, 'Here, drink this.' Then he walked round the van and climbed in the other side.

'Now, tell me all about it.'

A villain he might be, but Clive Forbes wasn't entirely heartless, and as he listened to the sad tale he put an arm round the girl and held her, giving her some comfort.

'Life can be tough, love,' he said, 'but it is better for your mum to go to a better place than to suffer in this one.'

'I know, but it doesn't hurt any the less for knowing that.' The tears trickled down her cheeks. 'I was supposed to be going to work, but can I just sit here instead?'

'Of course you can, but I'll have to leave you and take care of my customers, you realise that, don't you?'

She just nodded and sipped her tea.

As he worked he wondered just what he was going to do with the girl. He didn't want Jed to come round causing trouble, so he needed to get rid of her before he closed. He glanced across at Elsa – and wondered.

Towards the end of the day, Clive walked over to Elsa's pitch as she was about to pack her goods away. 'Can I have a word?'

'You don't usually ask,' she said.

'Look, I have a bit of a problem. Young Anne Sharp has been

sitting in my van all day. She's in a bit of a state as she's been told her mother is dying.'

'Oh, dear. I am sorry to hear that.'

'I've given her cups of tea and a sandwich, which she hardly touched, but she needs to go home, and it wouldn't be right if I took her.'

'Whyever not?' asked Elsa.

He grimaced. 'Her brother and me, well, we don't see eye to eye and he wouldn't be best pleased to think his sister had been with me all day.'

'Would you like me to have a word with her and see what I can do?'

'I would be grateful. If you give me the keys to your lock-up, I'll put your stuff away for you.'

She handed him the keys, then walked over to the van, opened the door on the passenger side and climbed in.

'Hello, Anne. I hear you've had some sad news.' She took the girl's hand.

Some time later they both emerged from the vehicle and Elsa said to Clive, 'I'm walking home with Anne. Thanks for putting my stuff away.'

Breathing a sigh of relief, Clive said, 'That's fine.' Looking at Anne he asked, 'You all right now?'

She gave a wan smile, and said, 'Yes. Thanks for letting me stay. I knew you would take care of me.'

Elsa looked at him and raised her eyebrow. 'I never figured you for a hero, Clive,' she said quietly, then walked away with her young friend.

I'm not a bloody hero, he thought, and the words 'I knew you would take care of me' sounded like trouble to him. Sorry as he was for the kid's predicament, he certainly didn't want her clinging to him for moral support. Anne was only a flutter for the moment, that was all. He didn't want her getting any daft ideas, oh dear me no.

When the girls arrived at the Sharpes' house, Anne caught Elsa by the arm. 'My brother wouldn't like it if he knew I was with Clive,' she said.

When Jed opened the door, Elsa said, 'Anne didn't feel like work after all, so she stayed with me in the market, but she's all right.'

Thanks,' said Jed. 'I was worried about her. Come in and have a cup of tea.'

The room was clean and tidy and there was an appetising aroma of hot food, which made Elsa realise how hungry she was.

'Stop and have a bite to eat,' suggested Jed. 'I bought a meat pie down the road and some chips, but there's far too much for the two of us.'

Anne murmured, 'I don't want anything.'

Holding out her hand to the girl, Elsa led her to a chair, saying, 'Now then, the best thing you can do to help your mother at the moment is to keep going. She doesn't need to worry about you, not at this time.'

Jed shot her a grateful look.

As she sat down, Anne said, 'That's the worst thing, you know, not being able to help her, not really.'

'You are so very wrong, love. Your mother, you tell me, has prepared herself for this journey she has to make, and you must do the same. Don't pretend it isn't going to happen. She's faced up to it and so must you. You just need to make her final days the happiest she can remember. Spend time with her. These will be precious moments to all of you, I promise. The memories you will have will be so much better than if you let sadness overtake you. The time for tears is later. Not now.'

Anne thought about it and said, 'Yes, you're right. At least now I know what I *can* do. Before I just felt numb.' Turning to her brother she said, 'We must do as Elsa says.'

'I agree. We can go to the hospital this evening if you like.'

Nodding, Anne said, 'Yes, let's do that. I'll pop to the corner shop and buy some magazines for Mum.'

When they were alone, Jed said to Elsa, 'Thanks. I didn't know how I was going to handle Anne. She was hysterical last night when I told her the news.'

'She's young, but I think you'll find she'll grow up quickly in the next few weeks.' Rising to her feet, she said, 'I must be off. If there is anything I can do, let me know.'

When she arrived home, she told her mother the sad news.

'They were always a sickly family,' said her father, who overheard the conversation. 'The aunt died of TB and from what I heard she wasn't the only one. And that Jed is as thin as a rake.'

'Wiry, I would say,' said Elsa firmly. 'There is a difference. Don't go wishing TB on him, for goodness' sake!'

George returned to his paper and Elsa pulled a face at her mother. 'Old misery!' she whispered.

A little while later, Peter called unexpectedly. 'Come down the pub for a drink, darling,' he said. 'I've something exciting to tell you about.'

They settled in the saloon bar with a small glass of bitter each before Peter explained. 'I have been given a special case to follow.'

'Really? Whatever is it? I don't know when I've seen you so excited.'

Glancing around, making sure they couldn't be overheard, he said, 'I am now a crime reporter! There are rumours of a smuggling ring operating in London and along the south coast and I am looking into it. This could be my big chance, Elsa.'

'Crime reporter! Isn't that a bit dangerous?'

'Nah! But it is far more interesting than local events. The editor said he felt I was the man for the job.'

'What's it all about, Peter?'

'Sorry, darling, but I can't divulge that kind of information . . . and anyway, it's better that you know absolutely nothing.'

Frowning, she said, 'Now stop being dramatic!'

'This could be big, Elsa, I'm not kidding, so the less anyone knows, the better.'

'You sound like a spy, and what's more you love it!'

'Bloody right I do. This is just the sort of thing I've been longing to get my teeth into. If it all works out, this could take me to Fleet Street and the big time, then we can get married.'

'I don't want you involved with anything dangerous,' she warned.

'Now just a minute, Miss Carter. You told me off the other day for telling you what you could and could not do. Well, the same goes for me. This is my job, this is what I want to do – and I will do it!'

Elsa smiled to herself. Of course he was right. Peter was good at his job and deserved to move up the ladder. Who was she to try to deny him that?

'Just be careful is all I'm saying.'

'You know me, love. A devout coward,' and he laughed.

'You are my hero and you know it,' said Elsa.

'I have always said you have impeccable taste, young lady. Give us a kiss!'

'Peter! Behave yourself,' she said, laughing, as he kissed her cheek. 'What will people think?'

'That I'm a lucky chap, that's what. Come on, let's find a park bench on the way home where we can have a cuddle.'

In the park he told her he would be away for a while.

'Away? Where?'

'I've got some leads to follow up in London and I'm not sure just how long it will take me.'

Frowning, Elsa said, 'These leads – are they to do with the story?'

'Yes. I have to meet someone who has information to sell, and then I'll take it from there.'

'Are you sure this isn't just too big for you? Aren't you afraid that you could be taking on too much, and be in danger, poking about looking for clues?'

'That's what a good reporter does, Elsa. They don't spend their lives reporting on dog shows and the Women's Institute, you know! And as for its being too much for me to handle, well, I thank you for the faith you have in my capabilities.'

She knew she'd hurt his feelings. 'No, of course not. I didn't mean that at all. You are good at what you do.'

'Yes I am, and this gives me the chance to show what I'm made of and no one is going take that from me.'

It was with a certain coolness that Peter kissed Elsa goodnight at her front door.

'Take care,' she said.

'I will. I'll let you know as soon as I'm back. Don't worry about me, Elsa. I can take care of myself.'

'Of course you can.'

But as she watched him walk away, she wondered what lay ahead for him and was filled with unease.

Fanny Braxton was absolutely livid. When a gentleman had entered her booth this morning she thought she had a punter.

'Sit down, my dear, and let Cassandra look into your future. But before I do, that'll be two shillings, please.'

The man had taken a seat, but had then handed over a printed letter to her.

'Mrs Braxton, this is a letter of notice from the council. You must vacate this pitch on the pier in seven days' time.'

'You what?'

'We have been inundated with complaints from your clients over a long period of time, and now we have to ask you to leave. The pier is a place of pleasure for the people of Southampton and of course a source of revenue for the town council. If the townsfolk who use the pier are unhappy it reflects on us, and your clients are very unhappy.'

'And what am I supposed to do to supplement my income if I leave here?'

He gave her a hostile stare. 'That, I'm afraid, is your problem, but let us get one thing very clear.' He stood up, towering over her. 'There is no *if* I leave here. You will vacate this property by noon seven days hence – the date is on the paper – or you will be forcibly removed by the bailiffs. Good day to you, madam.'

The gentleman walked away with expletives from the mouth of the fortune-teller ringing in his ears. Shaking his head in disgust, he carried on walking.

Fanny slumped into her chair, unable to believe what had just befallen her. What the blazes was she to do? How was she to earn a crust? Taking out a cheroot from a box on the small table beside her, she lit it and tried to think.

She was too old to get a job so whatever she did it would have to be from home. She puffed a smoke ring into the air, her gnarled hands on the table, fingers tapping as she racked her brains. Unable to gather her thoughts, she stepped outside and walked over to the railings, staring at the ripples lapping against the side of the pier. Nothing came to mind.

As she turned back to walk into her booth a torn scrap of paper blew around her feet. Tutting, she picked it up and looked at it. It was a piece out of the local *Echo*, and as she read it she realised it was a section from the Births, Marriages and Deaths column. At the foot were the entries under In Memoriam. As she read the entries she smiled. She now knew exactly how she would earn her living. Those who were grieving were always looking for a way to communicate with their dear departed, and she would be the one to help them! It was an inspired idea, and what's more she could charge a lot more money. People would pay anything to talk to or hear from those who had left them.

As she returned to the booth she thought she would change her name and advertise as a medium. Madam something would do; she'd think about that later. Besides, being at home could be a benefit. The summer weather wasn't always predictable and many a time she had sat and shivered in the strong sea breezes which had blown on to the pier. No, the council had in fact done her a favour. She'd close up and go and have a drink to celebrate.

'Bloody hell,' remarked the barman to his mate as he looked across at Fanny nursing a whisky mac, 'what's come over that old biddy? She's usually such a miserable soul, and look at her now, sitting with a smile on her face.'

'Perhaps somebody has died and left her some money.'

Madam Carlotta, thought Fanny. Yes, I like that. I'll dye my hair black and wear a mantilla, and a large cross on a chain round my neck. And she cackled softly to herself.

CHAPTER ELEVEN

Peter Adams rented a room in a bed and breakfast at the Elephant and Castle. The landlady seemed a pleasant sort who rattled off the house rules, and then offered him a cup of tea.

'I don't have no women in the rooms, young man,' she said, 'so don't you try sneaking one in when me back's turned.'

'Not me, missus. I'm engaged,' said Peter.

'Ah, ain't that nice? Well, you make sure you keep your nose clean, then. What you doing in the Smoke anyway? You ain't a Londoner.'

'Looking for a job,' he said. 'I fancy London wages will be better, then me and my girl can get married.' He had no intention of telling anyone his real reason for being in the city.

'Well, I always says, there's always work for those who really want it and who ain't too fussy what they does. Well, best be gettin' on. You keep your room tidy, mind.'

'Yes, missus, I certainly will, and thanks for the tea.'

After he'd unpacked his bits and pieces, Peter left the lodging house and made his way to a pub in Blackfriars, where he'd arranged to meet his informant. Peter was to carry a copy of the *Daily Mirror*, buy a pint and sit at a table near the door of the snug bar with the paper face up on the table in front of him

His fear as he entered the pub was that he wouldn't be able to carry out the instructions, as the place would be packed. Luck was with him. It was too early for the rush to begin, and he sat and waited in the designated area. His heart was pounding and he lit a cigarette to calm his nerves. I feel like a bloody spy, he thought as he sat looking round in what he hoped was an inconspicuous way.

Several people wandered in and out during the next half hour. Looking at his watch he checked that the timing was right. Whoever he was supposed to meet was late. He emptied the contents of his glass and was about to get to his feet and order another when a man who had been standing at the bar wandered over.

'You Adams?' he asked.

'Yes, that's right. Who wants to know?'

The man glanced down at the paper and said, 'Sorry you had to wait, but I needed to be sure you was alone. What's your poison? Bitter?'

'Yes, thanks.' He watched the stranger as he waited to be served. He was dressed in working clothes and was wearing a flat cap. If you walked into the bar the man would be almost invisible, so ordinary was his appearance. Peter smiled to himself. Very clever, he thought.

The stranger sat beside him. 'What I have to tell you has to be worth a few bob,' he said quietly.

'That all depends,' said Peter, 'and I'll have to be the judge of that.'

'There's a pretty well organised circle in the East End selling smuggled goods.'

'What kind of goods?'

'Furniture, paintings, faked antiques.'

'That's a pretty wide range of stuff,' Peter remarked.

'Well, you see, this is a big organisation. It stretches across the Channel to different parts of Europe. France, Germany and Amsterdam.'

'Bloody hell!'

'I told you, this is big stuff, and what's more I'm putting my bloody neck on the line even talking to you.'

'Then why are you doing it?'

The man sighed. 'Well, look at me. I'm a working class bloke, trying to scrape a living, always will be, but now, if I'm careful, I have a chance to earn a nice large bit of dosh and then for once in my life I can give my family what they deserve. Move to the country or by the sea somewhere.'

Still a little sceptical, Peter asked, 'How do you know about this scheme? As you say, you're an ordinary bloke.'

The man smirked. 'I work in a warehouse used for storage and some of this stuff is being hidden there. A lot of it is kosher, but some isn't.'

'But how do you know what is being stowed? I assume it is all highly secret.'

'Course it is. But I'm a nosy bastard, and I keeps me ears and eyes open. I came across some of it by accident, then I started to put two and two together. I know where they keep the two manifests for the goods.'

'Two manifests?'

'Yes. One for the Customs and the other for the bosses.'

'Have you seen any of the bosses?'

Shaking his head the stranger said, 'No, they don't show themselves. It's only the foreman and his mate. They runs it all.'

'You are putting yourself in great danger, er . . . what can I call you?'

'Charlie. Just Charlie.'

'Look, Charlie, I want this story badly, but then that's my trade, but you . . . do you realise just what can happen to you if this lot find out you've been snooping?'

'Of course I do. Think I'm stupid?'

'No, of course not, but are you sure you want to carry on with it?'

'Only if you can make it worth my while. How much are you prepared to pay me for this information?'

'I'll have to talk to my boss first,' Peter said. 'This is far bigger than we realised.'

'Fine. I'll come back here same time in two days' time. But now you listen to me, my young shaver. I want enough money to get out of the Smoke. If you do your job right and this all blows sky high, I need to be long gone, do you understand?'

'Yes I do, Charlie, and I must say this all sounds very genuine. But you must give me something to take to my boss, something that backs up your story. So far it's only been words. I've no proof of what you've been telling me. My editor won't even discuss money unless you can give me something concrete.'

'I thought about that, so I've got this.' He handed Peter a slip of paper.

'What is it?'

'It's an invoice. As you can see it's on the company's headed paper. It looks all right, and most of it is, but there are two paintings listed there.'

'So?'

'Well I happen to know that the actual paintings are quite different from those on the list. I overheard them talking about it.'

'But that could easily be detected by the Customs if they were opened.'

Charlie tapped the side of his nose. 'They wouldn't, because they've had another picture painted over them. That's easily cleaned off and then underneath you have something worth thousands.'

'But if the painting's well known, it can be traced.'

'Not if it's in a private collection, in a place nobody sees.'

Peter sat back and ruminated over the facts. He knew that some collectors would pay dearly for something that only they themselves could enjoy. He could never figure that. Surely if something was valuable and beautiful, you would want to show it off to your friends? But of course if it was stolen goods . . .

'I'll keep this,' he said, pocketing the sheet of paper. 'I'll ring my editor and I'll see you back here, day after tomorrow, at the same time, and for goodness' sake, Charlie, don't do anything rash!'

'No bleedin' fear of that. I already knows too much for me own good.' He downed the last of his beer and, getting to his feet, said, 'Cheerio, mate. See you later.'

Peter made for the nearest phone box, reversed the charges and spoke to his editor. He told him what had transpired in the bar.

'Do you think he's telling the truth?' the editor asked.

'Yes, I do. The invoice looks genuine enough, and don't ask me why because I can't tell you except to say it's a gut reaction, but I think we are on to something really big.'

'Call me tomorrow in the afternoon after I've talked to the boss.'

'Does anyone else in the office know what I'm here for?' Peter asked.

'Not at the moment. Why?'

'I'd like it kept that way, just you and the boss knowing, because if this is true blue, I could be in danger if I start to dig around. And the fewer people who know, the safer I'll be.'

'Yes, you're right. I'll keep a lid on it. Call me in the morning.'

Whilst Peter was doing his cloak and dagger stuff in London, Elsa's life was, by contrast, very quiet. She was busy at work, of course, but she was missing Peter already and he'd only been gone twenty-four hours. Anne had not been back to the market so she assumed the girl was at work, and hoped she was being brave in such sad circumstances.

Clive had just nodded over to her, but hadn't said anything more about the incident. Elsa was quite sure he wouldn't want to become involved either. Being a knight in shining armour in a young girl's eyes was only worth it if he got something out of it, and she hoped that Anne wouldn't turn to the market trader for comfort again, as Elsa wasn't at all sure she'd get it. Anne wouldn't be able to take rejection as well as her mother's imminent demise.

Later that afternoon, Elsa saw Jean-Paul approaching. She was in a quandary. What was she to do if she was invited out to dinner again? Peter hadn't liked the idea at all.

The Frenchman stopped by her stall. He kissed her hand and said, '*Bonjour, chérie*. I will come and see you in a moment,' and then walked over to Clive.

The two men walked round the front of Clive's vehicle and out of sight, where they stayed for several minutes before appearing again, still deep in conversation. The market trader, she saw, was holding a small bag, which looked as if it was made from leather, but he slipped it into his inside pocket as he spoke. Eventually the Frenchman turned and walked back towards her.

Elsa felt her heart begin to pound. Was it because he was smiling at her, or because she knew if he asked her out again, she would go?

'Will you have dinner with me again this evening?' he asked.

Thinking she really ought to consider Peter and his wishes a little, she said, 'Tomorrow is my half day. I could manage lunch then; would that be all right?' Surely lunch was safer than an evening meal, and she did so want to know more about this man. She told herself it would help her fiancé but in her heart she knew she was the curious one.

'That would be fine,' he said. We could spend the whole afternoon together. What time will you be free?'

'About one thirty.'

'I'll meet you outside the hotel, and we'll take a taxi to the Cowherds Inn. They tell me it is nice there.'

'Yes it is,' she said.

'I'll see you tomorrow then, unless you care to meet me for a drink later?'

'I'm sorry,' Elsa said, 'but my mother and I have plans.'

'Of course, I understand. *A bientôt.*'

As Jean-Paul left the market, Clive Forbes sauntered over. 'The froggy likes you.'

'Don't call him that,' she protested, glaring at Clive. 'He has a name. Or at least refer to him as the Frenchman . . . or gentleman.'

'Oh my, very touchy, aren't we? What would your young man say if he knew you were playing up to him?'

'I am certainly not playing up to him!'

'My girl, I think thou dost protest too much. Bet you didn't know I was familiar with Shakespeare? I am a man of hidden talents if only you would take the time to find out – and I'm not some bloody foreigner!'

Elsa was at a loss for words, because she was feeling somewhat guilty about accepting Jean-Paul's invitation, knowing that Peter would object if he knew. But there . . . he wasn't around and goodness knew when he'd be back, and as she'd told him, she could take care of herself.

'One day you'll realise that I'm not such a bad bloke,' Clive insisted. 'You'll come round, you see.'

As he walked away whistling, Elsa thought, Pigs might fly, Clive Forbes!

At lunchtime the following day, Elsa was sitting at a table at the Cowherds Inn, studying the menu and listening to the lilting voice of Jean-Paul.

'I see they have *moules marinière* on the menu. Why don't we have those to start with?'

Elsa studied the menu, and saw that the dish was mussels. 'I have never had them,' she said with a worried frown.

'Then you must try. We will share them and I'll also order 'ors d'oeuvres as well, just in case you prefer that.' His eyes twinkled. 'Come along, *chérie*, be adventurous. After all, I'm not asking you to eat frogs' legs!'

'I should hope not!'

He looked at her with amusement. 'If I suggested leg of lamb, you would not object, would you?'

'Of course not.'

'Of course not, how very British! But you eat that and enjoy, so why pull a face at frogs' legs? It doesn't make sense.'

Laughing quietly, Elsa said, 'It's only because we are not familiar with the idea. That's all.'

'Yes, the roast beef, well done, overcooked, served with watery cabbage. It makes me want to cry!'

'I can see you need educating into the English cuisine. You know nothing until you've tasted Lancashire hotpot, roast pork with lots of crackling, or pigs' trotters! And there's tripe and onions, toad in the hole, and my Dad's favourite, black pudding.'

'It all sounds very exciting, Elsa. You must take me in hand,' he said as he kissed her fingertips. 'You know, they say a way to a man's heart is through his stomach.'

Pulling her hand away, Elsa said, 'You really disappoint me, Jean-Paul. That doesn't sound French and romantic at all. I expected something quite different from you. Now you make the men in France sound exactly the same as the English.'

'But I would feed you strawberries, dipped in champagne. Is not that romantic?'

'Well, it's different.'

'You must come and stay with me in Paris. I will show you how the French live. You would love it!'

'You are an impossible man,' Elsa complained. 'As if I could do that. Think of my reputation – it would be ruined. My parents would disown me.'

He rocked with laughter. 'Oh, the stuffy English. Darling Elsa, wouldn't it be worth the excitement? Wouldn't it be wonderful to spend a few days in a different country, trying a different culture?'

'And staying with you? Do you live with your parents?'

'*Zut alors!* Of course not. I am not a child, I am a man. I have my own apartment.'

'Where you entertain your lady friends?'

'But of course, why would you doubt it?' He looked at her with just a hint of mischief in his eyes. 'I am French, *chérie*, I have a romantic soul. I need a place to love.'

Elsa started to laugh uncontrollably, tears streaming down her cheeks. Eventually she pulled herself together and looked at Jean-Paul, whose puzzled expression almost set her off again.

'What did I say that was so amusing?' he asked. 'What is so very funny about love?'

'Oh, Jean-Paul, love is many things. It is pure, like a mother's love for her child. It can be destructive and dangerous, it can be fleeting and it can last a lifetime. What made me laugh was you with your love nest. All most ordinary English blokes aspire to is a garden shed! I just found that funny.'

He shrugged. 'I will never understand the English!'

Later, having survived and enjoyed the mussels, Elsa ordered lamb for her main course, laughing as she did so.

'I bet you don't have mint sauce with this in France?'

'No, we have sprigs of rosemary; it is more subtle. But this halibut I ordered is cooked to perfection, I have to admit.'

99

'Do you think if you look at someone, you can guess what food they like to eat?' asked Elsa.

Shrugging, Jean-Paul said, 'Maybe.'

'What about Clive Forbes. What sort of food do you think he would like?'

'I would say bangers and mash!'

'Then he definitely is a garden shed man and not a man with an apartment for his lovers?'

'Ah, I think that Clive would like to drink champagne and eat caviar, although I doubt he would like or appreciate such fine things . . . He already has an apartment, but it is not quite up to the standard he would like, I suspect.'

'You seem to know a lot about him, yet I wonder how this could be as you are so different.'

'Business makes for strange bedfellows, *chérie*.'

Trying to be subtle in her digging for information, Elsa said, 'Don't tell me you are going to open a stall in the market?'

'Now you are being ridiculous! Come along and eat up before your food gets cold.'

She knew from his tone that the subject was closed. The rest of the meal was spent in the talk of fashion and France and the French way of life, as Jean-Paul tried to satisfy Elsa's curiosity about such things.

'It all sounds so colourful,' she said. 'In comparison, life here seems so dull.'

'Life is what you make it, *chérie*. You should be more adventurous. Hold it in both hands and live it to the full!'

Wryly she thought, For him it's fine. Money is no object, but for those without, in whichever country, things are always different. There was no colour in being poor.

After lunch, the Frenchman asked Elsa if she would like to see a film, but the thought of being in such close proximity with him, and in the dark, could be dangerous. He was a fascinating

man. What if he put his arm round her? Would it be a tempta-
tion? She quickly dismissed the notion.

'Why don't we get a taxi back to the town centre and walk
instead?' she suggested. 'The parks are looking lovely. We can
visit the aviary.'

He raised his eyebrows in question. 'Aviary?'

'Not sophisticated enough for you?' she teased.

Shrugging, he said, 'Well, a new experience, certainly.'

The next hour was spent watching the birds and walking
through the roses and the summer bedding, which was a riot of
colour, and sitting and watching the passers-by. After that, Elsa
suggested it was time to walk home.

When they eventually arrived back at the hotel, Jean-Paul asked
if she would like to take tea with him. When she refused he
seemed surprised.

'You don't want any?' he asked. 'I thought everything stopped
in England at four o'clock for tea!'

'Only in some houses,' she told him. 'Thank you for a lovely
time.'

He drew her into his arms. 'Elsa, we could have such wonderful
times together.'

'You behave,' she chided.

'Why would I want to do that?' he said. And then he kissed
her softly on the lips.

CHAPTER TWELVE

The lights were low and in the circle of chairs the sitters held hands, resting them on top of the chenille-covered round table. There was an air of expectation, consternation and fear in the darkened room.

'Is there anybody there?' Madam Carlotta asked as she shook back the mantilla that had fallen forward on to her face. 'Black Feather, chief of the Shoshone, are you there?'

'Who the hell is she talking to?' asked a voice in a loud whisper.

'He's my gatekeeper. Now shut up or he won't appear.'

There was a rustling as people shuffled in their seats, uncomfortable at the thought of a spirit being amongst them.

'I am here, madam,' intoned Carlotta in a deep voice.

'Do you have a message for anyone?'

'There is a young man in spirit, who died in the Great War.'

'That's my Bert,' came a cry from a woman at the table, who was immediately shushed by the others.

'Does this man have a name?' Carlotta asked.

'Albert or Herbert, I can't quite hear him.'

'That's my Albert,' came the whisper. 'Does he have a message for me?'

'If you are Albert Coleman, your wife is among us. Do you have a message for her?' Carlotta demanded.

'It's me, Bert. I want to say to my wife, Madge, I was sorry to leave you, my dear, but please don't worry about me, I am happy here. You take care of yourself.'

'Ask him what I should do about the money,' the woman said.

'What money?' Carlotta demanded sharply, before she realised what she'd done. 'I'm afraid Albert has gone, my dear; you'll have to come back again and ask at a later date. What seems to be the problem?

'My gran died and left me five hundred pounds. I don't know what to do with it.'

'We will have to ask Albert next time.' Carlotta smiled, mentally making note of what she'd just been told, knowing that at least one of her punters tonight would be returning.

Black Feather worked hard that night, bringing many folk from the spirit world into the front parlour of Fanny Braxton. She was always amazed at how much information people gave away about themselves, which was manna from heaven to the likes of her. But she had learned one lesson; she had stopped spreading doom and gloom through her readings. She needed these folk to come back and spend their money, and she had discovered that the spirit world was very lucrative. People would go without to find the fee to talk to their dear departed.

But there were times when she couldn't help being mischievous. She happened to know that Nellie, a barmaid from one of the local taverns, was having an affair with the butcher, despite being a young widow, and when she sat before Carlotta, for a private reading, Black Feather brought forth her late husband, Derek.

'Your hubby is standing beside you. Have a word with him, my dear,' suggested the medium.

'Hello, Derek,' Nellie ventured nervously. 'I miss you.'

'Bloody liar!'

Nellie was shocked and scared. 'What do you mean?'

'I know you are fornicating with that Fred the butcher. I'll have his balls if it don't stop!'

Nellie screamed, jumped to her feet, and ran for the front door like a greyhound out of a trap.

Fanny sat in her chair, rocking with laughter, tears streaming down her face.

There was no laughter for Jed and Anne Sharpe, who were sitting beside their mother's bed in the Isolation Hospital, knowing the end was near. Chrissie kept floating in and out of consciousness. Sometimes she would recognise her son and daughter and give a wan smile.

'How long is this going on for?' asked Anne. 'I don't think I can take much more.'

'Pull yourself together,' snapped Jed. 'You will sit here and be strong. It is the last thing you can do for her!'

'Yes. I'm sorry,' the girl said as she wiped the tears away. Leaning forward she said, 'I love you, Mum. I'm going to miss you so much.' She felt a slight pressure on the hand she was holding.

'She heard me, Jed,' she cried. 'She squeezed my hand.'

'They do say the hearing is the last to go,' he said, and, lifting his mother's hand to his lips, he kissed it. 'It's time to let go, Mum,' he whispered. 'You'll be going to a better place, a place without pain.'

Shortly after, Chrissie Sharpe passed peacefully away.

Elsa was placing some fruit on the front of the display, when a young lad came with a message telling her that Jed's mother had passed away. She was saddened by the news, but relieved that Chrissie would no longer have to suffer.

A little while later she walked over to Clive's stall. 'I thought I'd better let you know that Anne's mother has passed over.'

'I'm sorry to hear that. When did it happen?'

'About an hour ago. Anne will be devastated, so if she comes round, treat her with kid gloves.'

'Frankly I don't want her round here. I really don't want to get involved. She's just a young kid.'

'A pity you didn't think about that before you went out with her!'

'Don't lecture me, Elsa. She begged me to take her out.'

'And of course you couldn't say no, could you? Look, what's done is done; just don't make her life any worse than it is right now, all right?' She walked away without waiting for an answer.

Sorry as he was to hear the news, the last thing that Clive wanted at the moment was trouble. He'd looked inside the leather bag that Jean-Paul had asked him to hold and was shaken to the core when he saw the cluster of fine diamonds there. He didn't know much about gems but to him they looked glorious. He knew he needed to keep a low profile, because there was clearly a great deal of money involved . . . and he was on a percentage. They'd paid him for the two packages he'd held for a few days, which were collected by a stranger who produced the right papers. If this was to be the quality of the stuff he was going to be asked to deal with . . . well, he could see nothing but pound signs before his eyes. Now he could understand the Frenchman's warning about upsetting the people with whom he would be dealing. This was no small potatoes; it was way out of his league. This was the big time and he was part of it!

Jean-Paul was in the capital, in an antiques shop in Knightsbridge. He and the owner were ensconced in a small but plush office, looking at the icons he'd brought over from France. The owner was impressed. He studied them carefully through his eyeglass and touched them lovingly.

'They are in good condition,' he said. 'I know just the client who will buy them, if the price is right.'

Jean-Paul raised an eyebrow. 'Don't let us play games, *mon ami*. We both know their worth and how much we each want from the transaction.' Taking out a pen from his breast pocket, the Frenchman wrote on a card that was on the desk and handed it over to the other man.

'Here is my price.'

The owner looked at it, then at Jean-Paul. 'This is a lot of money.'

'*Oui. C'est exacte.* But you will make a lot of money.'

After a moment's hesitation, the buyer held out his hand. 'You've got a deal,' he said. 'I look forward to your next visit.'

'Of course you do.' Jean-Paul laughed. 'We always make money together, you know that.'

Later he went to Hatton Garden to one of the dealers in fine gemstones, where he had a quiet discussion with the owner. Jean-Paul took a diamond from his pocket and showed it to the jeweller, who examined it closely. After a short sharp conversation, the jeweller took the diamond, handed over some cash, and shook hands with the Frenchman, who left the shop looking very pleased with himself. He hailed a taxi and asked to be driven to the Ritz Hotel, where he sat in the bar until a very well dressed gentleman with a goatee beard joined him.

Shaking the man's hand, Jean-Paul greeted him warmly. 'Henry, how good to see you again.' He called a waiter over and ordered champagne. Smiling at his guest he said, 'After all, we have something to celebrate, *non?*'

'The paintings have arrived?'

'*Oui.* Waiting to be delivered.'

'Any problems?'

'Why should there be, *mon ami*? To the customs, they are of little consequence, just rather nice landscapes by an artist that the art-loving public choose mainly to ignore, and therefore of little value.'

'Then I suggest when we have drunk this rather good bubbly, we visit the gents' lavatory where I can hand over the cash to you in private.' Henry gave the Frenchman a smile of satisfaction, and, stroking his beard, added, 'I can't wait to see them.'

'They will be delivered in three days' time. Will you be there to receive them?'

'Of course, dear boy. I will cancel all my appointments for that day, and my man will be there to clean off the existing landscape.'

'You trust this person?'

'Of course! He's paid handsomely and he's good at his job. Drink up.'

When Peter met up again with Charlie in the pub in the Elephant and Castle, he found his contact all fired up with excitement. 'The pictures are being shipped out day after tomorrow,' he gasped.

'Well done, Charlie! Look, my boss is willing to pay you fifty pounds on account and then if it does come to anything, he'll see you get enough to get your family out of London. How's that? Sorry, but I can't do any better.'

With a nonchalant shrug, Charlie said, 'It's all right, mate. Fifty quid ain't to be sniffed at for the moment.'

'How can I find out where these paintings are going?' asked Peter.

'Only by following the vehicle delivering them. There is never an address on the invoice that's in the books and I might not hear them tell the driver where to deliver them.' Taking his flat cap off he scratched his head. 'Can you get hold of some vehicle to follow them? They are using a furniture van and dropping off a few genuine bits here and there first, to allay suspicions, making it look like a normal day's work.'

'I could hire a motorbike. That would probably be best. I can nip in and out of traffic and it isn't so big a thing to hide if need be.'

'You come with me, young shaver. My mate has a garage, and he sells second-hand bikes. Maybe he can help.'

Peter arrived at his digs later that day on the motorcycle he'd purchased. His landlady said he could keep it in the back yard.

'But no taking it to your room to clean!'

'As if I would!' said Peter.

'Yeah, well I knows all about men and bikes. My brother had one; it drove me poor mother crazy. He'd take it to pieces in her clean kitchen. It's a wonder she didn't swing for him.'

With a chuckle Peter promised that wouldn't happen to her. 'With any luck it won't need any work doing to it.' He certainly hoped it was in as good nick as Charlie's mate had said. It certainly sounded all right when he took it for a test drive, but he found the London traffic a bit hairy, especially as he wasn't familiar with the city streets. Still, he needed some form of transport if things were moving from the warehouse, and now he could leave at a minute's notice, as soon as Charlie gave him the nod. He was getting excited at the prospect.

There were not many people at the funeral of Chrissie Sharpe. Her neighbours were there of course to pay their respects, but apart from their children neither Chrissie nor Bob her husband had any living relations to swell the ranks.

Jed and Anne stood listening to the vicar standing over the open grave. Elsa, nearby, looked round and then up at the blue sky where the sun poured down upon the mourners. Oh, Chrissie, she thought. If only these poor souls could look through their sorrow and grief to see what a wonderful place awaits us all.

Jed Sharpe had organised sandwiches and tea to be served in the front parlour of their house. He and Anne had scrubbed and polished it the day before.

'It has to be spotless,' he proclaimed. 'We can't let Mum down, not on the day of her funeral.'

Anne had worked hard, but she'd scarcely said a word, and Jed was worried about her. Not only was he concerned, but also he didn't know how to cope with her. He was, after all, struggling with his own grief.

The little assembly after the funeral went well. Neighbours spoke to Jed and Anne about their mother and how good she'd been to them before she fell ill, and it was heart-warming for them both to see the high regard in which their mother had been held.

Elsa stayed behind and helped them to clear up after the last mourner had left.

'That was a fine send-off,' she said as they washed and dried the dishes. 'Your mother would have been proud.' She saw the silent tears fall on Anne's cheeks. 'Losing someone dear to you is never easy,' she said. 'And I'm not going to tell you it gets any better, but in time you learn to live with it, and you'll find the good memories more than the sad ones are the ones that live on in your mind.'

Suddenly Anne threw herself into Elsa's arms and wept bitterly.

Jed looked at Elsa and asked, 'What can I do?'

'At this moment, nothing, except take yourself outside with a cigarette and your own grief.'

Jed sat on a low wall, puffing on his Woodbine, but he couldn't shed a tear. He loved his mother dearly, and seeing her suffer had been dreadful, but now it was over he just felt empty. Maybe later he could cry, but not now.

CHAPTER THIRTEEN

Peter Adams was sitting on his motorbike, leather helmet and goggles covering his features, occasionally revving the engine as he waited for the van to leave the warehouse. The adrenalin was flowing as he watched anxiously. The gates opened and he saw Charlie looking at the traffic situation before waving the all clear to the driver. As the van moved out, Charlie glanced quickly over to Peter and surreptitiously gave him a thumbs up sign. Peter slipped in the clutch and set off.

The vehicle made several stops round the city before heading out towards the Berkshire countryside, which made Peter hope he would have enough petrol in his tank to last the trip. Had he not been on such an important journey he could have enjoyed the tree-lined roads, the opulent houses and the peaceful atmosphere denied him among the hustle and bustle of the city, but he had other things on his mind.

It was on the outskirts of Ascot that the van eventually pulled into the drive of a palatial residence. Peter drove past, stopping down the road where he stashed his bike and walked back, slipping in through the front gates and hiding in the shrubbery. From there, he observed two servants unloading the two wrapped pictures, closely observed by a well-dressed gentleman with a goatee beard. The two men from the warehouse went inside and the front door closed.

From the shrubbery, Peter marvelled at the grandeur of the building, which was huge, with a long sweeping drive up to the magnificently carved thick oak door. He desperately wanted a closer look, but realised that was impossible in daylight as he would be seen if he stepped on to the lawn. He would have to wait until nightfall. But if he were going to do that, he'd make good use of the intervening time. Slipping out of the gate, he walked to his bike, climbed on and rode to the nearest small parade of shops where he bought bread rolls, a lump of cheese, a bottle of milk, an apple and a toilet roll. Now he was prepared for all eventualities. Then he made for the local pub.

'Nice place round here,' Peter remarked as the landlord poured him a pint of bitter.

'We like it, sir.'

'I passed a rather palatial house along the road half a mile from here. I thought it looked very splendid.'

'That would be Lord Travers's place, I expect. His family have lived there for generations.'

'Must have plenty of money to own a pile like that, eh?'

'Oh yes. Army people over the generations, but not our Henry. Army didn't interest him; he became an explorer. He's retired now, but is interested in the arts, I'm led to believe. Dapper chap, wears a goatee beard. I'm not into beards myself, but I must admit it suits him.'

'Is there a Lady Travers?'

'Oh aye.'

There was something in the man's voice that made Peter ask, 'What's she like?'

'Very elegant, good-looking for her age.' He leaned forward. 'She has a taste for young men. Bit of a goer if you know what I mean.' He gave a knowing wink and walked away to serve another customer.

Interesting, thought Peter, who wondered what else he would discover during his late-night vigil.

*　　　*　　　*

Elsa was missing Peter dreadfully. Her father was spoiling for a fight; she had sensed it for days. What Elsa didn't know was the reason behind it. The detested Jenkins had been promoted ahead of him to a position that George Carter had certainly thought would be his, and what was worse it would make Reg Jenkins his senior. It made him furious and he had asked for an appointment to see his boss. The intervening days had been difficult, but at last he had his chance to voice his concerns.

'Come in, Carter. Sit down. I expect you've come about young Jenkins's promotion.'

'Indeed I have. I have been with the council for several years and that position was rightfully mine.'

'Come now, Mr Carter. There is no position in this entire building that is anybody's by right. I do agree you have the seniority, however,' he continued as George tried to chip in, 'but it was decided that we could do with a younger man on the job. Someone with perhaps a fresh mind, a few new ideas, and we thought that Jenkins fitted the bill. We have found him very efficient since he first started and I'm sure he won't disappoint.'

George knew he was beaten. He rose from his chair and begrudgingly said, 'Thank you for your time.'

Once back in the office, he glared at Jenkins. Bloody little creep, he thought. He's so far up the boss's backside it's amazing he can't see his tonsils. By the end of the day he was so fed up, he thought he'd pop into the pub and have a drink. Drown his sorrows.

As he sat with his first pint of beer, he went back over his working life. He had been proud to be a white-collar worker when most of his school chums had ended up working in the docks, doing manual work. He had been the one with a 'position'. He had done well, he mused, although he hadn't risen to any great heights, but he had expected to be promoted to office manager. He would have been satisfied with that. If he were honest, he wasn't really ambitious. The idea of being responsible for too much was a worry to him. But office manager would have suited him just fine. He took a long swig from his glass.

How he hated that oily Jenkins. Bloody little creep, always sucking up to the bosses. Well, he didn't trust the man! There was something about him that was suspicious. He would certainly watch him carefully from now on. Let's see just what sort of office manager he turns out to be. If he makes just one error, I will be on the little bastard like a ton of bricks. He downed the rest of his drink, rose to his feet and walked out of the bar.

It was now dark, and in the garden of the Ascot abode of Lord Travers Peter stood and stretched his legs. He had settled in the shrubbery, hidden from sight but able to watch the big house. He'd had his picnic and had a couple of cigarettes, hiding the lighting of the match inside his jacket so as not to give away his presence.

He'd watched the goings-on in the house with the aid of a pair of second-hand binoculars he'd purchased in a junk shop he'd found. He was amazed that no one had pulled the drapes, but he supposed with such extensive grounds the occupants wouldn't have to worry about privacy.

Peter had watched as Lord Travers and a few others, after changing for dinner, had seated themselves at a splendid dining table. A good time, Peter thought, for him to get nearer to the house, as everyone would be occupied with the evening meal.

Keeping low, he skirted the building, looking into all the windows, trying to learn the layout of the interior. Some rooms were in darkness, of course, but the others were lit in readiness for the guests to use. Peter marvelled at the comfort enjoyed by the aristocracy. The beautiful house, the elegant furnishings, the servants. He wondered if the butler earned more than he did. Perhaps he was in the wrong job? He chuckled, knowing that he would never want to do any other work.

As he was peering into one room, he drew back a little as an attractive middle-aged lady whom he had seen dining swept through the door. The skirt of her evening dress seemed to float out behind her, the material was so delicate. She seemed restless, marching up and down, until suddenly the door opened and a young man entered. The woman flung herself into his arms and they embraced. Peter was very surprised to recognise the Frenchman he'd seen with Clive Forbes. What had Elsa called him? Jean-Paul Devereux, that was it. Well, that was a turn-up for the books, he thought, and they were behaving like illicit lovers! The couple exchanged a few words and then the woman left. The Frenchman wiped the telltale lipstick from his mouth, checked his appearance in the mirror and left the room.

Peter walked along the wall and found he was looking into the dining room. Jean-Paul had just entered it and was taking his seat. Lord Travers and another gentleman were sitting at the table, drinking port, smoking cigars and chatting. Lord Travers said something that Peter was unable to hear and the three men rose from the table, and left the room.

Peter couldn't see where they were going, which was a pity because he would have found it more than interesting.

Henry Travers led his guests down some cellar steps and unlocked a door, hidden behind a heavy velvet curtain, which led into a large room that was softly lit. Round the walls were paintings of different sizes, encased in glorious frames, the small light over each illuminating the canvas for the viewer's enjoyment.

Jean-Paul approached one. 'This is a Monet.'

'Yes,' said Henry. 'I bought it several years ago. And next to it is a Goya and over there, an early Van Gogh. I have an eclectic taste.'

Jean-Paul stood back to enjoy a very large painting. He puzzled over it for a while then said, 'I last saw this in the Rijksmuseum in Amsterdam. It's Rembrandt's *The Night Watch*. This cannot be the original!'

'Alas no, it is a copy, but a good one. I just love the painting; sadly there is no way I can buy the original. But I can look at this and pretend.'

'It is a very fine copy I must say,' remarked the Frenchman, examining it very closely, running his hand carefully over the canvas.

'Yes, the man has a great talent.'

'Would you give me his address?' Devereux asked. 'I could use a man like that.'

'Yes, I'll give it to you before you leave.'

They looked at the rest of his artefacts, then decided to rejoin the ladies. Just as they were about to enter the drawing room, Henry caught Jean-Paul by the arm.

'A word, dear boy. We do business together; this does not give you the right to my wife also.'

Jean-Paul was visibly shaken.

Henry continued, 'I know that Virginia is like a bitch on heat, but remember, *mon ami*, business and pleasure never mix. Get my drift?'

'Absolutely. My apologies, but I am French: a little flirtation, it is what we do. It's in our blood.'

Lord Travers stilled him with a look that would have cut paper. 'Don't give me that. You are a predator who uses his nationality as an excuse to screw anything you fancy. That does not include my wife. In the country, if we find trespassers and poachers on our land – we shoot them. *Comprenez?*'

'Are you threatening me?'

'Absolutely!'

Jean-Paul was left standing, feeling as if he had been slapped. Had Henry thrown down a glove and offered a duel, he would not have been surprised. But Virginia wasn't going to like a cessation of the relationship, which was in its gloriously exciting early days, before disappointment and possession could possibly spoil things.

It was past midnight and Peter could see no reason to stay on watching the house of the aristocrat. He had discovered that the Frenchman was involved: that made his visit worthwhile, and he knew where the paintings were now housed, although he hadn't been able to see exactly where in the vast house they were stored. He was stiff and tired. He'd filled his petrol tank earlier in the day, so now he headed for his machine and eventually his bed. He thought he would go home tomorrow and meet his editor, get a change of clothing and see Elsa, making sure that she and the Frenchman were not still meeting. He didn't want her involved in any way.

Peter's editor and he were enclosed within a locked office, discussing the stolen paintings, Lord Travers, and Jean-Paul Devereux.

James Booth, the editor, spoke. 'We have to be very careful where we step here. We can't go off half-cocked to the police. We need plenty of indisputable evidence, which will hold up in court. We need to know who else is involved from the Continent, where the bosses are. We have this Devereux chap and one of his buyers, but that's all.' He looked at Peter. 'Do you have a passport?'

'Yes, sir.'

'When Devereux returns to Paris I want you to go too. Nose around; see what you can suss out. Meantime, write up your report, and as long as the Frenchman doesn't travel, take the weekend off. You've done well.'

'Thank you, sir.'

*　　*　　*

After finishing his work in the office, Peter made his way to Kingsland market and Elsa. He had missed her very much, but he was concerned that she may have been in touch with Devereux and now he knew so much more about him, he didn't want Elsa putting herself in any danger. He was therefore considerably concerned when as he entered the market, threading his way between the stalls and their customers, he saw Jean-Paul talking to his girl.

'I am returning to Paris on Monday, *chérie*, and I wanted to take you out for the evening. I thought a trip to the theatre and then, after, dinner somewhere?'

'I am sorry, my friend, but Miss Carter isn't free then or at any time in the future. You see, she is my fiancée, and I don't take kindly to strangers propositioning her. Do I make myself clear?'

'Peter!' Elsa was delighted to see him, but embarrassed at his outburst.

Jean-Paul apologised. 'Forgive me, I had no idea. I have the utmost respect for Mademoiselle Elsa.' Bowing in her direction, he left without another word and walked over to Clive's stall.

Clive, who had seen the exchange, was highly amused. 'Sent you off with a flea in your ear, did he?'

'I am not sure what that means but I can guess. That is the second time in twenty-four hours I have been warned off a woman!'

Clive's laughter was hearty. 'Losing your touch, are you?'

Shrugging, Jean-Paul muttered, 'It would seem so. For a Frenchman, that is a serious matter. Never mind, I have other things to think about. Tomorrow afternoon, a gentleman will call for the small package.'

'The diamonds, you mean?'

'You looked?'

'Don't be stupid, of course I did. I like to know what I'm

holding in case I'm nicked with the goods. I *must* know what I'm holding.'

Jean-Paul laughed and said, 'Show me the pouch.'

Clive went into his van and opened a locked steel box, then returned with the diamonds and handed them over.

The Frenchman counted the contents and, finding everything correct, exchanged them for another pouch.

'What are you doing?' Forbes asked.

'Do you really think I would trust a stranger with the real thing? I had to make sure you didn't take off with them. Well, you passed the test. And so, this gent will give you a note from me. His name is Jacobs. Just hand the stuff over.'

'Do I get a receipt?'

'No, I have already been paid.'

'Good. When do I get mine?'

'Tonight at the hotel. Nine o'clock.'

With a backward glance across at Elsa, who was in earnest conversation with Peter, Jean-Paul left the market.

Clive Forbes watched him walk away with a certain sense of relief. What would have happened if he'd nicked one of the so-called gems or run off with the lot, he wondered.

Elsa was furious with Peter. 'How dare you speak to Jean-Paul like that?'

He tried to take her hand but she shook him off.

'Elsa, I'm sorry, but I have learned a lot about the man over the past few days and he's a crook. I don't want you seeing him. It could be dangerous.'

'Whatever do you mean?' she snapped, still annoyed with him, and embarrassed as well.

'I can't tell you here. Look, I have the weekend off. I have to go home, have a bath, change my clothes and pack my bag ready for the off.'

'Off to where?' she demanded.

'Look, darling, I can't tell you anything here. I'll come round to your house at six o'clock and then we'll go for a meal somewhere and I'll explain.'

'All right,' she conceded reluctantly.

As it happened, Peter was a little early, which was just as well. George Carter, with a couple of pints under his belt and his promotion down the tubes, was feeling belligerent, and had started finding fault, building up to an explosion. Peter's arrival took the wind out of his sails, and as Elsa washed and changed and his wife washed up the dishes in the scullery, George was able to tell Peter about his disappointment. Getting things off his chest defused the situation.

Peter sympathised. 'I've seen that happen many a time, Mr Carter. Some little guttersnipe smarms his way round the bosses, feathering his own nest in the process. It's what happens, sadly, but I always say one thing.'

'What's that?'

'Whatever goes around, comes around. You wait and see if I'm not proved right.'

'Cup of tea, George?' asked Margaret.

'Yes please, and one for young Peter.' He smiled at the young man. 'You speak a lot of sense, and I appreciate your listening to me. Women don't understand such things,' he said quietly.

Peter frowned. He certainly hoped that Elsa would understand what he was about to tell her.

CHAPTER FOURTEEN

Elsa and Peter settled at a table overlooking the water, in a small restaurant near the Old Walls, relics of the original town boundaries.

'Now,' said Elsa firmly, 'what on earth is it that you want to tell me? The way you're behaving is a bit cloak and dagger, isn't it?'

'What I have to tell you, you must promise me you will keep to yourself.'

She gave him a suspicious glance. 'Very well, but you had better not be mucking me about!'

'As if . . .' He grinned. But then he became serious. 'I am investigating a large smuggling racket and I'm sorry to tell you that your Frenchman is deeply involved.'

'How do you know?'

Taking hold of her hand, he said, 'Darling, I can't give you any details, but I have seen it with my own eyes. He is also having an affair with a married woman.'

'Living up to his reputation as a Frenchman, is he?'

'It would seem so, but apart from that, Elsa, he is breaking the law. Now I know you think he's all right, but please, do keep away from him. He's a criminal.'

'What about Clive Forbes? Is he in this too?'

'To be honest I don't know, but it wouldn't surprise me. After all, ask yourself, what would Devereux want with him? Can you see them as friends, drinking buddies?'

Shaking her head, Elsa said, 'No, I can't see that. But Jean-Paul handed him something the other day. It was small; Clive put it in his pocket.'

'Mmm. Sounds a bit dodgy. Keep your eyes peeled for anything unusual, but that's all, Elsa. I hope you understand that I don't want you mixed up with this?'

With a chuckle she said, 'I love it when you're masterful.'

'Don't joke. I am serious.'

'I know, but I'm curious. So what is your next move?'

'I'm following the Frenchman to Paris.'

Elsa looked perturbed. 'Oh, Peter, I don't like that idea at all. What if you get hurt?'

Laughing, he said, 'What can possibly happen to me? I'm only watching, and making notes of his movements, who he meets, stuff like that. Where is the danger there?'

Elsa was at a loss for words.

'Anyway,' Peter said, trying to change the subject, 'how have things been at home with your old man?'

'They have been a bit dicey. He's been in a foul mood for several days, but when you talked to him tonight it seemed to help.'

He gently touched her cheek. 'Your dad has been passed over in a promotion, so he was very upset.'

'Poor Dad,' Elsa said. He was such a proud man, she thought, and she knew that that would really hurt him. And he was good at his job by all accounts, which would have made it much worse. What a pity he felt he couldn't talk to either her or his wife about it.

'Poor Dad,' she repeated. 'Not that I think he's terribly ambitious, but how are we to know if he doesn't talk to us about it?'

'You take after him then,' Peter said.

'Whatever do you mean?'

'Well, you're not exactly ambitious, are you? You have always

121

seemed happy with your lot and marriage to me to look forward to.'

Elsa looked at the satisfied smile on her fiancé's lips and was furious. 'Don't be so damned sanctimonious! How do you know what I want out of life? Have you ever asked me? You make it sound as if I'm not capable of anything more. How dare you!'

Peter was astonished at her anger. 'Bloody hell, love, calm down.'

'Calm down! Do you think that *all* I want out of life is to be your wife?'

His feathers were ruffled now. 'Is that such a bad thing?'

'No, of course not,' she said, 'but Jean-Paul said only the other day I was worth much more, and when I gave it some thought, he was absolutely right! He understands me more than you do.'

'What are you saying, Elsa, that you don't want to get wed?'

'No, not at all, but before that I want to do something with my life . . . like start my own business.'

'And where do you think you will get the backing to do that?' he scoffed.

'To be honest, I don't know, but then I haven't tried yet.'

'You have no collateral.'

She was even more angered by his negative attitude. 'I've got a good pair of hands, a working brain – and I've got charm!' She looked at him and laughed. 'I'll look for someone who wants a partnership. They can put up the money and I'll do the rest.'

'Are you serious about this?'

'Very, and you see, I'll make it happen. Anyway, enough of me and my dreams,' she said, wanting to get off the subject. 'How long do you think you'll be in France?'

Shrugging, he said, 'I'm damned if I know. It all depends what happens.'

'You watch out for those French women,' she warned. 'I've heard they are outrageous and without morals.'

'I've been looking for someone like that all my life.' He laughed.

'Listen to me, Peter Adams, you can look but you must definitely not touch.'

'You are saying you still want to be engaged then, despite trying to climb the corporate ladder?'

'Of course. Me being a success doesn't change that.'

'If you end up making more money than me, I can be a kept man. I quite like the sound of that,' he teased.

'I'll never keep any man so you'd best keep that in mind, you cheeky beggar.'

Later as they snuggled up on the settee together, Peter said softly, 'You really do still want to marry me, don't you, Elsa? You're not having second thoughts? I will be livid if that foreigner has unsettled you.'

Staring into his eyes, she said, 'Of course I do, you goose, but I do want to spread my wings a bit. At least I want to try. If I fail, well at least I've had a go.'

As he held her to him, Peter wondered what other ideas the Frenchman had put into his girl's mind. It was a bit of a worry, to say the least. He wondered also just what his trip to France would uncover. He also wished he spoke the language; if he ever needed help, it could prove a problem. He would just have to be careful. And now he was concerned about Elsa. It was great that she wanted to better herself, but she would be heartbroken if these unexpected plans didn't come to fruition.

When Peter left, Elsa went to her bedroom. She had surprised herself this evening saying she wanted her own business, but ever since Jean-Paul had said she could do better, the idea had festered in her brain. But whom could she ask to back her? The bank wouldn't without some guarantee, of that she was certain. As she lay in bed she racked her brains. Who did she know who had the money? She eventually fell asleep without finding a solution.

* * *

The following afternoon was busy in the market. Danny the pianist had had another row with his boyfriend and was telling Elsa all about it.

'Honestly, darling, I don't know what to do to please him. Whatever I do it isn't enough!'

'Give him his marching orders then,' Elsa suggested. 'There are always other fish in the sea.'

'You're right, of course, but sometimes the devil you know . . .' He picked up his bag of vegetables and walked away.

Ruby looked over at Elsa and grinned. 'Poor old Danny. He's such a lovable old queen. He doesn't deserve to be treated so badly. I'd kick the bugger out!'

'That's what I told him, but I think he's afraid of being lonely.'

'Listen, love, living with the wrong person is bloody lonely!'

Elsa had to laugh. Ruby was full of such pearls of wisdom.

Despite being busy, Elsa spotted a stranger speaking to Clive Forbes. The man was short and stocky. The fact that he was wearing a yarmulke, a skullcap, marked him as Jewish. The two men exchanged a few words and the stranger passed Clive a note. Clive read it, and then took something from his pocket and handed it over. The man turned away and unobtrusively looked at the contents, smiled at Clive, shook him by the hand and left.

Elsa was certain that what had changed hands had been whatever Jean-Paul had left with the market trader. She was intrigued, and Clive was looking very pleased with himself. Sauntering over to his stall, she asked, 'Good sale?'

He became watchful. 'What do you mean?'

'You look as if you have made a good deal . . . the little Jewish chap. Not your usual type of customer.'

He smiled arrogantly. 'I buy and sell to anyone who has the money to deal. That's what trading is all about,' he said.

'I just wondered what you had that he could possibly want, that's all.'

The smile disappeared. 'Why are you so interested in my business?'

'I'm not. But when a stranger comes into the market, I am curious.'

'Curiosity killed the cat, Elsa. And when people start asking questions about my trading, I get really pissed off.'

There was a definite hint of menace in his voice, which chilled her. But she pressed on. 'Whyever would you mind? Unless you have something to hide.'

Walking round the front of his display, he faced her. 'If you know what's good for you, my girl, you will keep your nose out of my dealings.'

'Are you threatening me, Clive?' she asked fearlessly.

'Take it any way you like, darling. But have a care, that's all.' And he walked away.

Elsa found her legs were trembling as she walked back to her own pitch. She had a feeling that these were not idle threats, and she knew she had to be careful in the future.

Later in the afternoon she saw Jean-Paul talking to Clive and wondered what else was going on between the two men, but she stayed behind her stall.

Eventually the Frenchman walked over to her.

'I'm sorry if I caused any trouble between you and your young man,' he said.

'You didn't.' She smiled. 'He misunderstood, that's all.'

'And you didn't tell me you were engaged. That was naughty of you, Elsa. It put me in a difficult position yesterday.'

'A man of your experience? I doubt that.'

'A great pity,' he said. 'I was so looking forward to an evening with you before I return to France.'

'Sorry about that. It would have been nice,' she ventured, 'but I'm afraid Peter wouldn't understand. When are you going back to Paris?'

'I'm catching the eleven o'clock ferry on Monday morning,' he said. 'But I will be back here soon. Until then, sweet lady,' and he kissed her hand, '*au revoir*.'

At least I can tell Peter when he's leaving, she thought. But she didn't like the idea of him following Jean-Paul around. If he was a criminal, as Peter said, it was bound to be dangerous.

Getting Ruby to keep an eye on her stall, she slipped to the nearest phone box and rang the office of the *Southern Daily Echo*, and passed on the information to her fiancé, making sure that Peter understood that the Frenchman just stopped to talk to her and that was all. She also told him about the Jewish man who had spoken to Clive. She omitted telling him of the threats she had received, not wanting to worry him.

'That's great work,' Peter said over the phone. 'But do be careful, darling. We don't know just what we are dealing with yet. I'll try to call round to see you on Sunday. I have a lot to do, so I won't be able to stay long.'

Jean-Paul was having problems of his own. Virginia, Lady Travers, had travelled down to Southampton and was waiting at his hotel for him. He took her into the lounge bar and bought her a drink.

'*Chérie*,' he began. 'We have to stop meeting.'

She looked distraught. 'What do you mean?'

'Your husband knows about us, and has warned me off.'

'Henry is an old fool,' she said dismissively. 'I'll come to Paris; we can meet there.'

'No, Virginia, we can't do that, I'm afraid. Henry and I do business together and I can't undermine that. We have had a wonderful time, but now it has to end.'

'You can't get rid of me that easily, Jean-Paul,' she said angrily.

'Don't be difficult, Virginia, it doesn't suit you.'

'I am not one of your women you can dismiss just like that.'

His voice was cold. 'But I can, Virginia. It's over. I'll call a taxi to take you to the station.' He took her firmly by the arm, stopped at the reception desk, asked for a taxi, and walked her to the hotel entrance and waited with her until the car arrived.

She was livid. As she got into the car she said, 'This is far from over, you wait and see.'

He watched the car drive away, wondering just what she meant. But he had bigger things on his mind. When he returned to Paris he was meeting the two other men who were part of his consortium. They had plans to make about a large shipment to be moved in the near future. Nothing must be allowed to interfere with that.

On her way home, Elsa called into the tattoo parlour and spoke to Jed.

'I've been wondering how young Anne is coping with the loss of her mother, and you too,' she said.

'Come and sit down,' Jed invited her. 'It's kind of you to ask. We muddle through each day. Anne is very quiet, which is more of a worry than when she was being wayward. How about a cup of tea? I've finished for the day.'

'That would be nice,' she said, and followed him into the back room.

Over the tea they chatted and she found herself telling Jed about her plans for her own business.

'That sounds a great idea,' he said. 'You are a good worker and you never make money working for somebody else.'

'You're the second person who has told me that,' she mused. 'But it's finding someone to bankroll me. It's probably just a dream.'

Looking at her, he said, 'I might be interested.'

She was flabbergasted. 'You?'

'Why not? I have a certain amount of money saved, and this business is enough for me, but I might be very interested in backing you, being a silent partner.'

'Oh, Jed, I don't know what to say.'

'There is a small shop coming empty soon in the parade on the east side of the market. I'll make enquiries if you like?'

'But that would mean I would be in competition with my boss, who would have to get someone else to run the stall.'

Jed gave her a hard stare. 'True, but if you want to run your own business, sentiment has little place in your decisions. You have your regulars who would come to you. Your boss might feel that it would be a waste of time to have a stall if you left.'

She looked dubious but then she said, 'He does have a large shop in the town. My stall is only a subsidiary of his.'

Jed smiled at her. 'See, you are already thinking with a business head.'

'I'll have to tell him at once if we get the shop . . . it's only fair, Jed.'

'Absolutely, I agree. That is a point of honour. Shall I make enquiries?'

'That would be wonderful.'

'Let's keep all this under our hats for now,' he suggested. 'If word gets out, the price of the rental might go up.'

Elsa was beside herself with excitement.

'Drink your tea, and I'll lock up, then we'll walk along and take a look at the premises.'

The shop, which was presently trading as an ironmonger's, was just the right size, they decided, as they stood outside looking through the window.

'It's in a perfect place: inside the market and yet you would be out of the bad weather. That would be an advantage,' Jed remarked. 'I reckon this would fit the bill. What do you think?'

'I think it's perfect,' said Elsa, eyes shining with excitement. 'We could keep the counter in the same place; on that wall we could put up shelves with baskets to display the fruit and veg. After all, it must look attractive to bring in the customers.'

'Well, you have a way with display,' said Jed. 'Your stall always looks inviting. The more I think about it, the more I like it.'

'I have no idea how much it would cost to set it up,' she said, suddenly fearful of the consequences.

'We can get together and sort those things out. Where will you buy the fruit and veg?'

'Oakley and Watling's,' said Elsa. 'That's where my boss gets his.'

'We will have to think of a name too.' Jed was warming to the idea as every moment passed.

'How about Carter and Sharpe?'

He grinned broadly. 'I like that. Leave it with me, Elsa. I'll find out all the details and we'll meet again. I'll call and see you in the market when I have any news.' He held out his hand. 'Partners?'

Gripping his hand firmly, she shook it. 'Partners!'

She walked home with a spring in her step. She wouldn't tell Peter about this until it was settled. After all, things could go wrong, but she hoped with all her heart that wouldn't happen. And criminal or not, it was the Frenchman who'd given her the idea that she was capable of running her own business, and she would always be grateful for that, even if it didn't come to fruition.

Unbeknown to Elsa and Jed, Fanny Braxton had been lurking round the corner, listening to their conversation. She was angry that the slip of a girl who had told her she was a fraud was now planning a business with Jed Sharpe. If only there was some way in which she could get her revenge. She wondered off, muttering to herself.

CHAPTER FIFTEEN

Young Anne Sharpe left Woolworth's on her half day. She felt as if she had been through a dreadful illness. Inside she was empty. She just about managed to serve her customers, but she felt like a zombie. Today, however, as she walked through the park, she felt the intensity of grief ease a little and she began to wonder about her future. Jed had said he would always care for her, which was very gallant, but she felt it was unfair; after all, he too had a life. What she desperately longed for was someone to love her. Someone of her own, to cosset and care for her, and the only person she felt anything for was Clive Forbes. Surely he felt something for her? After all, he'd made love to her, hadn't he? She decided to find out, and made her way to the market.

Clive Forbes saw the girl approach and inwardly groaned. After the day she had spent sitting in his van, she'd not been round and he'd breathed a sigh of relief, as he'd not wanted to be involved. Now as she walked towards him, his heart sank.

'Hello, Anne, how are you?'

'Not bad . . . well, you know. Day by day.'

Not knowing what to say, Clive muttered, 'Yes, it must be tough to lose your mother.'

'She was pretty sick for a long time, but I never expected her to die, which was very stupid of me, but I've had to do a lot of growing up lately.'

'Why are you not at work?' he asked.

'It's my half day. I wondered if you would be free later?'

'No, love, I'm afraid I'm really busy. Places to go, people to see, you know how it is.'

'I could come with you.'

'No, you couldn't.'

'I have done before,' she persisted.

'Anne, I told you no. This time it's different.'

She moved a little closer. 'Clive, do you love me?'

The market trader raked his hair with his fingers in agitation. 'Bloody hell, what's got into you, asking me such a thing?'

'I need you to take care of me, Clive. I really need someone.'

What a predicament, thought Clive, gazing at the girl. He didn't want to be unkind to the kid, but no way was he taking her on. But how to let her down lightly? Normally he would have told her to shove off, but her situation was different. Elsa had warned him to be gentle with her, but this was new territory to him.

'I'm sorry, love, but I can't do that. I don't plan to be permanently with any woman for many a year. You're a lovely girl, and we had fun, but you need to find a young man nearer your own age. Meantime, let Jed look after you.'

'But you made love to me!' she cried. 'Didn't that mean anything?'

He looked round, hoping no one had heard her cry of despair. 'Of course it did, Anne, but you must realise, men are different from women in their feelings .'

'In other words, you have sex without love, is that what you mean?'

'That's about it, yes!' He was beginning to lose his patience. 'I fancied a tumble and you were up for it, we both enjoyed it and that was that. It don't mean I've got to look after you now – or later, come to that!'

'You despicable bastard. I hate you!' She turned on her heel and ran away.

Elsa, who had been serving several customers, had been aware of Anne talking to Clive, and was dismayed to see her run past her stall, tears streaming down her face. Oh dear, she thought, that was bound to happen, but a pity it was now when the girl was so vulnerable. She glanced across at Clive who just looked at her and held out his arms, shrugging as if to say, What could I do?

Later in the afternoon when there was a lull in the market, she strolled over to him.

'Young Anne looked heartbroken as she flew past me earlier.'

With a frown he said, 'I know. She wanted me to look after her. I can't do that.'

'Or want to, I imagine,' said Elsa tartly.

'Look, I took her out a few times. That doesn't mean I'm obliged to her in any way.'

'Not if you just wined and dined her,' she said, looking straight at him.

Clive felt his cheeks redden.

'Just as I thought!' snapped Elsa. 'You stupid fool, do you think you can take a young girl like that, make love to her and then cast her aside?'

'Believe me, I didn't have to force her!' Clive was now feeling angry as well as guilty. 'Bloody hell, she kept on following me, inviting me. What else was I to do?'

'Be responsible, turn her down, look after her, talk to her, anything but take her virginity.'

'Saint bloody Joan you are, aren't you? Life isn't like that for a fellow. If it's on offer he takes it. It's being going on since the time when we lived in caves!'

'Precisely! But now we are supposed to be civilised. But like most men your brains are in your trouser pockets!' And she stormed away, outraged by his lack of sensitivity or moral standing.

Ruby came over to her. She too had seen Anne in her upset state and was concerned.

'What's going on?' she asked. 'That Clive been dipping his dick with young Anne?'

'You are very perceptive,' Elsa remarked.

'There's little that I miss in the market,' Ruby said. 'I saw the girl hanging round him. She's pretty and he's a feller, what can I tell you! But she's better off without Clive Forbes, that's for sure.'

'I don't know what to do. Anne is in a very fragile state right now. I'm worried about her,' Elsa confessed.

'You don't think she'd do anything daft, do you?'

'God! I hope not. Perhaps I'd better have a word with Jed, but the only thing is that may make matters worse. What do you think?'

'He'll go bloody mad if he thinks young Lochinvar has had his wicked way with his sister.'

'You're right there. Perhaps I'll try to talk to her.'

When she closed up her stall, Elsa walked round to the Sharpes' house, praying that Anne would be at home. As she wandered through the shabby streets of the poorer area of Southampton, she thought it was enough to undermine the spirit of those who lived there . . . except for the children. She watched some playing hopscotch, the spaces drawn on the pavement with chalk. Children always managed to rise above their surroundings, it seemed.

Arriving at the Sharpes' house, Elsa lifted the doorknocker and rapped it. After what seemed an age, a tearstained Anne answered the door.

'Can I come in?' Elsa asked.

The girl stepped aside and let her enter.

The room was untidy and dirty dishes were piled up in the kitchen sink.

'Good heavens,' remarked Elsa. 'Shall we try to clean up before Jed comes home? He won't be pleased to walk into this place after a day's work.'

Anne just nodded.

'I'll wash and you dry,' said Elsa as she filled the sink with hot water and green soft soap.

As they worked together, Elsa said, 'I saw you in the market this morning. You looked upset. Do you want to talk about it?'

Anne was only too pleased to unburden herself to another woman who seemed sympathetic to her needs.

'I miss Mum, and I'm worried about the future. I just wanted Clive to look after me. I thought he loved me.'

'Did he ever tell you that he did?'

The girl shook her head.

Wiping her hands, Elsa spoke softly. 'Clive Forbes is not the man for you, Anne. He's a chancer. He is only out for himself.' She took the girl's hands in hers. 'I know at this moment everything seems dark, but you are young and lovely, with your whole life in front of you. You don't want to throw it away on the likes of Mr Forbes. In time, you'll meet some nice young man who will love you, take care of you, and, what's more important, make you happy.'

'I'm so frightened and I feel so alone.'

'You are not alone, Anne. You have a brother who would kill for you. He really cares about you, and he too is suffering his own grief. You have lots of friends who care too. You are certainly far from alone.' She took the girl into her arms and held her as she sobbed.

After Anne had composed herself, Elsa made her a cup of tea.

'Look, I have an idea. What I'm about to tell you is a secret, but I am hoping to open my own business in the future. If everything works out, I'll need someone to work with me. Would you be interested?'

At last there was a spark of interest in the girl's expression. 'What sort of business?'

'A shop selling fruit and veg. Your brother and I hope to go into this together, but he would still be in his tattoo parlour, so I'll need someone in the shop.'

'Yes,' said the girl with a wry smile, 'I'd like that.'

'Fine,' said Elsa with a feeling of relief. 'Meantime you continue to work until everything is set up, then you can give your notice. But meantime, keep away from Clive Forbes.'

'I hate him!'

'Well, that's healthy.' Elsa laughed. 'I don't like him much myself.'

'He is attractive, though. The women like him,' said Anne.

'Handsome is as handsome does,' said Elsa. 'He only flatters them to sell his stuff. Now, are you going to be all right?'

'Yes. Thanks for coming round.'

'Listen, love, any time you are feeling down, you come and talk to me. I need you, so I don't want to see you unhappy. A miserable assistant won't sell my goods, you know!'

The girl managed a laugh. 'No, I don't suppose so.'

Elsa rose to her feet. 'I'd best be on my way. Look, my Peter is away for a while. Why don't we go to the pictures tomorrow evening?'

'I'd like that,' said Anne.

'I'll meet you outside the Odeon at six thirty. My treat.'

Anne hugged her. 'Thanks, Elsa.'

As she walked home, Elsa hoped she'd made the right decision. Anne only needed to be directed in her life and maybe she could be the womanly influence for the next little while. She could not, and didn't want to, take her mother's place. No one could do that, but she could help a little, give the girl at least some support and a shoulder to cry on.

* * *

Fanny Braxton, or Madam Carlotta, needed no support at all as she tried to ease her way into her client's confidence. The wife of Albert who lost his life in the Great War had returned for a private sitting. Fanny was playing clever, knowing the woman was in receipt of five hundred pounds.

The two of them sat in the semi-dark room as Carlotta called up her doorkeeper, Black Feather.

'Is Albert Coleman there? I have his wife Madge here and she wants to talk to him.'

There was a prolonged silence, then in a deep voice Carlotta said, 'Albert is coming . . . here he is. What question does his wife have for him?'

Madge, looking pale and hopeful, said, 'Bert, my gran has left me five hundred pounds. I don't know what I should do with it.'

'Now don't fritter it away, Madge. You are in a position to help others less fortunate than you. Look for a good way to spend the money. Find a good cause.'

'What kind of cause?' she asked.

'Ask Madam Carlotta; she will guide you. Do as she says. I have to go now.'

'No, please don't leave,' the distraught wife called.

Madam Carlotta said, 'Sorry, my dear, he has left us. So has Black Feather.'

Wiping away a tear, Madge said, 'He sounded different.'

'Things change in the afterlife,' said Madam quickly. 'He had a long journey to come to you.'

'Yes, I suppose so. What did he mean, ask you about a good cause?'

'Your husband is a good man,' said Carlotta. 'There are many who are in need in this life.' Like me, she thought. 'The most needy are the children. I do happen to know of a charity, Nazareth House; they could do with some money. I could see that they get it for you . . . that's what Albert meant.'

'How much?'

'A hundred and fifty pounds would buy food, blankets and beds for the little ones,' she said, holding her breath as she waited for a reply.

'I'll bring it round tomorrow, if that's all right,' said the trusting woman, 'but that leaves three hundred and fifty pounds.'

'I'll make enquiries meantime,' said Carlotta. 'That will be seven and six for the sitting.'

'Of course,' said Madge, and paid up.

When she was alone, Fanny crowed with pleasure. 'A hundred and fifty nicker! Bloody hell! And it was so easy. I'll get the rest in time, but I mustn't rush things.' Taking off her mantilla, she took herself off to the pub to celebrate.

CHAPTER SIXTEEN

Jean-Paul rang the number of the artist that Henry had given him and made an appointment to see him in London the following day. He had been so impressed by the copy of Rembrandt's painting of *The Night Watch*, he'd had an idea, but he would have to be very careful how he approached the artist. If he was agreeable to the plan formulating in Jean-Paul's mind, they could both make a lot of money.

Roger Johnson had his studio in the top floor of an old Edwardian building in Hammersmith. He was a middle-aged man and he smiled a greeting when he opened the door to the Frenchman. 'Mr Devereux?'

'Mr Johnson?'

'Please come in. I'm afraid you will have to climb three flights of stairs, but I need light when I paint and the attic has a window in the roof.'

After climbing the stairs, Jean-Paul saw that the attic was littered with paintings, which he looked at with interest. 'These are very good,' he remarked.

'Thank you. I sell a few here and there, but my copies of the masters are the things that sell the most. Ironic, isn't it?'

'Frustrating for you, I imagine?'

The other man shrugged. 'I make money where I can. That allows me the freedom to paint what I really like. You said on the telephone that Lord Travers gave you my number.'

'Yes, I saw the Rembrandt you painted. It was breathtaking,

and so accurate. Had I not known differently, I would have thought it authentic.'

'That's how I make my money. Buyers are unable to buy the original, so they commission me to copy their favourites.' He gave a wry smile and added, 'Sometimes they tell their friends it is the original.'

'I have a proposition to put to you, but you may not want to take it up. But I have to tell you it would make us both a lot of money.'

'I'm listening,' the artist said.

Peter, knowing that Jean-Paul was not in residence, made discreet enquiries at the reception desk of the Star Hotel, asking when Mr Devereux would be leaving, just to check up on Elsa's information.

'He was supposed to leave on Monday, but he's staying until Tuesday now. It seems he had to go to London on business,' said the receptionist. 'Can I give him a message?'

'No, I'll catch him another time,' said Peter quickly. 'But thanks anyway.'

He wondered just what was going on. He and Charlie had an arrangement that if anything were going on in the warehouse, Charlie would leave a message at Peter's lodgings, but when Peter rang his landlady he was told there were no messages for him. Well, he would have to pack his case, watch the hotel on Tuesday and follow the Frenchman. He would be able to pay a quick call on Elsa after all. He made his way to the market.

Elsa was surprised to see him. 'I thought you were off to France today,' she said.

'Your Frenchman isn't going until tomorrow after all. He changed his plans, it seems.'

'You're still going, then?'

'I have a job to do; I explained that to you. Now stop worrying. Do you want to meet up for a quick drink this evening?'

'I've arranged to go out with Anne. I thought you'd be away.'

'Never mind. How's everything at home?'

'Dad's a bit edgy, but behaving himself.'

'That's good.' He felt disappointed, as he'd looked forward to spending some time with his girl. 'I'd better be off then.' He kissed her on the cheek. 'I'll be in touch,' he said.

'Look after yourself. Don't do anything stupid.'

'As if I would. I'll see you as soon as I get back.'

As Elsa watched him walk away, she had mixed emotions. She had so wanted to confide in him about her plans for the shop, and to tell him about Jed's being involved. She longed for it to come to fruition, but now wasn't really the time to talk about it in case it all fell through. She felt disloyal keeping it from Peter as they usually shared everything and it didn't feel right, but perhaps by the time he returned she would have something definite to tell him. She would just have to keep her fingers crossed, meantime.

In the council offices at the Civic Centre, the atmosphere was very tense. The newly promoted Jenkins was strutting his stuff. He took great delight in undermining George Carter at every turn, making him do his own workload and half of his. Yet when the bosses were around, he was charm and efficiency itself.

George was having a hard time holding his temper. He managed it only by thinking that while it was bad enough to be passed over for promotion it would be far worse if he were fired. Besides, he was seeking revenge. Jenkins was all front really. He wasn't nearly as efficient as he made out and he, George, would hang on until he could prove this to those who had overlooked his own potential. He was not a patient man, he admitted to himself, but in this case he was prepared to make an exception.

Not only did he have this situation to cope with during his working day, but also, when he was at home, he felt he wasn't even in control there. What had got into his wife he had no idea. It was like living with a stranger these days; suddenly the down-trodden woman he'd been married to for years had become a different person. She seemed more confident, more assertive. Between them, bloody Jenkins and Margaret were doing his head in. He didn't like it a bit.

Margaret Carter, however, was enjoying her liberation. With each day her belief in herself grew. She liked who she was; after kow-towing to a man for years, she felt the joy of being an emancipated woman. Now she understood what the suffragettes had fought for years earlier. George still had the power to unsettle her when he arrived home until she was able to gauge his mood, but now she felt able to stand up to him even if after-wards she had to disappear and have a secret smoke to steady her. But each day she felt that bit stronger and each day her stature grew. No longer did she crouch through fear. Now she walked tall and it was all thanks to Elsa, her beloved daughter who had forced her to take hold of her life, and she would be for ever grateful.

Sometimes she even wondered if she and George would spend all their days together. She wondered if she even wanted to. But as soon as she thought that way, she shut her mind to the idea. It was more than she felt she could face at the moment, but she would bring the thought out again on occasion and mull over the possibility.

Jean-Paul Devereux and Peter Adams left Southampton on the Tuesday morning ferry, which would take them across the Channel to the coast of France. Peter, making sure that he kept out of sight of the Frenchman, was praying that Jean-Paul would catch the train to Paris when they landed, as he had no idea where his shop was. If the man went by road, it would make things difficult. His antiques shop might be in a different name and Peter would have to pound the streets to find him.

He was in luck, however, and he saw his quarry as he queued for a train ticket. Once on board the train, Peter sat where he could watch the man from a safe distance, and on their arrival, when Jean-Paul got into a taxi from the rank outside the station, Peter managed to explain with hand signals that he wanted the driver of the next taxi to follow the car in front.

The Frenchman's vehicle stopped in front of a very smart antiques shop and Peter signalled for his driver to drive past and stop some yards away. After paying for the ride, Peter strolled along the boulevard, staring into the window of the antiques shop as he slowly walked by. Looking into the windows of haute couture shops, cafés and bars, he observed that the area was classy. He grinned broadly when he saw two men wearing the black berets so typical of a foreigner's idea of a Frenchman. But where were the strings of onions, he wondered.

He found a waiter who spoke good English and asked where he could find a reasonably priced *pension*, and was recommended a nearby area, with an address written on a paper napkin. He finished his coffee and, picking up his case, decided that now he knew where Jean-Paul's shop was situated it would be advisable to get settled himself, then he would be free to do the job he was being paid to do. On the way, he bought a street map of Paris.

He found the *pension* easily. His room was small, but clean and adequate for his needs, but he hoped he wouldn't have to stay in Paris for too long. Everything seemed alien to him and he was already missing all that was familiar – especially Elsa.

In Kingsland market, Elsa was closing up after a busy day when she saw Jed approaching. He had a broad grin on his face as he stopped in front of her.

'If we want the shop, it's ours!'

Elsa let out a whoop of joy. 'Really?'

Jed nodded. 'Really, and I managed to get the rent reduced as it is in dire need of decoration, which I said we would do ourselves. We now need to sit down and discuss finances. Can you make it this evening, as we don't have much time? The man wants a definite decision in the morning.'

'I was taking Mum out this evening, but she won't mind me putting it off until another night, I'm sure.'

'Come round to the house as soon as you can.'

'I'll go home, get changed, have something quick to eat, and then I'll make my way over.'

He gave her the thumbs up and walked away.

Clive wandered across. 'He looks pleased with himself,' he remarked. 'Usually when I see him he looks a miserable sod.'

'It's the effect you have on him, I expect,' she said as she picked up the last basket of fruit and put it on the wooden cart.

'Thanks for nothing!' Clive called after her. 'One day you'll change your mind and come out with me, you see if I'm not right.'

'What a dreamer you are,' was her retort.

Once at home, Elsa almost flew through the front door of the house, so excited was she.

'Mum, come and sit down for a minute. I've something to tell you.'

Looking at the shining eyes of her daughter, Margaret wondered what was coming.

'I am going to start my own business!'

Margaret was speechless.

Elsa then told her of her plans for the shop and about her partner. 'Jed Sharpe is going to finance me. He'll be a silent partner, working still in the tattoo parlour, and I'll run the shop! What do you think of that?'

'Well, I don't know what to say,' said Margaret with amazement. 'Imagine!'

'We've got premises in the market – you know, in the parade. I am so excited I could burst! Look, I'm sorry, but I have to go round to Jed's house to make arrangements and I have to do it tonight, so I'm sorry but we'll have to go out another evening.'

'Good gracious, girl, what does that matter? Are you going to tell your father about this?'

Shaking her head, Elsa said, 'No, not yet.' She looked at her mother and added, 'There is a small flat above the shop too.'

Margaret understood the significance of the remark. 'Are you going to live in it?'

'Certainly not alone . . . we could share it, the two of us.'

'Or you could let it and take in more money,' Margaret suggested, unable to face the momentous decision.

'That too,' said Elsa. 'Look, I must wash and change, have a quick bite to eat and be off. I'll have more to tell you later, but not a word to Dad.'

When she was alone, Margaret sat with a cup of tea and pondered over the news. Imagine her daughter having her own business! She liked Jed Sharpe. He was a serious bloke but very reliable and she felt that Elsa could do no better than him for a business partner. She looked round the kitchen, at the room that was so familiar. Now she had the opportunity that had niggled at her. She had the chance of leaving the man who, until recently, had been so difficult at times to live with. However, she reasoned with herself, he wasn't always a bad husband. When he was sober he was fine . . . not that there was a great deal of pleasure in his company, if she was honest. She washed, ironed and cooked for him as she always had during their married life, and thank God she no longer had to sleep with him. She'd never enjoyed the physical side of her marriage anyway. For her there had never been any pleasure in it; she supposed most women felt the same.

'You just have to put up with it,' he mother had told her, so it hadn't been any good for her either. She hoped that at least Elsa would feel differently when she eventually married Peter. Now he *was* different. He wasn't shy of showing his affection for Elsa. George had never shown her any, but she had taken her vows in church . . . for her to walk away from that would be a difficult thing to do.

Jed Sharpe and Elsa spent the evening drinking copious cups of tea as they worked out how much money would be needed to open the new premises. There would be the cost of the paint to redecorate as well, but at least they would do that themselves which would save extra expense.

'I'll help too,' said Anne with enthusiasm. 'After all, I'm to be a member of staff.'

'Quite right,' Elsa said, and looking at Jed she explained, 'I told Anne I would need help in the shop as I couldn't manage on my own if I was busy, and she agreed to do it.' She could tell that he was pleased with the arrangement.

'Fine. May as well keep things in the family; at least then we know there will be no dipping into the till. What about your boss?' he asked.

'I'll have to see him in the morning and tell him of my plans. I'm not looking forward to that.'

'He's a businessman, Elsa. You have worked hard for him. Surely he'll want to see you get on?'

'At a certain expense to him, I'm afraid. Never mind; he's better off than we are and he had to start somewhere.'

Jed agreed, and then they worked the wage structure into their accounts. 'You can't not have an income until we open,' he said. 'You have to live.' They decided on an intermediate amount to keep Elsa afloat until opening day. And when they had at last worked everything out to their satisfaction, Jed poured them all a glass of stout to celebrate. 'Here's to Carter and Sharpe, best fruit and veg!' he said, and the three of them drank to the new venture.

But even as they did so, Elsa was filled with trepidation at the forthcoming meeting with her employer. However, she was determined that no one was going to spoil this chance to make something of herself.

CHAPTER SEVENTEEN

Early the next morning, Elsa made her way to the premises of her employer with a sinking heart. Ernest Turner was a shrewd middle-aged man, who through hard work and diligence had made a success of his life. Elsa liked and admired him, which made her task all the more difficult. She opened the door of the shop and walked in.

Mr Turner emerged from the back room and looked at Elsa with some surprise.

'Elsa! What on earth are you doing here? Is something wrong?'

Taking a deep breath, she said, 'Well, in a manner of speaking, yes there is. Could we have a word?'

Telling his assistant to watch the shop, her employer ushered her into the back room, which was set out as an office.

'Sit down. Now what is all this about?'

'I am sorry, Mr Turner, but I want to hand in my notice.'

He looked flabbergasted. 'Your notice? Whatever for?'

'I am opening my own business.' She explained how her idea had come to fruition with Jed Sharpe's timely intervention.

'But this is exciting. I'm sure you will do very well. I'll be very sorry to lose you, of course.'

'There is one thing, and I don't know quite how to tell you, but the shop we are renting is in the market, on the parade.'

The smile was no longer there as Mr Turner asked, 'Which shop is that?'

'The ironmonger's. They are closing down. We, Jed and I, are taking it over.'

'I see. You will be in direct competition with my stall.'

'I'm afraid so.' She looked earnestly at him and added, 'I am so sorry about this, but the shop is ideal.' Straightening her back, she added, 'It is too good an opportunity to let go. I do hope you understand? It isn't anything personal.'

He pursed his lips and Elsa held her breath, waiting for his next comment. Leaning forward, he said, 'If I was in your position, I would do the same.'

'You would?' she asked with surprise.

'Absolutely! Look, young Elsa, if you want to get on in this world, you have to take chances. After all, competition is good for the soul.'

'You'll keep the stall on, then?'

'Of course. And believe me, you *will* have competition. My youngest son can run the stall. You know Gill?'

Elsa's heart sank. She knew Gilbert Turner. He was a scheming, devious man, without any redeeming qualities, unlike his father. 'He's not working at the moment?'

'He's not happy in his present position, so this will be a godsend for him,' said Ernest. 'The change will do him good. When do you want to leave?'

'I can give you two weeks' notice if you like,' she suggested.

'Won't you need to clean up the shop interior?' he asked. 'If I recall, it needs at least a paint job.'

'Yes, it does. Jed, his sister and I are going to do it ourselves, but we don't take over until next week.'

'In that case, just give me till Saturday week. Gill can take over then. It will give him time to get to know the customers before you open,' he said, with a knowing look.

'Of course. Well, thank you, Mr Turner, for your understanding. I have enjoyed working for you. No hard feelings, I hope?'

Turner rose to his feet and shook her hand. 'No, my dear. You have done a good job and I wish you well, but don't expect an easy ride. We will be in direct competition and I do not intend to lose many of my customers. Nothing personal, as you said, just business.'

As she walked away, Elsa pondered on his remark. What would he do to make sure he kept his business? She sensed she wasn't going to like whatever the wily old bird had up his sleeve. The very fact that it was to be Gill Turner running the stall was bad enough. She wouldn't put anything past him!

Ruby was the first to greet her when she entered the market.

'Late again, miss! That's the second time lately, and unlike you. Anything wrong, love?'

'No, Ruby. I had to go and see my boss before I opened, that's all.'

'Well that's all right then,' and Ruby returned to her stall. A few minutes later she called over to Elsa, 'The ironmonger is having a sale. He's closing down, apparently.'

'So I heard,' was all Elsa said. It was too soon to let anyone in on her plans. When she left would be soon enough. If only Peter were here to talk to, now she would have something concrete to tell him. She wondered how he would take the news of her fledgling business. Would he be surprised . . . and pleased?

Elsa was a million miles from Peter's thoughts as he continued to watch his quarry in Paris. Things were not turning out as he would have liked. People came and went in the classy antique furniture shop. How on earth was he to know who they were or if they were genuine clients of the Frenchman? Anyone could walk through the doors and there was no way of knowing if they had anything to do with the smuggling ring. It seemed to him it was a complete waste of his time. All he could do was take pictures of everyone who entered in the hopes that they would be of use at a later date. He would give it to the end of the week and then decide whether to go home or not.

His persistence paid off, however, when two days later Jean-Paul emerged with two important-looking gentlemen. They walked towards one of the nearby hotels, and Peter followed. They made their way to the dining room and were led to a table.

Peter walked in a few moments later, asking the waiter for a table behind Jean-Paul's back from where he could watch and hopefully overhear the conversation without being recognised. Picking up the menu, his eyes opened wide at the prices.

'Bloody hell,' he muttered. His editor would have a fit when he put in his expenses. And the menu was in French! With the help of the waiter, he ordered soup and fish to follow, then tried to concentrate on the table with the three men, wondering if they were the ones involved with the smuggled goods. Charlie had said there were items from France, Germany and Amsterdam. One of the men was almost certainly German. His speech, though quiet, was very guttural. The other man? It was difficult to tell. He was certainly well dressed, but he spoke so quietly that Peter was unable to hear. Whatever they were discussing was very serious. This was no meeting of chums to have lunch and a laugh.

When they had all finished eating, they rose and left. Peter gave them a few minutes to get ahead of him, then followed. On reaching the shop, the two men he didn't know climbed into a chauffeur-driven car and departed. Peter had managed to take a couple of pictures of them from a distance, hoping they could be enlarged enough to recognise them when the film was developed.

He decided to return to England. He wasn't getting anywhere here. It seemed common sense to him to stay near the warehouse and Charlie. At least there he would be getting some feedback.

He returned to the *pension*, paid his bill, collected his clothes and, taking a taxi to the station, caught a train to the ferry port where he managed to buy an English newspaper to read on the journey.

As he settled himself and looked at the front page, he was appalled at the reports of so many people killed on the orders of General Franco, who had taken control of the insurgent forces in Spain. He recalled the remarks of George Carter about war spreading and wondered how prophetic they were. Would England be drawn into the hostilities?

Elsa was coming to the end of her final week on the stall. She had been watching the ironmonger's shop carefully during the last few days. The sale of goods was drawing some business, but she could hardly wait until Saturday, when the shop would close. On the Monday it would be empty and she and Jed could collect the keys. It was time for her to tell Ruby her news

Waiting for a lull in trade, she walked over to her friend. 'I've got something to tell you,' she said. 'Saturday is my last day on the stall.'

The older woman looked upset. 'You're leaving? Don't tell me that.'

'Yes, but I won't be moving far,' said Elsa, trying to hide a smile.

'You're talking in riddles, girl!'

'I'm taking over the old ironmonger's as my own, with Jed Sharpe. We are opening a fruit and veg shop.'

With a squeal of delight, Ruby said, 'My, you are a sly one. That's great, but what about the stall?'

'Mr Turner's son, Gill, is going to take over.'

'Gill Turner? I can't stand that man. My old man had a run-in with him once. Gill tried to shortchange him. He argued black was blue, but my Fred wouldn't back down and Gill had to pay up in the end. It nearly came to blows. Nasty creepy little toad he is.'

'I don't like him either, but old man Turner isn't giving up his stall.'

'Then you watch your back, my dear. That Gill will cause you no end of problems given half a chance. But I hope you do well, darlin'. All your customers will come to you, see if I'm not right.' And she hugged Elsa. 'I'll pop in for a cuppa if it gets too bloody cold out here in the winter.'

'You'll be more than welcome.' Elsa smiled.

The news soon spread and several of the stallholders came up to congratulate Elsa and wish her well. Clive Forbes wandered over later in the afternoon.

'I hear you are going into business for yourself, is that right?' he asked.

'Yes, that's right.'

'I wish you well then, and I am pleased you are staying in the market where I can still see your smiling face. Without that to lighten the day, my world wouldn't have been the same.'

Laughing, Elsa said, 'Your flattery is wasted on me. Surely you have learned that much by now.'

With a sly smile he said, 'Flattery is never wasted; I have learned that much about women. You'll think about what I said sometime, and even if you don't believe it, you'll be pleased I said it, mark my words, and maybe you'll want to hear more.' And he walked away.

Cheeky monkey, thought Elsa. Well, at least he keeps the market alive with his banter. The place would be quieter without him, and from her shop she would still be able to keep an eye on him for Peter.

Towards the close of the day, as she was putting the goods away from her stall, to her surprise Elsa saw Peter walking towards her. Her heart lifted with joy. She had missed him and had so much good news to tell him, but she saw the look on his face and wondered why he looked so angry. Before she could ask him, he told her.

'Waste of bloody time that trip was! How the hell was I supposed to know who the people were that went into the Frenchman's shop! I sat around for days, watching, taking pictures . . . for what?'

Elsa felt her hackles rise. 'And I'm pleased to see you too!'

'What? Oh, I'm sorry, love.' He put an arm round her and gave her a kiss. 'I'm just so bloody frustrated.'

'Well, help me put this stuff away and we'll go and have a cup of coffee somewhere and you can tell me all about it. By the way, I have some exciting news to tell you too.'

But so wrapped up in his own frustration was her fiancé, he hardly heard a word she said.

They made their way to a nearby café where they ordered some coffee. Peter began to tell Elsa about staying in Paris and regaled her with his opinion of the place.

'It's all right, I suppose. Not speaking the lingo made things difficult.'

'What's Jean-Paul's shop like?' she asked.

He glowered at her. 'Very snazzy. Full of expensive pieces, surrounded by posh shops, and plenty of cafés where I spent hour after hour watching the goings and comings.'

'So it wasn't successful?'

'No. A bloody waste of time. I didn't learn anything about him. Except he has a good business.'

Elsa was bursting to tell him about her new plans. 'I am finishing with my market stall tomorrow,' she said.

'Finishing? Whatever for? I thought you liked your job.'

'I am opening up my own business in the shop on the parade in the market that used to be the ironmonger's. They close on Saturday.'

'You what? How can you possibly afford to open your own business? Where did you get the finance?'

'Jed Sharpe. He is going to put up the money; I'm going to run the shop with the help of his sister. He will be a silent partner.'

Peter looked stunned. 'You did all this without consulting me first?'

Elsa stiffened. 'Well, first of all, you were not here, and secondly why on earth should I consult you about it?'

'Because we are engaged, or had you forgotten?'

'What's that got to do with anything?'

His face flushed with anger. 'It means, Elsa, that we are a couple who plan to spend our future together and surely such a move should be discussed between us.'

There was a sudden stubborn set to Elsa's mouth as she said, 'But this has nothing to do with you at all. This is my project, mine and Jed's.'

'And how come you've got so pally with Jed Sharpe that he is prepared to finance you?'

The fury within Elsa started to grow. 'I have not got pally, as you suggest. It so happened that I mentioned to Jed that I would like to start my own business but couldn't because of lack of finance, and it went from there.'

'And what does he get in return?'

'Peter Adams! I don't know what you mean. Jed is my business partner. We share the profits and that's all.' She rose from her seat. 'Just because your great story hasn't come to anything is no reason to take it out on me. No reason at all!' And she stormed off.

Peter sat dejected and sipped his coffee. Nothing was turning out as he planned. He thought he was on to the story of a lifetime. One that would take him to Fleet Street, clothed in gold for his achievement. Now it looked as if he was stuck here for ever, and now Elsa was spreading her wings. It wasn't that he didn't want her to succeed, he did, but it did nark him that she had done it without his knowledge. She was far too independent for her own good. He paid the bill and made his way to his office to see his editor.

CHAPTER EIGHTEEN

Peter Adams's boss was not a happy man. He flicked through the expense account before him and tutted loudly.

'What do you mean, you didn't find out any incriminating evidence?'

Peter struggled to explain how he spent his time in Paris, about the difficulties. 'But I took lots of photographs,' he said.

Looking at the receipts in front of him the editor remarked, 'And spent most of the days in various cafés by the look of it. What the hell were you eating in this bloody hotel, gold dust?'

'I had to follow Devereux there as the men with him looked important. I'm sure they were the two other men involved, the ones running the fraud in Germany and Amsterdam.'

'Have you any proof of that?'

Peter shook his head. 'I'm afraid not, but I do have photos of them. I'll try to discover who they are.'

'I dare not take this to the top without something concrete,' said his boss. 'Best thing you can do is get back to London tonight and keep an eye on the warehouse. Perhaps your contact there has some news, something we can really get our teeth into.'

'But I've only just got home,' Peter protested.

'You listen to me, young Adams. I'll give you another two weeks to come up with something or I'm pulling the story.'

'But you can't do that!' Peter protested. 'I know I'm on to something big.'

The editor rose from his desk. 'Two weeks!' he said as he strode out of his office into the newsroom.

Reluctantly Peter Adams followed him. He would have time to slip home, have a quick bath, change his clothes, pack some clean ones and catch the train to London. There would be no time to see Elsa and that concerned him as they had parted with cross words. Well, he'd have to write to her and explain.

The following day was Saturday, Elsa's last day on her stall. As usual the market was busy and she was rushed off her feet. She didn't notice she had a visitor until Gill Turner came and stood behind the stall beside her.

'Hello, Elsa. Thought I'd come and help you, get my hand in so to speak.'

What could she say other than 'Of course'. But it was slightly unnerving to have him working beside her. His banter reminded her of Clive Forbes. He chatted up the women but ignored the men. However, he lacked the charm and wit of Forbes and many of the women just glared at him. Elsa also noticed that when he was weighing the fruit and veg he was selling under weight. She pulled him up about it.

'I won't stand by and see you cheat the customers. The last three you served you sold short.'

'Did I?' He feigned surprise.

'Don't give me that old codswallop. You know damned well you did. You do it again and I'll show you up in front of the customer!'

This threat did not please him, but he gave the correct weight afterwards until closing time. He did not, however, attempt to help Elsa put the goods away but watched her lift the heavy baskets of fruit on to the cart and make several trips to the lock-up garage. When she had finished he held out his hand.

Elsa looked puzzled. 'What do you want?'

'The keys to the garage, of course. I'll need them to open up on Monday.'

She handed them over.

He grasped her wrist. 'Don't think you'll make a living opening up in opposition to me,' he said with a malevolent smile. 'I am going to give you a run for your money, you see if I don't.'

'What, by cheating your customers? They'll see through you in five minutes!'

'There is many a way to skin a cat and you just remember that.' He put the keys in his pocket and walked away.

Ruby, who had just closed her stall, walked over. 'Little bleeder! I'm really sorry he's going to be part of this market. He's a chancer, only out for himself, and he don't care how he goes about things. You just watch your back, girl,' she warned.

'Don't you worry about me, Ruby. I can take care of myself. Now don't you forget, you come over for a coffee when I'm open.'

'I'll be there. Are you seeing your young man tonight to celebrate your new career?'

Elsa hesitated. 'We had a bit of a row last night, but I expect he'll be round when he finishes work.'

'Course he will,' said Ruby. 'When are you opening up?'

'Next week. We have to clean up and paint the shop first, so Gill Turner won't have any competition for seven days.'

'Listen, love, all your old customers will come to you, have no fear. He'll really have to pull his finger out to keep them.'

'We'll have to wait and see,' said Elsa.

When Elsa arrived home she asked her mother if there had been a message from Peter.

'No,' said Margaret. 'Were you expecting one?'

'Not really. I expect he'll be round later. I thought we'd go out for a drink to celebrate.'

'Celebrate what?' asked her father, who walked through the front door in time to overhear her remark.

Elsa looked across at her mother, then said, 'I am going into business for myself. I'm taking over a shop in the market.'

'You what?'

She explained her plans for the future and her partnership with Jed Sharpe.

'You're getting a bit above yourself, aren't you?' George remarked coldly.

'Whatever do you mean?' Elsa demanded. 'I am perfectly capable of running my own business!'

'Of course she is!' Margaret snapped. 'She's run the stall virtually alone these past two years.'

'But Turner has done all the buying. You don't know anything about that side of the business.'

'But I can learn. I know about profit margins, that's common sense. You buy goods at the price that when you sell them will give you a profit.'

'You should be pleased for her, George, instead of putting her down like that,' Margaret stated angrily.

He rose to his feet and put his jacket back on. 'The trouble in this house is that the women in it are getting too big for their boots!' And he stormed out.

'Well I never!' Margaret said.

Elsa scratched her forehead. 'What is it with men, Mum? Peter was very put out when I told him my news because I had gone ahead without consulting him. We had quite a row about it.'

Putting an arm round her daughter's shoulders, Margaret said, 'Don't you worry about either of them. You will do well because you have the ability. Peter will come round, you'll see. He'll be very proud of you. As for your father, who knows, and frankly, who cares?'

*   *   *

George Carter cared a lot about the news that his daughter was making a success of her life while he had been sidelined for a lesser mortal. He was the man of the house . . . or used to be. Now it seemed the women in his family were running things and he was deeply resentful. He walked into the nearest pub and ordered a pint of beer.

Less than twenty-four hours earlier, Peter Adams had been sitting on the train heading for London, his mind in a whirl. He felt sure this was the story of a lifetime, but if he couldn't pull something out of the hat in the next two weeks all his hopes would have come to nothing, his one chance of making a name for himself. He was very worried. If there was no message from Charlie at his digs, he would make his way to the warehouse on Monday and try to catch the man's attention somehow. Two weeks wasn't very long. He also was worried about Elsa. They had parted with a row. His fault: he had been less than enthusiastic about her news. His masculine pride had got in the way, he realised, which was unfair to her, After all, she had mentioned her idea to him; it wasn't her fault he'd been away.

Elsa waited until the evening for her fiancé to call, but when he didn't arrive she told Margaret she would pop round to Jed Sharpe's house to make plans for the following week.

'We could make a start on clearing the shop in the morning,' she said. 'It would move things along, then on Monday we could start painting.'

'I'll come and give you a hand,' Margaret offered.

'Great, Mum! We need all the help we can get to have it ready to open.' Kissing her mother on the cheek, she said, 'I won't be long.'

*   *   *

In fact the discussions were varied and detailed, and Elsa was away much longer than she intended, so Margaret was alone in the house when George Carter stumbled through the door, reeking of beer.

As soon as she saw her inebriated husband, Margaret was filled with dread. She backed away from him and stood against the wall, waiting for the abuse to start.

Carter swayed on his feet, one hand holding the tall mantelpiece. He glowered at his wife.

'Well . . . nothing to say?' he slurred and waited, but she remained silent. 'You've had plenty to say recently, my dear wife. Ever since you and Elsa teamed up against me and enforced your new rules.'

Drawing herself up to her full height, Margaret faced him bravely. 'I wondered just how long it would be before you took to the bottle again. What's the excuse this time?'

All his frustrations poured forth. 'You have no idea what I've been through lately. That young creep Jenkins has been promoted over me to office manager. Office manager! That was rightly my position, but that young upstart was given it.'

'Oh, George, I am sorry.'

'I don't want your pity, woman! Who are *you* to pity *me*? You are just my wife – a nobody. A person I married to care for me, do my washing and ironing, cook my meals – clean for me.'

'I do all those things,' she said defiantly.

'But you're not a *proper* wife. You don't pleasure my bed.'

'To be honest, George, I never found any pleasure in you or your bed,' she said quietly.

This enraged him and he hurled himself at her, dragging her to the floor, tearing at her clothes, slapping her face as she struggled, yelling at the top of his voice.

'You will be a bloody wife to me if it is the last thing you do!'

Margaret struggled valiantly, but her husband was a powerful man. The drink and his unleashed fury added to his strength and she was helpless against his onslaught. When he had satisfied his animal lust, he rolled away from her, a drunken smirk on his face.

'Now you are a wife again.'

Margaret didn't move as he crawled to the chair, dragged himself to his feet and climbed the stairs, stumbling and swearing as he did so. The poor battered woman lay, tears rolling down her cheeks, unchecked, until she tried to sit up. Wincing with pain, pulling at her torn garments, trying to cover her bruised body. Hate in her heart.

'That's the last time, George Carter,' she vowed as she made her way to the scullery where she boiled a kettle, stripped herself and washed every inch of her body, muttering, 'I don't want to feel your hands on me anywhere.' From a pile of freshly ironed clothes she dressed herself, rolling her torn garments into a ball and putting them on the fire. She held them down with a poker to keep control of them as they burned. She was still doing this when Elsa returned home.

Elsa's eyes were shining and she had started to say something when she saw what her mother was doing. She then noticed the bruises on the swollen face and round the eyes which gazed at her. Rushing forward, she held her mother tightly.

'Are you all right? I don't need to ask what happened.'

'Your father raped me, here, in front of the fire!'

Elsa was so shocked she couldn't speak for a moment. Then tears filled her eyes. 'Where is he?'

'In bed, fast asleep I expect. I don't want to spend another night under this roof, because if I do I won't be answerable for the consequences. At this moment I want him dead.'

The venom in her mother's voice scared Elsa. She had never seen her like this. Taking the poker out of her hand, she made Margaret sit down. Once the burning bundle was safe to leave, Elsa stood up.

'You stay here, Mum, whilst I go and pack a few of our clothes. We'll go to a bed and breakfast for a few nights until I can get the flat over the shop ready. We'll move in there. Do you need to see the doctor?'

Shaking her head, Margaret said, 'No, but I would like to sit in a bath and soak, though. Do you think that would be possible?'

'I'm sure it would. We'll just tell the landlady that you have been in an accident. That will stop anyone being nosy and asking questions. I'll make you a cup of sweet tea first.'

Whilst she was packing for them both, Elsa was shaking with anger. That her own father could do this appalled her and she wondered if it was the first time. How must her mother be feeling at such degradation? Poor woman. Well, she would make it up to her from now on. Her father would have to fend for himself in future because she certainly wouldn't lift a finger to help him. If she were a man she would beat the living daylights out of him!

Elsa came downstairs and damped down the fire, then she and Margaret left the house. Along the road, they rang a bed and breakfast from the nearest call box, and when they knew a room was available they ordered a taxi to take them to their refuge.

CHAPTER NINETEEN

The kindly landlady at the bed and breakfast accepted the excuse that Margaret Carter had been in an accident and was only too willing to allow her to have a bath, and she gave her permission for Margaret to stay in her room the following morning.

'I usually like my lodgers out by ten o'clock so I can clean the rooms,' she said, 'but I can see you're poorly.'

'I'll see to it,' Elsa told her, 'but I have to go out on business in the morning and I would like my mother to rest just for the day.'

'That's fine,' the landlady said, and left them alone.

Margaret and Elsa settled in their twin-bedded room with a tray of tea.

'Your father will have the shock of his life when he wakes in the morning and finds us gone,' said Margaret with a certain satisfaction.

'Serves him damn well right!' Elsa exclaimed. 'I'll go and see Jed early and we'll find out just how much the upstairs to the shop needs doing to it before we can live in it.'

'Will you have to tell him why we want to live there?' asked her mother.

Elsa mulled this over in her mind for a moment. 'I think I must tell him the truth, Mum. After all, he is my partner. But don't you worry – he's very understanding and anyway, this is no fault of yours.'

'Washing my dirty linen in public has never been my habit, but you're right, it has to be done.'

'Jed won't say a word to anyone; I'd vouch for that. Now come on, let's try to get a good night's sleep.'

The following morning, Elsa went to Jed and told him her sad tale. He was shocked and angry that a man could treat his wife so, but didn't say too much, not wanting to upset Elsa.

'Come on then,' he said. 'Let's go to the shop and see what we have to do. Maybe we can make it habitable by tonight, or tomorrow anyway.'

The upstairs hadn't been lived in for a while, that was obvious from the dust and cobwebs, but the rooms were sound otherwise. Anne had come along to give a hand so between them they scrubbed floors and cleaned all day long, with Elsa slipping back to the lodgings with some sandwiches at lunchtime to check on her mother and report on progress.

'The only thing is, there isn't much furniture in it. There is a cooker in the kitchen which I've cleaned, but no pots and pans. Jed says he has a couple of camp beds we can use. But we'll have to go home and get some bedding.'

Margaret paled at the thought. 'I don't want to set foot inside that house again,' she said.

'Don't you worry about that, Mum. We'll sleep here another night and tomorrow when the old man goes to work, Jed and I will go and get what we need. I must fly; there are still things to be done.' She gazed fondly at her mother. 'Now don't you fret, it's all going to be fine. This is a new start for us all.'

George Carter was indeed surprised to find the house empty when he woke. He was not in the best of moods as he descended the stairs. His head was thumping and the taste in his mouth was foul. He needed a cup of tea, but he did wonder what sort of reception he would get when he entered the living room. But he was ready for a fight. Last night he had taken what was his by right and no longer was he going to live by the so-called 'new rules'. It was time he took back control of his home. He was therefore very surprised to see that the fire had gone out and he was alone in the house. He searched the downstairs, then went back up to the big bedrooms where he saw the bed hadn't been slept in.

'What the bloody hell is going on?' he growled. But there was no one to give him an answer.

At the end of the day, three weary and grubby people walked out of the shop in the market, delighted with how much they had achieved. Once the bedding and a few cooking utensils had been acquired, the flat was liveable in.

'Tomorrow, after we get your mother installed and collect what you want from your house, we'll start on the shop,' said Jed with a weary smile.

'I can't thank you both enough,' Elsa said, but was hushed by the others.

Anne said, 'We couldn't do much for our own mother; at least we can help yours.'

Elsa was deeply touched and hugged the young girl, then she returned to her lodgings.

George Carter had some bread and dripping and a pot of tea for his breakfast on Monday morning, still puzzled as to what had happened to his family, but in his heart he was sure they would be there when he returned home, and he set off for his office. When he got there he would have been startled indeed if he had known that Jed, Anne and Elsa had arrived at the house, and were packing up bedlinen, pots and pans, crockery and cutlery, and the rest of the clothes belonging to his wife and daughter.

They piled everything on to a cart belonging to Jed and pushed it back to the market, where it was all unloaded and stowed away above the shop. Whilst Jed and Anne started cleaning the ground floor, Elsa collected her mother, paid for their lodgings, and brought Margaret to her new home.

'Well, here we are, Mum. Not up to much at the moment, but in time we'll soon have it warm and cosy.'

Margaret sat on one of the two dining room chairs they'd taken and looked round. 'This is just like heaven to me,' she said. 'You go down and help the others while I unpack.'

'Are you sure you're up to it?'

'I'm fine,' she said. 'I'll make a cup of tea for you in a while . . . have we enough cups?'

'Jed brought some and a kettle this morning. They are in the kitchen. I'll see you later.' And with a brief kiss for her mother, she went downstairs.

'Your mum all right?' asked Jed.

'She's fine, thanks. Now let's get down to work.' And the three of them set to.

When George Carter arrived home he knew something was wrong. The fire was still out and two dining room chairs were missing. He ran upstairs and looked in the front bedroom, opening the wardrobe and the drawers. They were empty. Stunned, he sat on the bed. Margaret had left him! She had actually carried out her threat – he couldn't believe it. When he had gathered his thoughts, he stood up, walked downstairs and went out of the door.

Elsa and Jed were washing down the walls of the shop when there was a hammering on the door. They both stopped what they were doing and looked at one another.

'My father!' said Elsa. And she got to her feet and unlocked the door.

'Is your mother here?' he demanded.

'Yes, she is.'

'Then you tell her to get her things together. I'm taking her home where she belongs.' He made to step inside.

Jed Sharpe barred his way. 'Where do you think you are going, Mr Carter?'

George looked startled. 'I've come for my wife. Get out of my way.'

'These are my premises and you are never to enter them at any time. Mrs Carter does not want to see you, so please leave or I'll call the police and have you removed.'

George was speechless for a moment. 'You can't do this to me.'

'I can and I have. Now I'm sure you don't want everyone to know how you have ill treated your wife, but unless you leave now I'll have to tell the police exactly why Mrs Carter came to take refuge here. Her bruises will be enough proof to make them believe me.'

Carter turned pale at the thought. He paused for a moment, then turned on his heel and left.

Elsa found that she was trembling. 'Thank you so much, Jed. That could have been very ugly if you hadn't been around. Do you think he'll come back?'

Jed shrugged. 'Hard to say. He certainly wouldn't want anyone to know what he did, so perhaps not. We'll have to wait and see. If he gives you any trouble, you let me know.'

During the next seven days, Jed, Anne, Elsa and Margaret worked hard, painting and cleaning the shop ready for opening. Several of the stallholders poked their heads round the doors, which were open to eliminate the smell of the paint, to see how things were going. Ruby stopped by for a cup of tea and to gossip.

'That Gill Turner don't like it much in the market, I can tell you,' she said with some relish.

'Oh, and why is that?' asked Elsa.

'Well, love, he's a lazy git so the display is a mess, and he thinks he's a bit of a ladies' man but he don't stand a chance with that smoothy Clive. You know how he charms the ladies, well, Gill tries to do the same, but whereas old Clive gets away with it because he's got charm, with Gill it just sounds dirty and the women don't like it. I tell you, a few of them have given him a flea in his ear. Clive is lapping it up. It has made him ten time worse; now he really lays it on. It's better than being at the theatre, I can tell you!' She chuckled loudly.

'Is Gill losing business?'

'I keeps telling his customers you will be open next week. I tells them on the sly like.'

'Ruby, you are a star. Jed and I are off to Oakley and Watling's today to buy our goods. Then we'll put out the display.'

Looking round the shop with its newly painted white walls, Ruby said, 'It looks real nice, Elsa. You and Jed have made a good job of this. I saw your mother come out the other day. Has she been helping too?'

Yes,' said Elsa. 'We have moved into the flat above. We'll be living here now.'

There was something in her tone of voice that made Ruby leave the matter alone. She was a shrewd woman and she immediately twigged that there was more to this than met the eye, but it was young Elsa's business not hers.

'Better be off then, love. You take care and good luck on Monday when you open. I'll send as much business to you as I can.'

'Thanks, Ruby. See you later.'

Jed and Elsa went off to the fruit and veg wholesalers and opened an account. They wandered around the warehouse, which was packed with boxes of fruit and vegetables. It was all so colourful and inviting, Elsa was in heaven, as was Jed, choosing their goods and buying baskets in which they would display the produce. They ordered a big stock to start them off, which would be delivered the next morning.

When they saw the size of the bill, they looked at each other. Elsa frowned but Jed wasn't fazed.

'It will be our biggest outlay,' he assured Elsa. 'After all, we had nothing to start us off. From now on it will be just replenishing stock.'

'You will be in the shop for opening day, won't you?' she asked.

'Try to keep me away! I haven't made any bookings until mid-week in case we run into any problems.' He grinned broadly at her. 'Are you as excited as I am?'

'Oh, Jed,' she said, hugging him, 'you have no idea how much! For me it is a dream come true and I couldn't have done it without you.'

'That works both ways, you know. Now come on, we must put some shelves up before the stuff comes tomorrow, or we will be in a mess.'

That night, Margaret and Elsa sat in the bare kitchen, using an upturned wooden crate as a table, and ate their supper. They were tired yet triumphant.

'I don't know when I've enjoyed myself more,' said Margaret. 'Or when I've been so dirty. Thank goodness we have some hot water, as I need to soak in a bath. I ran the water and got all the rust out of the pipes, so now it's fine. You can have one after.'

'You know that Dad came round here the other day, don't you?'

'Yes, I heard everything. That Jed is a real man. Your father won't come back . . . unless he has a skinful of beer, that is, but you know, Elsa, you have so many friends in the market, they would take care of him, I'd stake my life on it. Anyway, we are going to forget about him. Next week is very important and we won't let thoughts of him spoil it.'

'No, you're right. I'll wash up while you have a bath, then I'll have mine and after that I'm off to bed, I am so tired.'

Both women slept soundly that night, which was more than George Carter had done all week. Jed had scared him off. At the moment, it was more important to George that he keep his good name at work. No one there would know his wife had left him and that was how it would remain. He would have to do his own washing, or send it to the laundry, and he could go to a café for meals. He would carry on as if things were normal. Fortunately he wasn't chummy with his neighbours, but if anyone did ask about Margaret he would just tell them she was helping out her daughter until she got on her feet. Yes, that's what he would do. But he didn't like it one little bit.

CHAPTER TWENTY

It was a bright sunny day when Jed and Elsa opened the doors to their shop. The sign writer had finished his job the day before and so the new name of Carter and Sharpe was emblazoned across the shop frontage. Outside were displayed a few goods set off by a colourful display of flowers, steeped in buckets of water. It had been Elsa's idea.

'There is only one trader in the market who sells flowers,' she said to Jed, 'and he is at the far end of the market, so let's give it a try. Buy just a few to start with and see how it goes.' He had agreed.

They were soon busy. Elsa's old customers poured in to see her – and to buy.

'We've missed you,' one lady said. 'We don't like that man on the stall. He's rude and impolite, and we think he cheats us when he weighs stuff. He puts veg on the scales and before you have the chance to check, it's all whipped off and bagged.'

Elsa didn't comment except to say how pleased she was to see them all.

At one time she briefly looked through the window at the market outside. Women, old and young, as usual surrounded Clive but Gill Turner was not doing a lot of business. Elsa allowed herself a smile of satisfaction and turned to serve yet another customer.

At eleven o'clock, Margaret come down with cups of coffee for everyone.

'I've been watching out of the upstairs window,' she said,

172

'and all I could see were people coming through the door.'

Jed grinned at her and said, 'It's been bloody marvellous. We haven't stopped. How would you like to help out, Mrs Carter? I won't be here after tomorrow, and if business keeps up the girls will need a hand.'

Margaret looked across at Elsa to get her approval.

'Do say yes, Mum. At this rate Anne and I will have difficulty finding the time to spend a penny.'

'I'd love to!' she said gleefully. 'I can't think of anything I would like better.'

'You'll be paid, of course,' said Jed, 'so you'll have a bit of money of your own.'

Knowing how significant this was to her present situation, Margaret really appreciated the offer. 'Thanks, Jed, that would be great. You are such a gent,' she added, to his embarrassment.

He dismissed her compliment. 'Not at all. Why don't you stay for a while now and help? It will give you an idea of what is required.'

And she did and enjoyed every moment of dealing with the customers. She had covered what remained of her bruises with a little make-up, so felt able to face the public. It was from her mother that Elsa had inherited her charm and so the customers immediately took to her.

Anne too was enjoying herself. She hadn't time to be sad and once or twice when a couple of the men flirted with her, she showed a little of her old sparkle.

At the end of the day when the market was quiet and all the stallholders were packing up, Clive Forbes popped into the shop. Looking round, he said how nice it was.

'You have been busy,' he said. 'Whenever I've glanced over you have been going full pelt. Well done! Your old stall has suffered, I can tell you.'

'You say that with such relish.' Elsa laughed.

'Well, I can't stand that Gill Turner. He thinks he can outshine me with the ladies, and he fails miserably. He just gets up my nose!'

'I don't know why,' Elsa said, smiling. 'No one outshines you when it comes to the ladies.'

'Except when it comes to you.' With a broad grin he said, 'Why don't I take you out for a drink tonight to celebrate?'

Knowing that young Anne was hovering in the background and that Clive had ignored her presence, Elsa cut him short. 'No thanks, and we have to close now, Clive.'

'Giving me the bum's rush, are you?'

'Something like that, but thanks for dropping in.'

When he'd left she said to Anne, 'I hope it didn't upset you seeing Clive and listening to his flannelling. You know it means nothing.'

The girl shrugged. 'I know. Don't you worry about me.'

But as she put her coat on ready to go home, Anne knew in her heart she still was fascinated with the market trader, and hated herself for it.

Jed and Elsa locked up and counted their day's takings.

'Well, Elsa,' Jed said, 'if this keeps up, we have a good business on our hands. A sure success. No wonder old man Turner wants to keep his stall going.'

'But what will he do if he's losing money? He said he would give me a good run.'

'We'll just have to wait and see,' said her partner. He put the takings in a bag, leaving a float to start with the following day. 'I'll bank this in the morning,' he said, 'so I'll be a bit late.' As he opened the door to leave, he held up the bag. 'We did well. Long may it continue!'

As Elsa locked up behind Jed and made her weary way upstairs she wondered why Peter hadn't come to see how they had managed. She hadn't heard from him for a week, and it hurt her that he hadn't shown up. She had really wanted to share all the excitement with him. Surely he wasn't sulking? It would be so unlike him.

Peter Adams had not forgotten Elsa, but he had been trying to find Charlie. There had been no message from the man over the weekend and so he'd gone to the warehouse on Monday and stood outside all day, but there had been no Charlie amongst the comings and goings of the staff, and Peter was worried. He couldn't go up and ask one of the other employees about him and jeopardise their contact; all he could do was wait. There was no sign of Charlie all week, and Peter was starting to feel frantic: half his time had gone already and he had achieved precisely nothing. He spent the weekend trying to think of ways to find Charlie that wouldn't compromise their arrangement, and on Monday was immensely relieved to see the man walking towards the warehouse entrance. He put his fingers in his mouth and whistled shrilly.

Charlie looked up and saw Peter standing across the road. Looking around furtively, he gestured with his hand as if he was drinking and then motioned one o'clock, then he walked into the warehouse entrance.

At noon, Peter was sitting in the bar of the pub where he and Charlie had first met, eating a pie whilst he waited. Just after one o'clock, Charlie walked in, went to the bar, ordered a pint of beer, and sipped at it, looking around for a while, before he came and sat next to Peter.

'Where have you been?' asked Peter anxiously.

'Been off sick,' he said. 'Nasty chest infection.'

'So what's the latest news? Any movement lately?'

'Not really, but something's in the air. The foreman and his

175

mate have been behaving shifty, like, so something is cooking. Now I'm back, I'll keep my eyes skinned.'

Peter didn't tell the man he only had five days left to get his story. He had decided that he was going to see this through to the bitter end anyway. If it took longer than five days, he'd quit his job, if his editor insisted on pulling the story.

'I'll come in here every day at one. If something breaks you'll know where I am, or leave a message with my landlady.'

He would have been very surprised if he had been in Kingsland market the following day, as Elsa had an unexpected visitor.

Business on the second day of opening wasn't quite so frantic and Elsa was replacing the goods in the display that had been sold when she was startled by the sound of a voice from behind her.

'*Bonjour, Mademoiselle Elsa.*'

She spun round and looked into the smiling face of Jean-Paul. 'Good heavens! What are you doing here?'

He kissed her hand and said, 'I'm not sure if that means you are pleased to see me or not?'

Somewhat confused by this unexpected encounter she said, 'Of course I am pleased to see you, it is just such a surprise.'

He looked round the shop and with a broad smile and gesticulating with his hand said, 'As is this. I am told that this is your new business. Congratulations, Elsa. I am so happy for you.'

She was thrilled by his enthusiasm. 'Isn't it wonderful, Jean-Paul?' She introduced him to Jed. 'This is my partner, Jed Sharpe. I couldn't have done it without him.'

The Frenchman shook Jed by the hand. '*Bonne chance*, my friend. The place looks very inviting. I will certainly be shopping here myself.'

Jed left to serve a customer and Elsa, now filled with curiosity, asked, 'Does that mean you will be around for a while?'

'For a little. Does that please you?'

His enigmatic smile was unsettling and Elsa felt the colour rise in her cheeks. 'Of course. Have you been in England long?'

'No. I arrived late last night. I have several business meetings in London, but I hate to stay in London for too long. I will be staying at the Star Hotel for a while until all my business is complete. Elsa, *chérie*, please come and have dinner with me this evening and tell me all about your good fortune. We will celebrate and drink to your success.'

How could she refuse? 'I would love to,' she said.

'Shall I send a taxi for you?'

'Certainly not,' she said. 'I'll walk. I live above the shop now so it isn't very far.'

His eyes glistened. 'Are you telling me that you have a love nest of your own?'

She burst out laughing. 'No, I am not! I am sharing the flat with my mother.'

He looked disappointed. 'A pity. It would have had such possibilities! I will look forward to seeing you this evening. We'll dine at the hotel if that is all right with you? Only I am waiting for a telephone call.'

'That'll be fine,' she told him.

'*Au revoir, chérie.* I look forward to our meeting.'

When he'd gone, Anne sidled over. 'Who was that?'

'Jean-Paul Devereux, from Paris.'

'What a beautiful man. His clothes, and that voice, the accent. It made my toes curl!'

'Anne! Behave yourself.' But she had to admit, he was dangerously attractive. If only Peter would show up, she could tell him the Frenchman was back, but she certainly was *not* going to be the first one to make a move. Peter had been horrid and she hadn't yet forgiven him. The fact that her fiancé had forbidden her to see Jean-Paul again gave her a fiendish satisfaction. Besides, perhaps she could be more successful in finding out what was going on. Wouldn't it be a scream if she did better than Peter at his own game! It would really show him that she could stand on her own two feet!

The dining room of the Star Hotel was nicely laid out; many of the tables were already taken when Elsa sat with the Frenchman and ordered from the menu, letting him choose the wine. He insisted that they start with champagne to celebrate her new business. After the waiter opened the bottle and filled the two glasses, Jean-Paul held his up.

'To success in your first business,' he said.

'My *first* business – what do you mean?'

'Success leads to further business, perhaps to a chain of shops,' he said as he clinked glasses.

Elsa sipped from hers and wrinkled her nose at the bubbles. 'A chain! That is too forward-thinking for me at the moment.'

'You have the ability, of that I am certain,' he said, 'you just need to believe in yourself more.'

'It is very early days,' she told him, 'and my old boss still has the stall I used to work at. His son is running it and he promised I wouldn't have an easy ride.'

The Frenchman frowned. 'Was that some kind of threat, *chérie*?'

'To be honest, I don't know. Gill Turner is not a very nice man.'

'I see.' His frown deepened. 'I don't like the sound of that at all. We can't have this man causing trouble for you.'

The sudden change in his voice unnerved Elsa. 'What on earth do you mean?'

His voice lightened immediately. 'Nothing, nothing at all. But if he becomes a problem, you must tell me, Elsa.'

'But all this is nothing to do with you,' she protested. 'It is my business.'

'I have just made it mine,' he said. 'Ah, here is the food. I am so hungry. Let's eat.' And the subject was changed.

Just as they were eating their dessert, Jean-Paul was called away to take a phone call. He returned to her full of apologies.

'I am so sorry, *chérie*, but it was important. Would you like to have our coffee in the residents' lounge after we have finished?'

'That would be nice.'

They sat comfortably on a settee and ordered more coffee.

Jean-Paul put his arm along the back of the seat and gazed at Elsa. 'You are so very charming, *ma chère*,' he said. 'You have such a delightful air of innocence about you which is so appealing.'

Elsa was at a loss for words and a little embarrassed by his flattery. 'I can't be innocent now I am a business woman,' she protested.

He stroked the back of her hair. 'I have a bottle of champagne on ice upstairs in my room. Why don't we go there and have a nightcap?'

With a soft chuckle, Elsa refused. 'You cannot use your charm on me, Jean-Paul. I think that you would become quite dangerous if I was to agree.'

He laughed and said, 'How right you are to refuse, because I think I just might be.'

But when he insisted on taking her home and kissed her outside her new premises, she knew for a certainty that whatever Peter said she would see Jean-Paul again. No one had ever kissed her the way he did. It seemed to turn her legs to jelly. Nevertheless, despite her subtle questioning, she realised she had learned very little about the Frenchman. She also realised just how clever he was at fielding her queries.

'Bonsoir, *chérie*. That was an enchanting evening, the first of many more, I hope?' Before she could answer, he kissed her again and then insisted he watched to see her safely inside her door 'I'll be in to see you tomorrow,' he promised.

As she undressed, Elsa was pleased her mother was asleep because her emotions were in turmoil. She loved Peter, yet here was a stranger who had walked into her life who both disturbed and fascinated her. She seemed to be under some kind of spell when she was with him. Surely such a man wasn't mixed up with this business that Peter was involved with. He could be wrong, couldn't he?

Elsa was even more perplexed when mid-morning the following day she saw Jean-Paul in deep conversation with Clive Forbes, especially as they both were looking across at her old stall where Gill Turner was working. Had she heard their conversation she would have been even more concerned.

Jean-Paul questioned Clive about Gill. Who was he? What was he like? Did Clive think he was capable of making trouble for Elsa now they were in competition? Clive made his feelings about the man very clear.

'He's a conniving little bastard, and yes, I do think he could be trouble.'

'I want you to keep a close eye on him,' Jean-Paul told him. 'If you think that Elsa or her business are in any danger from the man, you must let me know. I'm off to London for a couple of days, but after that I will be around for a while. Call me or leave a message at the Star Hotel. I will of course pay you for your trouble.'

Clive would have done it for nothing, such was his dislike for Gill Turner. 'Fine, it will be a pleasure. You got the hots for our Elsa then?' he asked.

Jean-Paul stared hard at the market trader. 'That is my business. You do yours, that's all that need concern you.'

'All right, keep your hair on. You got any business coming my way soon?'

'Probably in the next few weeks. I'll let you know,' he said.

The Frenchman entered Carter and Sharpe and walked up to Elsa. 'I have to go to London on business; I'll be away a couple of days. I'll contact you when I return, *chérie*. You take care of yourself.' He kissed her hand and left the shop.

CHAPTER TWENTY-ONE

Jean-Paul Devereux booked into a London hotel and asked the receptionist if Mr Borchets had arrived yet. Apparently he hadn't. Jean-Paul took his key and made his way to the lift and his room on the third floor, where he unpacked, ordered some coffee from room service, and waited. A while later, his telephone rang.

Picking up the receiver, the Frenchman listened and then said, 'Ask him to come up.'

A few minutes later he answered the knock on his door. 'Günter! Come in.'

At one o'clock the same day, Peter Adams was waiting in the bar of the pub, wondering if Charlie would arrive with some good news for him. His time for getting the story was running out. It was with a feeling of relief that he saw the door open and his informant hurry in. He ordered a beer and came straight over to Peter, his eyes bright with excitement.

'Here! The old foreman and his mate are all fired up. It seems a couple of the blokes who ship over this stuff are due at the warehouse later today. I overheard them talking when I was taking a slash.'

Peter felt the adrenalin begin to pump through his veins, but from past experience, he knew that just waiting outside the place and watching was of little use. He needed proof.

'Can you get me inside the warehouse somehow, Charlie?'

'Bloody hell, mate, that's going a bit far, ain't it?'

'I've got to be there, Charlie. I could hide away and listen to what they say.'

'What if they find you? I'll be for the bloody chop!' He looked terrified.

'If they do find me, I'll tell them some tale or other. I promise I won't implicate you in any way.'

'What'll you say?'

'At the moment I don't know, but I'll think of something. You've got to get me inside!'

A little later, Charlie and Peter arrived at the back entrance to the warehouse. Charlie opened the door carefully, looked round the interior and beckoned Peter in. The place was huge, filled with packing crates and labelled boxes piled high one on top of another, set out in aisles with a narrow walking space in between.

'The foreman and his mate are up there,' said Charlie, pointing to a staircase leading to some offices.

'Where is the stuff we have been talking about?' Peter asked.

The two men crept on tiptoes to another area of the store. Looking around, Peter spied a pile of boxes opposite the ones in question, and seeing the possibility he pulled at the other man's sleeve.

'I can climb up there,' he said. 'If I lie flat, they won't be able to see me, but I can listen to their conversation. You go on. I'll be all right.'

Charlie hurried away.

The crates, piled high, were of slightly different widths, affording Peter a foothold on each layer. He made his way skywards somewhat precariously, and lay on his stomach where he could peer over the edge. If he were lucky, he could listen to a conversation, but if the men spoke in a foreign tongue he knew he would be scuppered. He crossed his fingers, quietly wishing for some luck in his endeavours.

An hour passed and Peter Adams was more than a little uncomfortable. His shoulders ached and his neck was stiffening. He dared not move, having positioned himself well, in case the foreman or his mate were now prowling around. Eventually, he heard the sound of footsteps . . . and held his breath.

The footsteps came closer, then stopped. He recognised Jean-Paul Devereux's voice as he spoke to the foreman.

'Which crates are ours?' he asked.

'This lot here,' he was told. 'Here is the manifesto.'

'That will be all for now,' said the Frenchman, dismissing the foreman.

Peter lay still as he heard the man walk away. He then craned his neck to peer over the edge. Below him stood Jean-Paul and the German-looking man Peter had seen dining with him in the restaurant in Paris.

'So, Günter. What do you think? Is it time to distribute the goods?'

In a deep guttural voice, the other man spoke. 'Yes, I don't think we should keep them any longer. Where are they going?'

'The French bureau has been aged to perfection and is sold to an antiques shop in London's West End. The other pieces have been similarly treated, and are being sold around the English countryside,' Jean-Paul told him. 'We don't want all these fakes to be in one place, that is dangerous, but a piece here and there is safer. I defy even the experts to discover they are not genuine.'

'Your men are masters at their craft, I must say, which is good, as I don't want to waste my life serving a prison sentence for fraud.'

'There is always that risk, *mon ami*, but we have had much success in the past and I am very confident about the future.'

Jean-Paul chuckled and said, 'It is very lucrative, I'm sure you'll agree?'

The German nodded. '*Ja*. It keeps my wife happy.'

'And your mistress?'

The German laughed loudly. 'Oh, yes, she has no room to complain.'

'Right,' said the Frenchman. 'I'll have the bureau delivered tomorrow, and the rest the following day.'

'When is Hans bringing over the diamonds?'

'Thursday of next week. He'll take them straight to Hatton Garden.' Jean-Paul grinned broadly. 'The Customs and Excise will know nothing of them and they will make us all a nice profit.'

'Excellent,' said Günter. 'I have a fancy for a nice little house I've seen, just outside Hamburg. The money we make will allow me this extravagance. I leave it to you to make the arrangements.'

'I'll go and speak to the foreman now. I'll meet you back at the hotel and we will have a drink to celebrate. Will you stay for dinner and return to Hamburg in the morning?'

'Yes, I'd like to. Let us go to a nightclub this evening. I would like to have a little fun before I leave.'

'An excellent idea,' agreed Jean-Paul. And the two men walked away.

Peter lay in his hideaway for some time after they had left before he moved his cramped limbs and then tried painfully to climb down, but he misjudged the last step and slipped. He landed with a loud clatter, bumping his head, which stunned him for a moment. Therefore, he was unaware of the approaching footsteps.

'What the bloody hell do you think you're playing at?'

The burly foreman hauled Peter to his feet and thumped him on the chin, which sent him flying.

'I haven't stolen anything,' Peter cried, holding his sore face. 'I had a row with the missus last night and she chucked me out. Your back door was open and I hid in here.' He held his breath, hoping he had lied sufficiently well to get away with being on the premises.

The foreman's mate came rushing over, followed by Jean-Paul.

'What's *he* doing here?' the latter asked, staring at Peter, prostrate upon the floor.

The foreman looked at the Frenchman. 'You know him? Then what *is* he doing here?'

'We had better find out,' Jean-Paul said grimly.

'He told me he'd had a row with his wife and she'd kicked him out. Lying little bleeder!'

The men dragged Peter away. Out of the corner of his eye, he saw Charlie peering out from behind a packing case, horrified at what he saw.

The three men sat Peter down in the office in front of the large desk.

Perching on the front of the desk, Jean-Paul said, 'What are you doing here?'

'I was just passing and saw you come in,' Peter said.

Jean-Paul slapped him hard across the face. 'Don't play games with me!' he snapped. 'I ask you again, why are you here?'

Peter knew he was in deep trouble. He racked his brains for a likely story.

'I thought you looked an interesting character when I saw you in Kingsland market, and I wondered if there was a good feature story about you. You know the sort of thing . . . a Frenchman's views on England, and so on.'

'You have been following me?'

Peter just shrugged.

Glaring at the reporter, the Frenchman said, 'You are a very foolish young man.' He said to the foreman, 'Take him to the cellar and lock him up. Make sure he's secure . . . and teach him a lesson.'

'Then what?'

'You keep him shut away until I tell you any different.'

'You'll never get away with this, Devereux. I'll be missed,' Peter protested.

Jean-Paul laughed. 'If you are worrying about the lovely Elsa, I'll make sure she isn't lonely!'

Peter leaped to his feet in his anger and made to strike Devereux, but was swiftly overpowered by the other two men.

The Frenchman stood up and said, 'You have no idea what you are dealing with, but by prying into my affairs you have become a problem, *mon ami*. I can't have that. You will not spoil what I have worked so hard for.'

The menacing look he gave Peter made the young man's heart sink. How on earth was he to get out of this? Before he could think, he was dragged away and taken to the cellar beneath the building.

The room was dark and dank. A small round barred window, grimed with the dirt from the street above, afforded little light. He was pushed on to a rickety chair, his hands bound behind him, a gag put in his mouth.

The foreman looked at him and said, 'You had better make your peace with your maker, my son, because you'll be seeing him very soon.' And he hit Peter again and again.

Eventually, left alone in the semi-dark room, despite the pain from his beating, Peter struggled with his bonds, to no avail. Sweat beaded his forehead with the effort. He nearly tipped the chair over which was the last thing he wanted. On his side he would be even more useless. His one hope was Charlie. He wondered if his contact would know what they had done with him. The stench of damp and mould filled his nostrils. Outside he could hear the sound of traffic and footsteps as people passed by, but he was helpless to call out for assistance.

Upstairs in the office, the foreman suddenly remembered the third member of the staff in work that day. 'Where the hell is Charlie?'

Charlie had watched the proceedings from a hiding place and was fearful of the consequences. He knew that he would have to be very careful to stay out of trouble himself, so he had taken himself outside to the back yard and started tidying up old and damaged crates. There he stayed until the two men searching for him eventually found him.

What are you doing?' the foreman asked.

'Tidying up, guv. I thought this place was becoming a hazard with all these crates.'

'How long have you been out here?'

'About an hour. Why, do you need me for anything?'

'No, you carry on until it's finished,' he was told.

As the two men returned to the office, the foreman said, 'That's a bit of luck. He didn't see anything, or we would have two bodies to dispose of.'

At the end of the day, to Charlie's great relief, he was dismissed as usual. Once outside he lit a cigarette to calm his nerves and walked casually out of the yard and round the corner into the street, where he stopped opposite the window of the cellar. He bent down and pretended to tie his shoelace, then when he was sure he wasn't being watched he tapped on the window of the cellar before moving away. At least by doing this he was letting Peter Adams know he knew where he was. What he could do about it he had not the slightest idea.

Trouble was also looming in Kingsland market. Gill Turner was pissed off. He watched the steady flow of customers entering Carter and Sharpe and watched his daily takings dwindle.

'Bloody woman!' he muttered. He even cut his prices, but it made little difference. Some came looking for a bargain, but his takings did not increase by any great margin. What could he do?

During a quiet lull in the afternoon, he wandered over to take a look for himself at the new premises.

Elsa was very surprised to see Gill. She and Anne were serving customers when he walked in. Keeping one eye on him she saw him glancing round, studying the layout, and looking more furious with every moment.

'Can I do something for you?' she asked as her customer walked out of the shop.

'Just having a look round,' he said.

'So what do you think?'

'It's all right,' he grudgingly admitted.

'Thanks. How's business?'

'You trying to take the piss?' he snapped.

With a laugh, Elsa said, 'That bad, eh?'

He glared at her. 'Think you're bloody smart, don't you?'

'No,' she said in a steady voice. 'There is room for both of us, if you were to be pleasant to customers and stop giving them short measure.'

'Don't you talk to me like that, missy.'

'Look, Gill,' she said, trying to reason with him, 'you could have a good business too, but people don't like being cheated. They think you are underestimating their intelligence, that's all. Just a word to the wise.'

'I don't need some smart alec of a woman to tell me how to run my business!' And he stormed out, passing Clive, who was standing in the doorway.

'He giving you any trouble?' he asked.

Shaking her head, Elsa said, 'No, not really. Just rattling his cage, that's all.'

Clive turned on his heel and walked back to his stall, glancing over at Gill Turner as he passed. The other market trader looked like thunder.

Gill was fuming as he stood behind his stall. He should have a shop like that. Why hadn't his father thought of renting that one for him? After all, he could afford it. But no, he would rather his son stand around in the open. Well, he certainly wouldn't be doing this in the winter; his old man could find some other patsy to do it then. The more he watched the customers coming and going from Elsa's shop, the more his resentment grew.

Fanny Braxton, who had observed the anger and frustration of Gill Turner, seized the opportunity.

'Getting above herself, that girl,' she declared.

'You can say that again!' snapped the trader.

'Are you going to let her get one over on you and do nothing about it then?'

He looked at the old crone with interest. 'What do you mean?'

She moved nearer. 'I have an idea as to how you can get your own back.'

In the early hours of the morning, before the dawning of the day, a shadowy figure crossed the market heading for the parade of shops.

CHAPTER TWENTY-TWO

Kingsland market was cloaked in darkness, the street lamps affording little light to the square. The man approached the parade of shops, stopping in front of Carter and Sharpe, where he stooped down. Pulling a large piece of rag from his pocket he took the stopper out of a bottle and soaked the rag, putting the stopper back in the bottle before striking a match. The rag ignited. He stood up and approached the shop door, searching for the letterbox. As he put out his hand to push it open, he was grabbed from behind and sent flying on to his back, dropping the blazing rag as he fell.

His attacker picked it up and held it close to Gill Turner's face. The market trader screamed in terror. All he could see were two eyes staring at him from behind a balaclava. The other person laughed and removed the rag, but held it so that Gill's coat caught alight. As Gill tried to scramble to his feet, he felt the sole of a boot at his throat. The pressure caught his breath. As he tried to grab hold of the leg of his attacker, he was kicked in the face. He trembled as he heard a voice warning him.

'You try anything like this again, and you're a dead man!'

The boot was removed which allowed him to get to his feet, gasping for breath, desperately trying to remove the burning coat. His hands were scorched in the process and his arm was burnt as he tore the garment free. He stamped on it to try to put out the flames, setting the leg of his trousers alight in the process, at the same time looking round to see where the next blow was coming from, but the square was empty. He managed to beat out the flames on the trousers, and stood, trembling, blowing on his hands trying to lessen the pain. His arm and leg felt as if they were on fire. Pieces of fabric fluttered across the tarmac in the breeze. He looked carefully round again, before sloping away.

Fanny Braxton, hidden in the darkness, fumed when her planned act of revenge failed. She slipped away, cursing under her breath.

Earlier the same evening, Jean-Paul Devereux and Günter Borchets were celebrating in one of the more classy nightclubs in London's West End. The Frenchman had kept to himself the problem that had beset him earlier that day and so they had dined well and supped on good wine and were now awaiting the start of the cabaret when Jean-Paul felt a light touch on his shoulder. Turning round he was not pleased to see Virginia Travers smiling at him.

'Hello darling,' she said as she bent to kiss his cheek. Both men rose from their seats. He introduced Virginia to Günter, who bowed.

'Is Henry with you?' asked the Frenchman.

'Yes, he's over there talking to our friends. I was on my way to the powder room when I saw you.' She sat in an empty chair beside him, and taking his hand said, 'I have missed you, darling.'

'I am sure you have found plenty of men to distract you, Virgina my dear. Now run along; your husband will be worried.'

'As if I care,' she said.

'But I do,' said Jean-Paul coldly. 'We are good business acquaintances. I wouldn't let anything spoil that.'

'You didn't always think that way,' she snapped.

'Jean-Paul, how lovely to see you!' Henry Travers stood beside them. 'Go along, Virginia, I want to talk business to our friend.'

The woman rose to her feet, and, with a sulky expression spoiling her good looks, walked away.

The Frenchman introduced the two men.

The aristocrat lowered his voice and asked, 'Do you have anything in the pipeline for me, dear boy?'

'Not at this moment, Henry, but I have not forgotten you.'

'Good, good – and I appreciate the fact that you took my words about my wife to heart. It simplifies everything, don't you think?' Without waiting for an answer he rose to his feet and said, 'Hope to hear from you soon.'

Günter leaned forward. 'What a beautiful woman,' and with a significant look he asked, 'You know her well?'

'Too well. She is nothing but trouble.'

'I can see that there would be compensations, my friend,' said the German, chuckling softly.

Such compensations were easily forgotten, thought Jean-Paul. There were always other women to fill his needs; Virginia would not be allowed to become a problem. Fortunately she could be discarded without too much trouble, unlike the young reporter who had wandered into his life. The cabaret started and any further conversation was impossible.

The following morning, Kingsland market was buzzing with rumour. Gill Turner's stall was bereft of all produce, standing strangely bare among the others. Elsa had noticed this as she set up the fruit and veg on display outside her shop, but it wasn't until Ruby called in for a quick cup of coffee that she heard the reason why.

'Heard about Gill?' Ruby asked.

'Heard what?'

'Seems he had to go to hospital in the early hours of the morning, suffering with burns.'

'Burns? Whatever happened to him?'

'Nobody knows for sure but rumour has it that he was got at.'

'What for?' asked Elsa.

'Who knows, love? That bastard has a few enemies, of that I'm certain.'

Elsa was intrigued about Gill Turner. She instinctively knew that Clive and Jean-Paul were at the bottom of whatever had befallen the trader and that it had something to do with her. And when she wandered over to Clive's stall later in the day she saw that his fingers were bandaged on one hand.

'Had an accident?' she enquired.

'Cut myself opening a tin,' he explained.

'You didn't burn them by any chance?'

She knew by the shocked expression on his face that she was right, although he denied it, but what worried her more was the disturbing dream she'd had the night before. She couldn't remember the details except that Peter was in some kind of danger. The feeling had stayed with her all morning.

Anne Sharpe had been watching Elsa talking to Clive and had seen his hand was bandaged. Later in the morning she slipped out to buy biscuits for them to have with their coffee. She paused in front of Clive's stall.

'What have you done to your hand?' she asked.

Clive glowered at her. 'Did Elsa send you over to ask?'

'No, why would she? I was worried about you, that's all.'

'Nothing about me is your business! When will you get that through that thick head of yours?'

Anne hurried away, tears of anger brimming in her eyes. That Clive Forbes was such a bastard. Could he ever be persuaded to change towards her? God, she hoped so.

Charlie arrived at work that morning with some trepidation. He dared not stay away in case it caused the foreman to become suspicious. To his surprise and great relief, work carried on as normal and he was given his duties for the morning, stacking cases and crates as they arrived. So the two men had believed his story. What a relief that was.

Later that day, one of the largest crates belonging to Jean-Paul was removed and driven away. Charlie overheard the directions given to the driver and hurriedly wrote down the address where the delivery was to be made, then carried on with his work. When he was sent out for sandwiches at lunchtime and was asked to get more than usual, he was certain the extra ones were for Peter, their prisoner. He couldn't hang about as he always went to the pub at lunchtime and he needed to behave as he normally would. As he walked outside he racked his brains as to how to help the lad.

Peter Adams had spent an uncomfortable night. He'd been desperate to relieve himself and cursed the beer he'd drunk the previous day, so it was with some relief he heard the key turn in the lock.

'I'm going to untie you,' said his jailer, who showed him a heavy wooden stake. 'Any trouble I'll bash your brains in . . . understand?'

Peter nodded.

When his hands were free, he almost ran over to the corner to relieve himself in a bucket his warder pointed to. When he'd finished he indicated the gag.

The man retied his hands then untied the gag, saying, 'Not a word!'

'I need a drink,' Peter said when the gag was finally removed. His mouth was dry and sore from being bound.

He was given a tin mug filled with water and a sandwich the man had brought with him, after which the gag was replaced and he was once more left alone.

Peter's heart sank as he heard the key turn in the lock. He felt dirty, hungry and frustrated. Locked away, he was unable to warn the authorities – or write his story of a lifetime. He had no proof now, as he knew the goods were being shipped out and it was obvious that he was being held here until then. But after? Cold shivers ran down his back as he thought about after. He knew he was going to die. How would they kill him, he wondered. His thoughts wandered to Elsa. She must be wondering where he was, but they'd fallen out at their last meeting and he knew how stubborn she was. She certainly wouldn't call the office to talk to him. Their last words to one another were spoken in anger and he deeply regretted that. What a bloody mess!

Elsa was fretting that there had been no word from Peter. Eventually she used the telephone in the shop and called the *Southern Evening Echo*, asking for her fiancé. She was told that he was out on a job and couldn't be contacted, which only increased her anxiety. To add to her worries, she found young Anne in tears in the room at the back of the shop.

'Whatever is the matter?' she asked. 'Aren't you well?'

Anne, her tear-stained face showing her abject misery, looked at Elsa. 'I'm pregnant!'

Elsa held her to her and closed her eyes. Oh my God, this is all we need, she thought. She was certain that Clive was the father, which would send Jed crazy. 'How far are you?' she asked.

'I've missed two periods. Jed will kill me. Please don't tell him!' the girl begged.

'I won't, but you can't hide it for long. He'll have to know some time or other.'

Anne just sobbed uncontrollably.

Margaret popped her head round the door, but withdrew when she saw what was going on. But she wasn't too surprised, as she'd heard Anne being sick once or twice.

Elsa made Anne a cup of tea and said, 'Drink this, then wash your face and come into the shop. We'll talk about it after closing

time.' Back behind the counter she told Margaret what had transpired. 'I don't know what to do,' she said. 'Jed will do his nut
when he finds out.'

'Poor girl,' said Margaret. 'She's had enough to cope with
losing her mother . . . and now this. Look, I know that the situation isn't desirable, but maybe having a baby would be the
making of her.'

'Whatever do you mean?' asked Elsa with surprise.

'It will give the girl someone to love . . . and to care for. A
purpose in life. What has she got at the moment?'

'Her whole life in front of her, Mother! An illegitimate child
is a hell of a burden to carry, or don't you agree?'

'Of course I do. However, I still think I'm right. Anyway,
wouldn't the father of the child marry her?'

'If it's who I think it is, she's got no chance.'

The arrival of some customers allayed further conversation for
a while and as Anne eventually joined them, nothing more was
said until closing time

Upstairs in the somewhat bare flat, Anne poured her heart out.
Clive was the father, of course, and the girl was beside herself
with worry.

'Do you think Clive will marry me when I tell him?' she asked.
'Only he snapped my head off when I spoke to him this morning.'

Taking Anne's hands in hers, Elsa said quietly, 'I think we both
know the answer to that.'

'I did love him,' Anne said, wiping her tears. 'I suppose if I
was honest, I still have feelings for him.'

'Do you want to have this baby?' asked Elsa.

'What other choice have I?'

'I hope you're not thinking of abortion?' Margaret said, looking
anxiously at her daughter.

'I'm just thinking of all the alternatives, of Anne's future.'

'And you think some back street woman is the answer? I'm ashamed of you!'

'Of course not! Really, Mum, what's got into you? I was thinking of taking her to the doctor, telling him the situation. With Anne suffering the loss of her mother, maybe he could find a medical reason for her to have the baby terminated legally, in hospital.'

'Kill my baby?' The note of anguish in Anne's voice made them turn and look at her. 'I couldn't do that, it would be sinful. I've already lost my mother. I can't lose my baby too!'

Margaret shot a look at Elsa. *I told you so* was obvious in her expression.

'That's a decision only you can make,' said Elsa. 'And of course we will help you in any way we can. Jed will be a problem, I'm afraid.'

'The baby will be his niece or nephew, after all!'

'That won't be his problem, Anne, his problem will be Clive Forbes.'

'Perhaps he will make him marry me!' the girl said hopefully.

'You wouldn't want to be married to a man who was forced into it,' Margaret interrupted. 'Believe me, it's bad enough when you marry a man who *is* willing!'

'Mother!' warned Elsa. Then, looking at Anne, she said, 'We can make sure that Clive makes some payment towards the upkeep of his child. That at least will be a help.'

The young girl looked brighter. 'As he watches the baby grow, maybe he'll feel differently?'

Elsa was silent. It was sad to see Anne clutch at such an unlikely straw.

'You must make an appointment to see the doctor soon,' said Margaret, and seeing the troubled look on Anne's face she added, 'I'll come with you if you like.'

'Would you, Mrs Carter? I would be so relieved if you did.'

'We'll wait to see what he has to say before we think of telling your brother,' Elsa suggested.

'When the time comes, will you tell him?' begged Anne. 'You could talk sense to him. Stop him doing an injury to Clive. He is the father of my child, after all.'

Elsa agreed, wondering just how she would cope with Jed's hatred of the market trader. But she had to defend Anne as best she could for her sake and that of her unborn child.

She wondered just what Clive's reaction would be when he was told he was to be a father. It probably wouldn't be the first time. A man like him could father half a dozen children and not give a damn! Never mind Jed, she could kill him herself at the moment, she was so angry. But she would have to be diplomatic when she told her partner about his sister's predicament. The last thing young Anne needed was for her brother to cause more trouble.

CHAPTER TWENTY-THREE

The problems of the Carters were further compounded when at lunchtime the following day George Carter walked into the shop. Margaret faced him alone, as Anne and Elsa were in the back of the premises, collecting more vegetables from the stock room.

Margaret noted that her husband's shirts were not as well ironed as they used to be, and although he still looked dapper there was an air of neglect about him, which saddened her.

'Hello, George. What can I do for you?' she asked.

'You can stop this nonsense and come home where you belong!' he retorted.

'Have you come here just to bully me?' she said calmly, not rising to the bait.

He was at a total loss. Before him stood a different woman.

Margaret Carter had found herself working with her daughter – mixing with people. The customers respected her opinions in their various discussions whilst she served them, which built her confidence, and what's more she was popular. She had blossomed more as each day dawned. She liked who she was now and cursed the years she had wasted with a man who had just treated her as his possession, and she was in no way going to take a backward step.

'Well?' she demanded.

'I need someone to look after me and the house,' he said.

'Get a char. After all, that's all I was to you. It might cost you a few bob, but there are plenty of women looking for jobs; you won't have any trouble.'

'How can you treat me like this? I am your husband, after all!'

'The only good thing you ever did for me, George Carter, was father our daughter . . . and you couldn't have done *that* without me!'

'I don't understand you at all.'

'You never have, but then you have never tried. I don't need you, George. In truth, I'm very much happier without you. I should have left you years ago!' Looking at her watch, she said, 'You had best be off or you'll be late back at the office, and that would never do.'

Speechless at her dismissal of him, George spun round and left hurriedly as two customers entered the shop. He couldn't stand being humiliated in front of strangers.

George admitted to himself that he was useless at living alone. There had always been a woman to care for his needs. First it was his mother and then Margaret, both excellent housewives, serving his every whim. Now, he was having to cope alone and he wasn't good at it. The house was a mess, which he hated being by nature a tidy person, but he seemed unable to manage the housework. When he came home from work, he was tired; consequently things went from bad to worse. He ate out most days but felt lonely sitting in a café as opposed to the comfort of his home with a wife to fuss over him. His work was suffering, which suited the jumped-up Jenkins who did his best to belittle him in front of his boss. George Carter was at his wits' end, especially now that Margaret had sent him packing. He walked into the nearest pub.

'A large whisky,' he told the barman.

An hour later, George walked somewhat unsteadily into his office. Jenkins was sitting at his desk in the room they shared. He pointedly looked at his watch.

'What time do you call this? You're late – this will not do.'

George ignored him and picked up some papers. The words blurred as he looked at them.

'Did you hear what I said?' Jenkins demanded.

'Yes. I'm not deaf.' His speech was slurred.

'Have you been drinking?' His associate rose from his seat, walked over to George's desk and bent towards him, immediately recoiling in disgust.

'You smell like a brewery! I will have to report this behaviour.'

George stood up so suddenly his chair was sent flying. Grabbing Jenkins by the lapels he roared, 'Report this too!' And he punched the other man on the chin, knocking him backwards and senseless.

As he gazed at the prostrate figure of the man who had caused him so much aggravation in the past, George was filled with a feeling of euphoria. Picking up his chair, he set it upright, sat on it, lit a cigarette and stared at Jenkins.

The door flew open and their boss rushed in, having heard the commotion. He looked with horror at the form on the floor and then at George.

'What happened here?'

'I hit him!'

'You what?'

Puffing on his cigarette George repeated casually, 'I hit him. Ever since he was promoted he's been a bastard to me and he pushed me just too far.'

Jenkins moaned as he began to come round.

Looking at the man with contempt, George said, 'You think he's so great, well let me tell you he is an idle sod. I do all my work and half of his whilst he sits on his backside feeling important.' He gave a lopsided grin and added, 'So now he's where he should be, flat on his back!'

'You're drunk!' his boss accused him.

'I am, and I will be back in the pub when I leave here tonight!'

His employer helped Jenkins to his feet, then glared at George.

'You won't have to wait until tonight; you can go to the pub now. You're fired! You can pick up your cards and money in the morning.'

'Suits me!' Picking up the pile of papers on his desk, he thrust them at Jenkins. 'Here, you can do your own work from now on!' he said, and left the room.

As he walked down the steps of the Civic Centre, he felt free. The man Jenkins had ridden him hard for the past weeks and every morning he had hated the thought of going to work; well, now he wouldn't have to. In his drunken state he wasn't worried about being unemployed – he didn't even consider it. He rubbed his scraped knuckles and smiled. He felt good and made his way to the pub to celebrate.

Fanny Braxton was donning her mantilla, ready for her Madam Carlotta role. This evening, Madge Coleman was coming for another private sitting where Fanny was all set to relieve her sitter of the remains of her money. So far she had taken four hundred of the five Madge had been left by an aunt, under the pretext of funding various children's homes, as instructed by the woman's dead husband. It had all been so easy.

The old woman cackled with glee. Some of the money had been spent on clothes and much of it in the pub, but now she fancied a day in London, which the poor fool would provide unknowingly.

The doorbell rang and Madam Carlotta opened it. To her surprise, Madge was not alone.

'This is my brother, who's lost his wife,' she said. 'Can he come to the sitting too?'

Money signs floated before Fanny's eyes. Her clients spent

more on a private sitting so tonight would be very profitable.

'Yes, that's fine,' she said, and ushered them into her front room, where the chenille-topped table was cleared in readiness.

The three of them sat down and Carlotta put out her hands, palm down on the table top, and closed her eyes. 'Are you there, Black Feather?'

There was a long pause.

'Madge Coleman is here and wants to communicate with her husband Albert.' She listened and then smiled at the woman. 'Albert is here, and he's pleased to see your brother. Now what do you want to ask, my dear?'

'I have one hundred pounds left of my legacy. What does he want me to do with it?'

'Ask Madam Carlotta, dear. The children at the homes you sent the other money to are benefiting greatly from your generosity. I have to go now.'

'Albert,' called Madge, 'don't leave me.'

Carlotta placed a comforting hand over her sitter's. 'He's gone, I'm afraid. Now then, I know that Nazareth House needs new beds and bedding, so if you give me your money I'll see that they get it.'

'Just a moment,' said her brother. 'I would like to see the receipts for the other money my sister gave you before she lets you have any more.'

'Receipts? What receipts?'

'Surely when you donated the money on behalf of my sister, the organisations gave you a receipt for the money?'

Carlotta sat up straight in her chair and oozed outrage. 'No, as a matter of fact they didn't.'

'No, I'm sure they didn't,' said the man, 'because you never handed it over.'

'What do you mean?'

'I have been to all the charities you told this woman you gave the money to and not one of them has any knowledge of such funds. How do you explain that?'

Fanny Braxton was flustered and nervous. 'I can't explain it. They have made a mistake, that's all.'

'Strange that they all made such a big error, don't you think?'

'I don't like what you are implying,' she cried.

From his pocket, the man withdrew a warrant card. 'I am Jack Johnson of the fraud squad, and you, lady, are nicked!'

'I thought you were her brother!'

'So did Albert. Don't you think that's strange?' He stood up and held out a pair of handcuffs. 'You will come quietly or I will have to use these,' he threatened.

Knowing that she was beaten, Fanny Braxton stood up. Taking off her mantilla she said, 'There's no need for those.'

The three of them walked outside to the police car that was waiting.

The London warehouse was busy with crates being moved out and others arriving. Peter Adams could hear the commotion from the cellar, where he remained a prisoner. He'd been given a cup of weak tea and a piece of bread and butter early that morning and a toilet break. Once he'd been settled back in the chair and bound and gagged, the foreman's mate leered at him.

'Best say your prayers, mate, 'cause you don't have long for this world!' He laughed heartily as he climbed the stairs to the door.

Charlie was getting desperate. It was nearing the end of the day and the last crate belonging to Devereux was about to be moved. Time was running out. The crate was an awkward size, so whilst the foreman, his mate and the carrier were trying to cope with it, Charlie sped upstairs to the office and grabbed the key to the cellar off the board of keys, then ran down the stairs and unlocked the door.

With his penknife he cut through Peter's bonds with some

difficulty, swearing softly, sweating with nerves. Taking off the gag, he shushed Peter, who was about to speak.

'Shut up, mate. We have to leg it out of here double quick.'

The two of them ran up the stairs, peered round the door and seeing the coast was clear ran as softly and as swiftly as they could for the warehouse door and freedom.

Outside, Peter stopped, only to be dragged on by Charlie. 'Don't stop, you bloody fool!' They jumped on to a passing bus and collapsed on a seat.

When he eventually recovered his breath, Peter clasped Charlie's hand. 'I don't know how to thank you,' he said. Then with a frown he asked, 'When they discover we have both scarpered, won't they go round to your house looking for you?'

'I thought of that,' he said. 'I sent the missus and the kids off to Southend to her mother last night. I'm coming with you to your digs until we work out what to do next.'

'There's not much I can do,' Peter wailed. 'All this was for nothing. The stuff has been moved out and I have no idea where it's going.'

With a broad grin Charlie said, 'But I have!' He produced a scrappy piece of paper from his pocket. 'I've got all the addresses here. I listened to what they told the driver!'

Peter was delighted. 'Charlie, I could kiss you!'

'Not until you've had a bath if you don't mind, mate.'

'Look,' said Peter, 'We'll go back to my digs and freshen up and then I'll think of our next move.'

Peter's landlady saw him when he returned to his digs. She looked at him with disdain.

'Been out on the razzle, have we?'

'Something like that,' he said. 'Would it be a lot of trouble to make my friend and me a pot of tea to have whilst I get changed and have a bath?'

'As long as the pair of you aren't going to drink. I don't have drunks in my house.'

'I promise the tea will be sufficient, and thank you.'

Charlie pulled a face when they were alone. 'Bit of an old battleaxe, that one, isn't she?'

Laughing, Peter said, 'No, she's all right. Make yourself comfortable, I'm going to clean up.'

The bath felt wonderful. He'd purchased some bath cubes on the way home and had put all three in the hot water. He lay back soaking, his brain working overtime. God bless Charlie for taking the addresses of the recipients of the fake antiques. And then there was the knowledge that the Dutchman was coming into the country carrying diamonds. If he only knew that man's name. All he had was a Christian name to go on. Would all this be enough for the Customs and Excise fraud squad? He had made up his mind to go to see them in the morning and put before them everything that he had, in exchange for the promise of an exclusive story if they were successful. If he were lucky, all would not be lost. But he would have to protect Charlie. If a case could be made, he prayed the paper would pay his informant enough to get away with his family permanently, because it would be obvious that it had been inside information that had set the ball rolling. He would know more when he'd spoken to the authorities.

When he was clean and wearing fresh clothes, he told Charlie of his plan as they drank their tea.

Charlie was horrified. 'You go to the authorities and I'll be in the frame too!'

'No, I promise you won't. Hopefully by the time it all comes out you'll be long gone.'

'What do you mean – hopefully?'

Peter tried to explain that everything hinged on what the

customs could do: if they would have enough proof to bring charges.

'Fuck me,' said Charlie, 'you had better make sure I'm in the clear after all I've done for you.'

'You have my word that you'll be protected,' Peter assured him. 'You can go to Southend with your family meantime. Give me your address so I can keep in touch.'

'That's all very well,' Charlie protested, 'but I'm out of work now. How will I manage?'

Peter put his hand in his pocket and took out his wallet. 'Look, I've got to pay for my digs, but here's a fiver to be going on with. I'll get some more from my editor when I get back to the paper. I won't let you down, I promise.'

Margaret Carter sat in the waiting room of the doctor's surgery in Southampton with a very nervous young lady.

'Now don't worry,' she said to Anne Sharpe. 'Doctors deal with this sort of thing every day.'

'I'm not wearing a wedding ring,' Anne said. 'They'll know I'm not married!'

'That's not important now. The main thing you have to think about is your baby.'

'I know, but then I keep wondering what Jed will do when he finds out. He hates Clive and he'll half kill me!'

'What, when you're pregnant? I don't think so. He's bound to be angry at first, but you'll see, he'll come round.'

The girl didn't look convinced and sat with her hands clasped so tightly her knuckles were white.

They returned to the shop in Kingsland Square a little later, where Margaret went and made them all a cup of coffee.

'How did you manage on your own?' she asked Elsa.

'I was fine, but never mind me. What did the doctor say?'

'Anne is almost three months gone and everything is fine . . . well, with her and the baby, that is. She's terrified of what her brother will say or do.'

'I'm wondering who we should tell first, Jed or Clive.'

'You'd best ask Anne about that,' Margaret suggested.

When the question was put to Anne she urged Elsa to tell Clive. 'He might want to make an honest woman of me,' the girl said wistfully.

Putting an arm round Anne's shoulder, Elsa said, 'Don't expect him to do that, love. Clive is certainly not the marrying sort – well, not at the moment anyway.'

'But I would make him a good wife.'

With a wry smile Elsa said, 'No doubt, but would he make you a good husband? I very much doubt it. I'll have a word with him at the end of the day as he packs up. You had better stay on with Mum until I've spoken to him.'

Clive Forbes was very surprised when Elsa strolled over to him as he packed his goods away.

'Well, I'm honoured that you should leave your ivory tower to talk to me. I'm intrigued. To what do I owe the pleasure?'

'As a matter of fact it is your pleasure we need to talk about.' At his puzzled look she said, 'Young Anne Sharpe is pregnant.'

'Oh, shit!' His eyes narrowed as he asked, 'Who's the father?'

'Don't try to get clever with me, Clive. You are the father and you know it.' As he started to bluster, Elsa said, 'Don't try to talk yourself out of this. You are responsible for her condition.'

'I did it all by myself, did I? She was perfectly willing, you know.'

'No one is disputing that. What are you going to do about it?'

'Well I'm not bloody marrying her, that's for sure.'

Elsa was incensed by his attitude. 'You really are a callous bastard!'

'Does her brother know?' he asked.

The sudden anxious look gave Elsa a certain satisfaction. 'Not yet, but of course we will have to tell him, and then all hell will be let loose.'

Clive's attitude changed. 'Look, I am sorry I put her in the club, but what can I do about it?'

'You can pay maintenance for the child when it's born. After all, you do have a responsibility here.'

He did not look pleased. 'All right. But that's as far as it goes! I don't want to know anything more. Don't expect me to take an interest in the brat.'

Elsa could hardly control her anger, she wanted to strike the man. If only his women customers who clung to his every word could hear him now, they would never shop with him again.

'Your main worry is what interest Jed will have in you when he knows,' she retorted before walking back to her shop.

'What did he say?' asked Anne hopefully.

Elsa decided that to lie and spare the girl's feelings was about the worst thing she could do for her, so she told her the truth.

Anne looked crestfallen and tears brimmed in her eyes.

'Don't you fret over him,' said Margaret, 'he's not worth the salt of your tears. You have plenty of others who really care about you. There's Jed, Elsa and me. We'll see you through all this, and when you've had the baby you'll be able to bring it to work. Between us we'll take care of you both, won't we, Elsa?'

'We certainly will.'

Looking at the two women, Anne said, 'You are both so kind. When will we have to tell my brother?'

Elsa gently said, 'I would suggest we do it now; get it over with. He'd be even more annoyed if he found out some other way. I'll come home with you if you like.'

The girl looked terrified. 'Does it have to be today?'

'If you put it off you'll keep looking for an excuse. Come on, how bad can it be? He won't murder you.'

'It's not me I'm really worried about,' said Anne as she put on her coat.

CHAPTER TWENTY-FOUR

'She's what? I'll kill the bastard!' was Jed's immediate reaction when Elsa broke the news of Anne's pregnancy. Elsa was relieved that the girl was in the kitchen making them a cup of tea, giving her a chance to reason with her brother.

'Jed, listen to me, please, before you do anything. Your sister has been through enough already; don't make things even worse. Clive has agreed to pay towards the cost of the baby.'

'When did he do that?'

'Today, when I broke the news to him.'

'He didn't offer to marry her, I'll bet!'

'No he didn't, and at least be grateful for that. Can you imagine what sort of husband he would be?'

Running his fingers through his hair, Jed said, 'I don't know what to say. I feel so guilty.' Glancing at Elsa he said, 'I've failed in my duty to take care of her, haven't I?'

'Not at all. You must never think that. Look, Jed, Elsa was searching for love because her father was away and her mum was in hospital. Besides, Clive has a way with women and she was vulnerable.'

'And he took advantage of that.'

Shaking her head, Elsa said, 'Sadly he did. However, Anne wants to keep the baby, and my mother says she needs someone to care for.'

'But an illegitimate child?' His look of anguish saddened Elsa. 'She'll be marked for life. You know what people think.'

'She'll cope with our help. She's got a job so she'll earn money, and after the child is born she can bring it to the shop. We'll take care of both of them between us, but please be kind to Anne. She's terrified of what you'll say and do.'

At that moment, his sister returned with a tray of tea and an anxious expression as she looked at him.

'Jed?'

He rose from the chair, took the tray from her trembling hands and held out his arms to her. 'Come here, you stupid girl.'

She ran to him with a sob in her voice as she said, 'I'm so sorry I've been so stupid. Don't be angry with me.'

Elsa watched the pair of them as the brother tried to assure his wayward sibling that everything was all right. Knowing Jed as she did, she wondered when he would be paying a visit to Clive.

It was mid-morning the following day and Clive was in full flow, with a large gathering of females listening intently to his sales spiel. He had turned his back for a moment to produce some fresh stock from his van when he was grabbed from behind and hurled across the table, where lots of his goods on display were sent flying in every direction.

There were loud screams from the women as Jed Sharpe bent down and hauled Clive to his feet before punching him squarely on the jaw, sending him sprawling once again.

'You know what that's for!' said Jed. 'Now, apart from paying up on a regular basis for the baby, you keep away from my sister or I'll kill you!' And he strode away.

There was an excited buzz among the spectators who had rushed over to see what the fuss was all about. Clive got to his feet, somewhat unsteadily. One of the male stallholders called out, 'You been undoing your flies in the wrong place again, Clive?'

'Perhaps that will teach you a lesson to leave the women alone in future,' called another. 'If you got my sister in the club, I'd bloody well string you up!'

The women who were Clive's customers looked at one another and started to move away.

'Ladies, ladies!' called Clive. 'No need to let a misunderstanding stop you buying. Look at this . . .'

But no one was interested.

Hearing the commotion, Elsa had walked over to her shop window and had witnessed most of the scene. It was time that swine got his come-uppance, she thought. Fortunately young Anne, who was in the back, hadn't seen anything and Elsa prayed that having vented his anger Jed would not cause another scene. Just as she was turning away from the window, she saw her ex-boss approaching.

Ernest Turner walked into the shop and looked round.

'You've done a good job here,' he said brusquely.

'Thank you,' said Elsa, but she sensed he was here for a reason. 'Is there something I can do for you?'

'You can tell me what is going on in the market.'

Somewhat puzzled, she said, 'I don't know what you mean.'

'My son was attacked here late one night. He's been in hospital in the burns unit.'

'So I heard. How is he?'

'Fortunately he's improving. His arm, hand and leg were burnt, so he'll be needing treatment for some time. I want to know who did it and why.'

'I have no idea, and what makes you think I would know?'

'He was your opposition, that's what. I imagine your business has increased since the stall has closed.'

Elsa did not take kindly to his accusation. 'Your stall wasn't the only one selling fruit and veg in the market,' she retorted. 'My business has thrived from the day I opened and Gill's has

214

suffered. He cheated his customers and they knew it. I'm sorry to have to say this to you, Mr Turner, but he was disliked from the moment he stepped into the market. Believe me, his stall offered no competition to me.'

Ernest Turner was no fool. Gill might be his son but he knew his character and his faults and was not surprised at what he was being told. He had hoped that by making his son work for him the boy would have changed. It would seem it hadn't.

'I'm sorry to hear about him cheating the customers. That does nothing for my good name and he won't be coming back.' He gazed round the shop again. 'I see little point in reopening the stall; it would be wasting my time and money. I like the idea of the flowers, by the way. Do they sell well?'

With a smile Elsa said, 'Yes they do, I'm happy to say.'

'Mm, might do that in my shop.' He stared at Elsa and said, 'I don't know who was behind Gill's attack, and I have no idea what Gill was doing in the market at the time, but if I'm honest, he was probably up to no good. You and your shop are the centre of all this, I'm certain.'

Elsa immediately thought of Jean-Paul and the conversation she had with him about Gill's giving her trouble. He had spoken afterwards to Clive, who'd had a bandaged hand the day following Gill's attack. It all added up to her, but she wasn't going to say so.

'Well, whatever it was, I'm really sorry to hear your son was hurt.'

'It was probably a painful lesson. I am his father, but I know my son. I'll sell the space to someone else. Take care, Elsa. Glad things are working out for you.' And he left the shop.

As she watched him walk away, Elsa thought about their conversation. Was Gill going to burn down her shop, was that the reason for his being in the market? She'd not even considered that until now and the idea filled her with horror. She and her mother could have been killed! Maybe she had good reason to thank the Frenchman . . . and Clive Forbes, after all.

As if on cue, Jean-Paul entered the premises. '*Bonjour, chérie.* How are you?'

'How strange,' she said. 'I was just thinking about you.'

'I am flattered. And what were you thinking?'

'Gill Turner was attacked in the market a few days ago, and I wondered if it was at your request?'

The smile faded. 'Attacked? What happened? I have been in London, so I have heard nothing.'

Elsa related the story. 'Did you have anything to do with this?'

'How could I? I wasn't here.'

'Perhaps you asked Clive Forbes to look out for me?'

'You are letting your imagination run away with you, *chérie*, but I am pleased that dreadful man is no longer a problem to you. That makes me very happy.

Elsa wasn't convinced, but what more could she say? As several customers arrived at the same time, the Frenchman took his leave. 'I will see you later, Elsa.'

He sauntered over to see Forbes. 'Good heavens, what has happened to you?' he asked, looking at Clive's bruised face.

'I got a girl into trouble and her brother gave me this,' the trader growled, pointing to his jaw.

The Frenchman roared with laughter. 'Haven't you ever heard of contraception?'

'Of course, but this time I forgot.'

'Your stall is not busy, that is unusual.'

'Lots of my customers saw the commotion and left,' he gave a lopsided grin, 'but they'll be back!'

'You are such an arrogant young man,' the Frenchman chided. 'Now tell me about Gill, the stallholder.'

Clive related the story and how Gill was trying to burn Elsa's shop down.

'I taught him a lesson. He's in hospital.'

Jean-Paul was angry when he heard the details. 'You did a good job. I will see you are well rewarded. Elsa suspects us both, but I don't think we will hear any more about it. She is probably grateful. I am in Southampton for two days then I have to return to London, so I'll settle up with you before I go.'

As he walked away Jean-Paul was pleased that the problem of the market trader had been solved. If his men in London had carried out his wishes, her young man would also be out of the picture, leaving his way clear with the girl who fascinated him so much.

The Frenchman would not have been so self-satisfied had he known that Peter Adams was in the office of the Customs and Excise, telling the officers his story, giving them all the addresses where the fake antiques had been delivered.

'Are you certain that these men were going to kill you?' he was asked.

'Too bloody right! Fortunately I was able to escape so I didn't have to wait around to see if I was wrong.'

'How did you escape?'

Peter thought long and hard about giving them Charlie's name, but he decided that his informant wouldn't be in trouble with the authorities. After all, it was Charlie who first put him on to the fraud and who had saved his life, so Peter told them how it all started. He also told them about the paintings that were taken to the home of Lord Travers.

'I have photographs of the men who are involved,' he told them, and handed over the photographs he'd had printed.

The customs officials looked at them, discussing their contents. Peter had the impression that the men in the pictures were no strangers to them. They rose from the table and walked to a corner where in low tones they talked together for a while before sitting down again.

The senior man spoke.

'Well, Mr Adams, you have been a great help. We have been watching these men for some time, gathering information, looking for proof, building a case against them. The foreman and his mate will be apprehended immediately and put into custody. It would be wise for your friend Charlie to stay in Southend for the time being, until we have enough proof to arrest Devereux and his associates.'

'What sort of proof?'

'We will visit these antique shops and confiscate the furniture and we will get in touch with the French authorities about Devereux's premises in Paris.'

'What about the man coming in with the diamonds?'

'Don't you worry about him; we'll have our men watching every port. We think we know who it might be.'

'And Lord Travers?'

'We didn't know about him,' Peter was told. 'That will have to be handled with kid gloves. If Lord Travers has got rid of the pictures, we could get into a lot of trouble if we go in with a warrant, so we'll keep that one on a back burner for the moment. But I need a statement from you today.'

'Then I can go home?'

'Certainly not. Devereux thinks you are dead. If he sees you, he'll make his escape. You must lie low, stay at your digs, and whatever you do, do not contact your family or friends, not even a girlfriend. Do you understand?'

Peter desperately wanted to talk to Elsa to tell her he was all right, and he was worried that Jean-Paul would make a play for her, which could be dangerous for Elsa. He told the customs men what the Frenchman had said to him about Elsa and how she had already been out to dinner with the man.

'I understand your concerns, but don't worry. We will be working with the police on this and someone will be watching

Devereux's every move, so Miss Carter will be protected if she is with him at any time. You will have to trust us, Mr Adams.'

'I don't have much choice, do I? Just one thing, gentlemen. When this all breaks, I want exclusive rights to the story. After all, that's where all this started and I almost got killed doing it.'

The officer grinned broadly. 'I don't see why we can't accommodate you. I'll have a word with my superior. Now off you go. Leave your address and we'll be in touch.'

'How long will I have to hide out?' Peter asked.

'As long as it takes. We can't jeopardise the case now, we've been working too long on it, but with your information we should be able to move fairly quickly. Now one of my officers will take your statement.'

Peter Adams did make one phone call after he left the customs. It was to his editor.

'Don't say my name,' he told his boss, 'but I need to see you in London as I can't be seen in Southampton.' And he gave the address of his digs.

CHAPTER TWENTY-FIVE

When Jean-Paul returned to his hotel it was to be told that there were two messages for him. When he read the first one he frowned. It was from Virginia, bemoaning the fact that Henry, her husband, had sent her packing after one affair too many, and asking Jean-Paul to call her. He looked at the telephone number, then screwed up the piece of paper, throwing it in the nearest waste paper bin. The other message, which was from Roger Johnson, brought a slow smile to his lips. He pocketed the slip of paper and went to his room, where he picked up the telephone and asked the receptionist to arrange for a dozen yellow roses to be sent to Elsa.

The staff of Carter and Sharpe were taking advantage of a welcome lull in business to enjoy a cup of tea when the florist arrived with the bouquet.

As Elsa took delivery of the perfect blooms, Anne and Margaret crowded round her as she read the enclosed card.

Blooms for my English rose. I have to go London unexpectedly, will call on my return. Jean-Paul.

'Blimey,' said Anne, 'he's got it bad . . . lucky devil, you!'

Margaret gave her daughter a questioning look. Elsa shrugged her shoulders. 'Well, that's the French for you,' she said.

'Romantic gestures are never for nothing,' Margaret said dryly. 'They always want something in return.'

'Like what?' asked her daughter.

'You'll find out soon enough, I'm sure,' Margaret said and walked away. 'I'll put the kettle on for another cuppa.'

As Elsa steeped the roses in water she was more than disappointed. She had thought it had been Peter who had sent them. She was getting really perturbed about his absence. The fact that he'd made no contact at all worried her and she wondered just what he'd got himself mixed up in. She began to wonder if Jean-Paul knew. After all, it was Peter who said the Frenchman was part of whatever he was investigating. It was very unsettling.

Jean-Paul caught a train to Waterloo and then took a taxi to the artist's address, where he was ushered inside. The two men walked up the stairs to the studio. There, on an easel, stood a picture. Jean-Paul studied it from a distance, then moved nearer to examine it more closely.

'This is incredible!' He put out his hand and gently touched the canvas. 'It is cracked with age; how did you manage that?'

'To make it brittle like that, you bake it at eighteen degrees for a day, spray it with vinegar and then apply urine to the surface. That will accelerate the deterioration to make the painting look older.'

With a wry look Jean-Paul asked, 'Did you do that yourself?'

Roger Johnson laughed loudly. 'Of course. I could hardly ask someone else to pee on my picture, could I?'

'It is amazing! Will it fool the experts?'

'I'll stake my life on it,' said the artist.

The Frenchman studied it again for a long time, then said, 'Pack it up, my friend, and I'll take it to Sotheby's. We'll soon find out. But from now on we will not meet. I'll contact you by phone only.'

Jean-Paul waited until the painting was ready to be moved. The two men shook hands, and the Frenchman left, hailed a passing taxi and asked to be taken to Sotheby's.

*   *   *

Clive Forbes was in a bad mood. It wasn't enough that he'd been caught out with fathering that stupid bitch's child, but his business had suffered ever since Jed Sharpe had given him a thrashing. Rumour had spread around the market that he'd got young Anne into trouble, and his customers, mostly female, had given his stall a miss, showing their disapproval. And what's more, Miss Goody Two Shoes had given him the cold shoulder after she broke the news to him.

He had noticed that her boyfriend, the reporter, hadn't been around lately but Jean-Paul had, and he wondered if Elsa's engagement was off. He'd seen the flowers being delivered and guessed the Frenchman had sent them. It stuck in his craw that the smooth frog had managed to get closer to Elsa than he ever had. Searching in the back of his van, he found the cocktail watch he'd bought for her weeks ago. Opening it, he wondered if he should try his luck.

After closing, he went home and had a bath, then put on his smartest clothes and made his way back to the market, stopping on the way for some Dutch courage in the nearest pub. He had rather more than he'd planned so he was well into his cups when he rang the bell outside the shop.

'I'll go,' Elsa called to her mother. As she made her way downstairs, she cursed the fact that there was no separate entrance to the flat upstairs. Any visitors had to walk through the shop to get to their private quarters.

She was very surprised to see Clive Forbes waiting on the doorstep and looking so smartly dressed.

'Hello, Elsa,' he said politely.

'What on earth are you doing here at this time?' she asked.

'I feel that we have always misunderstood each other . . . got off on the wrong foot, so to speak, and I wanted to make amends. Look, do you mind if I just step inside?' And he did so before she could refuse. He closed the door behind him.

'I'm not the bad lot you seem to think I am,' he began.

Annoyed at the way he pushed his way in, Elsa said, 'You are exactly the man I thought you were, Clive. Now I must ask you to leave.'

'Now don't be so hasty,' he said, taking the box from his pocket. 'Look, I bought this for you ages ago and I thought now was the time to give it to you.'

He opened it so she could see the contents.

Elsa looked at the watch and then at him. 'It's very nice, I'm sure, but no thank you, Clive. I want nothing from you.'

This further rejection infuriated the trader. He snapped the lid of the box shut. 'Amazing, isn't it? You turn away every kind gesture from me, but you flutter your bloody eyelashes at that French bastard every time he calls on you. Don't mind two-timing your boyfriend for him, but me, oh no. I'm not good enough!'

'You've been drinking!' she accused him.

'I've had a couple, yes.' He glared at her. 'Would you believe it – me, Clive Forbes, felt the need of some Dutch courage before seeing you! No other woman treats me the way you do.' He cast the box and watch aside. 'You are so bloody stuck up. What you need is a real man.'

He grabbed at her, holding her firmly, and assaulted her mouth with his.

Elsa struggled to be free of him, but his superior strength over-powered her and before she knew what was happening, Clive had pushed her to the floor.

She clawed at his face with her fingernails, drawing blood.

'You stroppy bitch!' he said and pinned her hands with one of his, pushing up her skirt with the other.

'You rotten bastard,' she cried, 'I'll kill you for this. Let me go!'

He just laughed at her. 'If you won't come to me of your own free will, I'll take you any way I can. I'm sick of you ignoring me. I am going to teach you a lesson, my girl!'

'Over my dead body you will!'

Margaret Carter, hearing the commotion had come downstairs to investigate. Now she picked up an empty metal bucket, used to stand the flowers in, and smashed Forbes over the head with it. He slumped to the floor, unconscious.

'Oh my God, Mother! You've killed him!' Elsa looked horrified.

Bending over the market trader, Margaret said, 'No I haven't. He's still breathing.' Taking the flowers out of another bucket she threw the contents over the still figure. Water splashed everywhere.

Elsa picked up a knife they used in the shop and stood over Clive Forbes as he moaned and regained consciousness.

He sat up slowly. 'My bloody head,' he said, holding the painful spot.

As he staggered to his feet, Elsa threatened him with the knife. Looking at his open trousers, she stared at him with disgust.

'Put it away, Clive, or I'll cut the bloody thing off!'

The water had sobered him a little and he looked embarrassed as he tidied himself, closing his flies. Then he held out his arms where his wet clothes hung on him.

'I'm soaking wet!' He looked from one woman to the other. 'I paid good money for this suit!' he complained.

Elsa pushed him towards the door, opened by her mother, and shoved him outside.

'Go home. And if you come within five feet of me ever again, I'll go to the police and tell them about tonight!' And she slammed the door shut. Once her assailant was safely outside, she started to shake from head to foot, almost collapsing against the counter.

Margaret rushed over to her. 'Are you all right, love?'

With a wry smile, Elsa answered, 'A bit bruised and shaken,

but a lot better off than I would have been if you hadn't made such a timely arrival.' She tidied her dishevelled garments with trembling fingers.

'One rape in the family is more than enough,' her mother muttered. 'Come along upstairs. We both need a drink, but let me mop the floor first.'

In their living room a few minutes later, she poured two glasses of sherry. 'Are you sure you don't want to report Clive Forbes to the police?'

'And have to go to court and tell them what happened? No thanks,' she said, rubbing her sore wrists. 'Fortunately it wasn't as serious as it could have been. Clive will be more frightened of me now, in case I do. He was drunk, otherwise he wouldn't have dared to call.' She chuckled softly. 'He certainly won't want to take on the battling Carters again! You swung that bucket with such vigour, Mum. I couldn't believe what I was seeing!'

'I should have done the same thing to your father years ago!'

They both started to laugh at the thought, until Elsa stopped, saying, 'Not a word of this to Anne, because if Jed got to hear of it, well, I dread to think what he would do.'

As she climbed into bed that night, Elsa longed for Peter. Had he been around, this would never have happened. Clive would never have thought of calling. Where the hell was Peter and why hadn't he been in touch?

Peter Adams had spoken to his editor who had travelled to London at his request, and given him all the relevant details of the case. His boss had sat listening intently.

'The customs have promised me an exclusive,' Peter said proudly, 'but I have to wait until they give me the all clear. As far as the Frenchman knows I'm dead.'

'Good work, Peter. You were right to pursue the story, but my God, you almost pushed your luck too far.'

'Thanks to Charlie, I'm alive. The paper will see he's rewarded, boss, won't they? Only the poor sod is now out of a job through me.'

'Give me his address and I'll get some cash to him.' He put his hand in his pocket, and taking his wallet out he handed Peter some notes. 'Here, you'll need this to keep you going. Let me know what's happening.' He rose to leave. Shaking Peter by the hand, he said, 'Good job. Well done! Call me if you need anything.'

Alone again, Peter felt pleased that his editor had been happy with him, but he desperately wanted to see Elsa. He couldn't bear the thought of her worrying about him any longer.

The next day he threw a few things in a bag and left his digs.

Just as Elsa was closing, the phone rang. Picking it up, she said, 'Carter and Sharpe, can I help you?'

'Don't say anything, just listen,' Peter said.

Elsa could hardly hide her excitement as she heard the familiar voice. When she put down the receiver she hurried upstairs and quickly changed.

'I'm going out, Mum,' she called. 'I may be some time as I'm going to the pictures. I'm meeting a friend there.'

'Have a nice time,' her mother answered.

Elsa made her way to the cinema and bought a ticket for the back circle. The usherette showed her to a seat in the back row as she requested. This part of the cinema was quiet with lots of empty seats. Before long a figure sat down beside her.

'Hello, Peter,' she whispered.

He took her into his arms and kissed her soundly.

In low tones they spoke.

'I've been frantic with worry,' she told him. 'Where on earth have you been?'

She listened intently as he told her what was going on. She was astounded at what she heard. He warned her about Jean-Paul.

'He's being watched,' he said, 'so keep out of his way.'

'That's difficult,' she said, 'because he comes into the shop.'

'That's all right,' he said, 'but, darling, please don't agree to see him, if he asks you out. I don't want you mixed up with him in any way.'

Elsa didn't tell him about the flowers the Frenchman had sent to her. Peter had enough to deal with as it was.

'I have to return to London tonight,' he told her. 'But I had to see you.'

'But isn't it dangerous for you to be here, after what the customs men said? If Jean-Paul sees you it will ruin everything.'

He took her into his arms. 'When you love somebody as I love you, tonight was worth the risk.'

'Oh, Peter. I love you too. I've missed you so much.'

'Look, darling, when this story does break, I may just get a job in Fleet Street. If I do, let's plan an early wedding?'

'Let's do it even if you don't get it.'

'Do you mean that?'

'Of course I do. I need you, Peter.'

He kissed her again. 'I must go. I'll be in touch when I can. You take care of yourself.' And he slipped quietly away.

Elsa sat in the cinema alone, hugging herself, delighted that her beloved Peter was safe after all. She went over the details of his story and still found it hard to come to terms with Jean-Paul's part in all this. She felt somewhat guilty about the flirtation with him, now she knew what sort of man he really was. She thought she was pretty smart at reading people, but her intuition had let her down as she had been taken in by his charm. He had said he would get in touch with her after his trip to London so she would have to find an excuse to keep away from him. Then she began to wonder if he had been followed to London.

*   *   *

The Frenchman had indeed been followed. Two plain-clothes policemen caught the same train as he did. They followed him to the artist's address and then on to Sotheby's. After that they split up. One followed him whilst the other went into the gallery to discover why the Frenchman had entered with a painting and left without it.

CHAPTER TWENTY-SIX

Hans Van der Haar walked down the gangway of the ferry in Harwich, his small suitcase in his hand, and headed for the 'Nothing to Declare' exit. As he passed through it, two Customs and Excise officers stopped him.

'Could I see your passport, sir?' one of them asked.

The Dutchman produced it and handed it over.

'What is the purpose of your visit?'

'Just visiting a friend,' Hans answered.

Looking at the size of the case the Dutchman was carrying, the officer said, 'Just a short stay, is it?'

'I can only spare a few days.' The jeweller felt his stomach tense as the man stared at him.

'Just bring your case over here please, sir.'

'Of course,' he said, trying to behave naturally.

The officers took out his pyjamas, two clean shirts and changes of underclothing. They searched his toilet bag. There was nothing untoward in anything. The clothes were returned to the case.

'Take off your jacket,' he was told.

'This is preposterous,' the man protested. 'I am here to stay with a friend, that's all.'

'Your jacket,' he was told sternly.

Reluctantly he removed it.

The officer took a lighter and a handkerchief from the pockets.

'There you are!' said Hans defiantly.

The officer began to feel the lining, the lapels and finally the collar. As he ran his hands along the material, he stopped and glared at the Dutchman.

'I would like you to accompany my colleague and me to a room nearby,' he said.

There the two men carefully removed the stitching to reveal several diamonds, carefully hidden among the stiffening of the collar. The customs official held them in the palm of his hand.

'You, Mr Van der Haar, are in deep trouble!'

Elsa Carter went about her work with a spring in her step. Her mother, watching her, remarked on it.

'You are walking on air this morning. Something has given you a new lease of life. What is it?'

Taking Margaret to one side, she whispered, 'I saw Peter last night.'

'Where has he been all this time, for goodness' sake?'

'He's working on a story, but I can't tell you about it at the moment. But the main thing is he's fine.'

'I'm glad to hear it,' said Margaret. 'When will you be seeing him again?'

'I really don't know, but you mustn't tell anyone he's been around. If anyone should ask you must say you haven't seen him.'

Intrigued, Margaret said, 'It all sounds very mysterious, but all right, I'll say nothing.'

Elsa decided to buy some cream cakes for them to have with their coffee as a treat for them all. To get to the baker's she had to pass Clive Forbes's stall. The market trader glowered at her. On the way back her friend Ruby waylaid her.

'Hey, love, have you seen Clive's face? It's all scratched down one side. I wonder what he's been up to this time?'

'I have no idea,' said Elsa, 'but I'm sure he deserved it, whatever the reason.'

'That boy will come to a sticky end, mark my words,' said Ruby. She lowered her voice. 'How's young Anne?'

The girl's pregnancy was no longer a secret among the traders, who whenever they saw her treated her kindly, which gave her the confidence to carry on with her daily life.

'She's fine,' Elsa assured the woman.

'Shame she got caught, though. It is a burden for a youngster to carry.'

'Well at least she has lots of friends to support her,' said Elsa. 'Jed has been really good with her.'

'After he had a go at old Clive, there.' Ruby chuckled heartily. 'I can't tell you the pleasure it gave me to see that arrogant bugger taken down a peg or two.'

'Must get back,' Elsa said, not wanting to be drawn further into a conversation about the man who tried to rape her. As she walked towards the parade, she saw her father skulking around, watching the shop from a distance. She walked over to him.

'Hello, Dad,' she said. 'What are you doing here? Why aren't you at work?'

'I got fired,' he told her.

'You what? Why on earth did they do that?'

'Because I punched that bastard Jenkins, that's why.'

Elsa looked horrified. Her father had worked for the council for many years without a stain on his character. 'Why on earth did you do that?'

'Because he pushed me too far one day.'

She frowned and asked, 'Had you been drinking?'

He hesitated and then said, 'I might have.'

She was furious with him. 'You never learn, do you! Your drinking drove us from the house and now it's cost you your job.'

'Thanks for your sympathy. A fine daughter you are, I must say.'

231

'Sympathy! You used to beat my mother . . . and you raped her!'

He paled at her onslaught. 'I'm sorry,' he wailed, 'I'll change, I swear I will, I just want you both to come home.'

Looking at the pathetic creature before her, Elsa was outraged. 'You had plenty of chances, Dad. Mother is happier now than I have ever seen her and I won't let you spoil that for her. Go home. Go and find another job!'

She decided to keep his presence from her mother. Why spoil her day? She felt she had made the right decision when she watched Margaret serving several customers. She was chirpy, looked years younger and was happy, which gave Elsa the greatest pleasure. She thanked the Lord that her Peter was so different from her father.

Virginia, Lady Travers booked in at the Star Hotel in Southampton's High Street. After signing the register she asked the receptionist if Mr Devereux was in the hotel.

'No, my lady, but we are expecting him today.'

'When he does arrive, will you let me know?' said Virginia, smiling sweetly. 'Please don't tell him I'm here, as I want to surprise him.'

'Very well, madam.'

Virginia took the lift to the second floor, tipped the porter, ordered a tray of tea and started to unpack. She ran a bath, after which she changed her underwear, smoothing the ivory cami-knickers over her body, pulled up her stockings and slipped into a dress. She sat the dressing table, brushed her blonde locks, sprayed herself with perfume and applied fresh make-up. She smiled slowly at the thought of seeing her ex-lover.

The telephone on her bedside table rang. It was the receptionist telling her that Mr Devereux had just arrived and was going up to his room, which was next door but one to hers.

* * *

Jean-Paul removed his jacket, loosened his tie and poured himself a whisky from the side table As he helped himself to a splash of soda, he was surprised to hear a knock on his door.

'Who is it?' he called.

A muffled voice answered, 'Room service, sir.'

Puzzled because he hadn't ordered anything, the Frenchman opened the door.

'Hello, darling,' said Virginia as she pushed the trolley with its ice bucket and champagne past him. 'I thought I'd give you a nice surprise.'

'Virginia, whatever are you playing at?' Jean-Paul was exasperated. When would this woman realise that their relationship was over?

Walking over to him, she played with the neck of his shirt, removing the loose tie. 'Why don't you make yourself comfortable whilst I open the bottle, then we can have a nice time together.'

'Those days are in the past. I thought I made that very clear!'

The cork popped and Virginia poured two glasses of champagne, then handed one to him. 'Don't be such a sourpuss. Good heavens, I've had enough with Henry laying down the law.' She moved closer to him and caressed his cheek. 'Be nice to me, darling. You know you won't be sorry.'

He pushed her firmly away. He sipped the contents of the glass and stared coldly at the woman opposite him. 'I'm not a fool, you know. You want to make use of me, now that you are on your own. Where have you been staying after leaving Henry?'

'At our place in London. Henry will have to make some provision for me and I want to keep the flat. Come back with me and we'll have a good time going out to dinner, to a few nightclubs. You can stay with me.'

'And be cited in your divorce case? No thank you!'

'Why are you being so difficult?' she cried.

'You no longer interest me,' he said cruelly.

She was furious. 'You men, you make me sick. Henry was too busy to spend time with me, yet he objected to my having any other friends.'

'Lovers, you mean.'

She ignored him. 'He has offered me a pittance as a divorce settlement.' Her eyes narrowed. 'You and he should be very careful how you treat me.'

The threat in her voice did not go unnoticed. 'And what exactly do you mean by that?'

'Well, darling, I know all about his private art collection, the genuine buys, and the few that are stolen. I also know who purchased them for him.'

Jean-Paul caught her by the wrist, making her wince. 'Don't ever threaten me, because I would be sad if I heard you had an unfortunate accident in the near future.'

'What do you mean?'

'You are a beautiful woman, Virginia, with your life before you. You will soon find another rich fool to take care of you.' He stroked her face. 'It would be a great pity if you were to lose your looks, don't you think?'

Putting her hands to her face, she asked, 'What are you saying?'

'Stay out of what doesn't concern you, or face the consequences – if you forgive the pun!'

She looked horrified. 'You wouldn't dare!'

He leaned towards her. 'Then don't push me too far!'

Virginia stared at Jean-Paul, who met her gaze with a coldness she'd not seen before. She knew that he meant every word – and she was afraid.

'Go back to your London flat, Virginia. You know lots of people from your social circle, you'll still have a good time, but keep out of my way, that's all.' He walked to the door and opened it.

She rose from her seat and walked out. In her room she repacked her bag and rang reception for someone to collect her suitcase and call a taxi to take her to the station. She wanted to get away, feeling that it would be safer to put a distance between her and her ex-lover as soon as possible.

Jean-Paul sat and contemplated the meeting he had just had with Virginia, trying to judge whether he had convinced her to keep silent. Women were so unpredictable. Could he take a chance? As he sat pondering the problem, he heard someone knock on Virginia's door and heard a man speak.

'I've come for your case, my lady.'

So Virginia was leaving. Good. He had obviously frightened her. He decided that she was far too vain to become a threat, as she wouldn't want to lose her looks: they were her future, after all. No, she wouldn't hinder his plans, which were going so well. Soon he would be able to return to Paris with his latest round of business complete, a much wealthier man.

The Frenchman wouldn't have been feeling so secure had he over-heard the conversation between Peter Adams and the officers who were investigating the case. Peter had been summoned to the customs offices to be updated on the latest results.

'The two men from the warehouse have been only too happy to talk to us to save their necks,' he was told. 'This fraud has been going on for some time, it would seem, but at Sotheby's Devereux was clever enough to ask their advice about the authenticity of the painting he took to them, so we can't hold him on that.'

'I thought he was a pretty smooth character when I met him,' said Peter. 'But what about the furniture?'

'We have all the pieces he sold. I must say, they were well aged; it would take a clever man to see that they were fakes, and of course the antique dealers who bought them were all certainly fooled. The Frenchman has a good name in the antiques world, but then we must remember much of his business is on the level. This other stuff is a sideline, although a very lucrative one, which, it seems from the information we received from the men in the warehouse, has been growing. And by the way, we picked up the Dutchman.'

'Did he have the diamonds on him?'

'He did, but so far has not named his accomplices. In time he will, no doubt.'

'People get greedy, don't they?' Peter remarked.

'And that's when they make mistakes.' The officer paused. 'Devereux had an interesting visitor last night at his hotel. A Lady Travers.'

Peter raised his eyebrows. 'Really?'

The officer nodded and with a broad grin said, 'It seems that Devereux and she were lovers at one time, but he cast her aside. Probably didn't want to upset her old man.'

'Then why was she there?'

'London gossip has it that she is a lady with a voracious sexual appetite and I suspect that his lordship has had enough. He is divorcing her.'

'Is she still in Southampton?' Peter asked.

'No, the Frenchman sent her packing, but we are going to pick her up for questioning. It should be interesting.'

'When will you pick up Devereux? I want to go home.'

'Give us a couple more days. We'll let you go back to Southampton as soon as possible, I promise.'

'Don't forget I have an exclusive story about all this,' Peter said.

'We won't forget. After all, you have helped us tremendously.'

As Peter left the office, he stopped at a telephone box and made a long distance call to Southampton. He would tell Elsa that things were going well and hopefully he would be home soon.

Elsa was delighted with the news.

'I believe that the Frenchman is in Southampton, darling,' he told her. 'If he comes to see you, be very careful what you say and for goodness' sake don't accept any invitations from him, will you?'

'Of course not! I want nothing to do with him, although in all honesty I still find it difficult to believe he is the criminal you say he is.'

Her reluctance worried Peter. 'Now listen to me, Elsa, this man is dangerous, despite his Gallic charm. If he suspects that you know about him and his dodgy dealings, goodness knows what he would do. Don't you forget it was him who told his men to dispose of me. He is ruthless beneath all that charm.'

'I'll be careful,' she assured him.

It was towards the latter part of the afternoon that Elsa saw Jean-Paul talking to Clive Forbes. She saw the Frenchman hand over a package, which by the shape looked like a picture or a mirror, but it was well wrapped, so she could only guess at the contents. The two men were talking with their heads close together, and then Clive nodded, and climbing into his van placing the article at the back.

To her dismay, Jean-Paul turned and made his way towards her shop. Elsa waited, her heart pounding.

'*Ma chérie*, he said, smiling at her. 'You look as beautiful and fresh as ever. How are you?'

'Fine, thank you, and you?'

'I am feeling good also. How is business?'

'The shop is doing well. Both Jed and I are pleased.'

'I am so happy for you. I told you you could do it, didn't I?'

'You did indeed.'

'You and I must have dinner tonight and catch up with everything.'

'I am sorry, Jean-Paul, but I have made other arrangements.'

As she looked at the Frenchman she still found it difficult to see him as a criminal. He was so charming, so smooth.

'What about tomorrow?' he asked.

'I am sorry, but I am really busy this week,' she said with a smile.

The Frenchman stared hard at her and asked, 'Has your fiancé been making trouble between us?'

There was something in his tone that made her watch her words carefully. She met his gaze. 'Peter? No, I've not seen him for a while; he's away on an assignment.' She noted the look of relief in his eyes.

'Are you trying to tell me that you don't want to see me any more, *chérie*?'

No, I am telling you that I am busy,' and trying to lighten the situation she added, 'What is the matter, Jean-Paul? Is it unusual for women to turn down your invitations?'

Chuckling softly, he said, 'As a matter of fact it is, but you are unlike any woman I know. I will have to ask you again, later this week, before I return to Paris.'

'But you will be back soon, won't you?'

Shrugging, he said, 'Probably not for some time. That's why I'm anxious to see you before I leave.'

Playing for time, she said, 'Maybe towards the weekend I might be free.'

'Then I will return, my sweet Elsa. You take care of yourself.' To her relief, he left the shop.

Anne sidled over and said, 'Why didn't you go to dinner with him? Any other woman would jump at the chance.'

'I have too much to do to go gallivanting about,' Elsa told her. 'Besides, you seem to forget that I am spoken for. Now then, help me to put out these fresh apples. Make sure there are no bruised ones in the box.'

*   *   *

238

But Jean-Paul Devereux was not so easily fooled. He sensed the tension in Elsa this afternoon. Something was different about her attitude. Oh yes, she had tried to hide it, but the difference was marked enough to make him suspicious. He would return to his hotel and make some phone calls.

CHAPTER TWENTY-SEVEN

Lady Travers had arrived at her flat in Chelsea, poured herself a drink, and had settled to read the paper, which was full of the news that the *Queen Mary* was due to dock in Southampton after winning the Blue Ribbon for the quickest crossing of the Atlantic Ocean on her voyage to New York, when there was a ring on her interconnecting telephone.

'Hello, who is it?'

'Detective Inspector James from Scotland Yard,' said a male voice. 'I would like to speak to you, Lady Travers.'

'You'd better come in,' she told him. But as she waited to open her flat door, she felt decidedly nervous. Scotland Yard? That sounded serious. She had no further time for contemplation as the doorbell rang.

The tall plain-clothes officer flashed his badge at her and introduced his colleague. 'This is Detective Inspector Baker.'

Virginia ushered the two men into her living room.

'What can I do for you, gentlemen?' she asked.

In Southampton, Jean-Paul sat on his bed making telephone calls. He rang the warehouse but received no answer, then he rang the artist who had painted the forgery. To his relief the man answered.

'Roger Johnson.'

'Roger! Devereux here, just wondering how you are?'

'Fine, thanks. Any news of the painting?'

'No, not yet, but you know how it is, it takes time for the

experts to go through their procedures. I just thought I'd give you a courtesy call.' The two men chatted for a while, then the Frenchman put down the receiver. There was obviously no trouble there. Maybe the men in the warehouse were on a delivery themselves. It was not unknown when sometimes the crates needed extra hands. Perhaps he was becoming paranoid, he told himself, but even so, he was unsettled.

Tomorrow he would collect the painting he had acquired from an art dealer from Forbes and take it to Henry Travers, then he would be free to return to Paris when he'd heard from Hans. He had half expected a call last evening but the Dutchman enjoyed the bright lights of London's nightclubs, he knew, so he assumed he would hear soon enough. He didn't know where Hans was staying or he would call him. Maybe the jeweller would wait until he returned to Holland. They had made no definite date, only that he would be contacted when the deal was completed. But to settle his troubled mind, he would pay another call on the lovely Elsa after he'd delivered his painting to Henry Travers.

The following morning, Elsa was taking the buckets of flowers to display outside the shop when Jean-Paul took her by surprise.

'*Bonjour*, Elsa. How are you this morning?'

Somewhat flustered, she said, 'I'm fine, but what on earth are you doing here so early?'

'I have to go to London unexpectedly, but when I return I will be round to see you and I will not take no for an answer this time. We will spend the evening together.'

Elsa felt his comment was more of a demand than an invitation. If she refused yet again, it might make him suspicious. 'Very well, Jean-Paul, I'll look forward to it.'

'Then, *au revoir, ma chérie. A bientôt.*'

She watched him walk over to Clive, retrieve the package he'd left with him, and leave the market.

As the Frenchman left, Clive looked up and saw her watching him. He glared at her, tapped the side of his nose and then turned away. Elsa, annoyed at his implication that she was nosy, glanced at the retreating figure of Jean-Paul and observed that an unknown man seemed to be following him at a discreet distance and wondered if it was a plain-clothes policeman. Peter had said the Frenchman was being watched. She gave an involuntary shiver as it made her realise the seriousness of the situation.

Later that day, Henry Travers were sitting with Jean-Paul in the aristocrat's drawing room, sipping champagne and unwrapping the painting. Henry was delighted as he studied the canvas.

'I have only one other Van Gogh, but this is exquisite. Look how he captures the light. I think many of his paintings show his depression, but this . . . this is so beautiful.'

'I am happy that you like it.'

Travers placed it lovingly on an easel. 'I will have to decide where to hang it in my gallery later – but now I will just enjoy it here.' Picking up his glass, he said, 'Did you know that Virginia and I have separated?'

'I heard,' said the Frenchman casually. He had no intention of telling Henry about Virginia's visit.

'I couldn't put up with her indiscretions any longer without becoming a laughing stock. I have the family name to consider, after all. But she won't be alone for long.' And he cast Jean-Paul a look that was full of meaning.

'She will not be with me, Henry, if that is what you are thinking.'

'I was just curious, that's all.'

The butler entered the room. 'The gentleman's car is here, my lord.'

Jean-Paul rose to his feet; pocketing the cheque that Travers had given him. The two men shook hands and walked to the front door.

'I'll be in touch,' said Devereux.

As he was driven away, Jean-Paul decided that it would be wise to let time pass before he did business with Henry Travers again. He would wait until the man's divorce was finalised, as he didn't want to become involved in any way. Women could be a distraction and a delight but they could also be an inconvenience and Virginia was certainly that.

Jean-Paul Devereux should have realised that a scorned woman could also be a danger. Despite her ex-lover's threats, after speaking to the men from Scotland Yard, Virginia agreed to accompany them to the station and make a statement.

The Frenchman asked the driver to take him to the warehouse in London's East End. He wanted to check that all was well there. He'd still been unable to raise the foreman on the telephone, which made him uneasy.

The car pulled up outside and Devereux, having asked the driver to wait, walked to the door. He turned the handle, but it was locked. He rang the bell, but no one came. He walked round the building but the big gates at the back were padlocked. Whatever was going on? Climbing back into the vehicle, he instructed the driver to take him to Waterloo Station.

Once on the train he racked his brains as to the reason for the closure of the warehouse. Could it be for a holiday period? He'd never enquired about shut-downs, as when he'd had goods stored there there had never been any difficulties about dates. The foreman and his associate had always been accommodating. Well, at least all his goods had been delivered, so for him there was really not a problem. He sat back and began reading the day's edition of *The Times*.

In the council offices at the Civic Centre, the auditor frowned as he pored over the figures before him. He flicked back two pages and started again. There was something definitely wrong here. There had been no problem when he started checking the accounts earlier that week. Figures for the beginning of the year all married together, but after mid-year he discovered one discrepancy after another. At the end of the day, he'd discovered that there was a shortage of almost a thousand pounds. He took his papers along to the head of the department.

Kingsland Square was busy and Jed Sharpe was standing in the shop talking to Elsa.

'We are doing really well,' he told her. 'We've well covered the rent for the month and believe it or not are breaking even, which is amazing for a new business.'

She was delighted. 'All my old customers have come here,' she told him, 'and we have new ones every day now that they've discovered our prices are still competitive. Some thought they would be more expensive, but they have all been delighted with the larger variety we offer. The extra, more expensive vegetables on offer, like the asparagus, have brought in the upper class people who have the money for them. The strawberries are going well, and the longer we keep our stocks at a reasonable level and turn them over quickly, the better we'll do. Later on, I thought of taking a florist's course, so we could do wedding bouquets and funeral wreaths, but that will have to wait a while.'

Laughing, Jed said, 'I do admire your get up and go, Elsa. You're full of ideas.'

'It's called spreading our wings,' she said with a broad grin. 'After all, look at the flowers: they sold well which allowed us to buy even more. Perhaps we should sell house plants too. What do you think?'

'If you go on like this,' he said, 'we'll have to get another shop, as we won't have room here for all these extras.'

The words of the Frenchman came to mind and she recalled his talking about a chain of shops. Who knows, she thought, in time if all goes well, why not? But what if she and Peter were married and he moved to Fleet Street to work – what then? Would he expect her to move there too? Looking around at the premises, and the colourful displays, her mother chatting away happily as she served the customers, and young Anne with her ever expanding girth, she knew she couldn't leave them or the shop. What would Peter have to say about that?

She served another customer and decided that Peter would have to commute every day. After all, lots of people did and it wasn't a long journey. There was no necessity for her to move. It wasn't as if he was being sent to the other end of the country. Having made her decision, she felt more settled about the future – but she would feel happier when he'd finished his current assignment. How would it all end, she wondered. Would Jean-Paul be arrested?

Henry Travers was sitting alone in the dining room of his Ascot home when the butler announced that there was a detective at the door, asking to see him.

Looking somewhat puzzled, he said, 'Take him into the library. I'll see him there when I've finished my meal.'

When eventually the aristocrat walked into the library, he was surprised to see several uniformed policemen standing there and a plain-clothes man with them. The tall detective held out a paper and said, 'Lord Travers, this is a warrant to search your premises.'

'A warrant? What the bloody hell is going on?'

Without a change of expression the detective said, 'I particularly wish to see the room in which you keep your art treasures. It's downstairs I believe.'

Henry started to protest until he was threatened with arrest for obstructing the police. 'Come along, sir, we can do this the hard way or the easy. It's up to you.'

Travers gave in, knowing that he really had no choice.

* * *

That evening, as Jean-Paul walked out of the lift in the reception area of the Star Hotel, he was stopped by the police.

'Jean-Paul Devereux, I'm arresting you on a charge of fraud for selling fake antiques.'

The Frenchman looked astonished. 'There must be some mistake,' he said.

A detective read him his rights and then said, 'We have a car waiting outside, sir. We don't want any fuss – it might upset the hotel residents.'

'I am one of the residents!' he replied indignantly.

'Not any more, sir, I'm afraid. Now do I have to handcuff you?'

'Certainly not! I am a gentleman, not a common criminal.'

'That remains to be seen,' said the man. 'Come with me, please.'

As they walked through the front door, Devereux saw the police car waiting, but what shook him was the figure of Peter Adams standing by the vehicle.

'You!' he said.

Peter gave a wry smile and said, 'Yes, no doubt you are surprised. You thought I would be dead by now, didn't you?'

'I have no idea what you mean.'

'Don't lie, you bastard. You told your men back at the warehouse to get rid of me – they even taunted me about it. And you told me not to worry about my girl, because you would look after her.'

'And I have done so, in your absence, *mon ami*. A lovely girl, much too good for you.'

This was too much for Peter. He lunged at the Frenchman, but Devereux was too quick for him. He pushed the policeman beside him into Peter, sending them both sprawling. In the mayhem, the criminal fled.

'Go after him,' yelled the detective. 'Don't let him get away.'

Jean-Paul was fast on his feet. He ran into the entrance of the nearby Dolphin Hotel, just as a wedding party was leaving. The sudden influx of people, blocking the way, hampered the progress of the police, which enabled the Frenchman to run the length of the drive of the hotel, past the Dolphin Tap Bar, and heave himself over the wall at the bottom. From here he ran on until he came to the side door of Holy Rood church, where he slipped inside and found himself in the vestry.

Out of breath, he paused, looking for somewhere to hide. He peered round the door very carefully to find one or two people sitting in the pews. He retreated back inside the vestry and looked about him. He saw a cassock hanging on a hook and quickly put it on over his suit, then took a dog collar and placed it round his neck, tucking in the large bib front. Picking up a bible from the side table, he walked out into the main body of the church. Keeping his head down, he headed for the church door.

Once outside he jumped on to the platform of a moving tram, heading towards the docks.

'Blimey, Father,' exclaimed the surprised driver, 'taking a chance like that will find you in heaven sooner than you think!'

Jean-Paul smiled and nodded to him, and sat down on the nearest empty wooden bench, paying his fare to the conductor. He had no idea what he was going to do, but he must not be caught.

He alighted at the dock gates and walked towards them.

The policeman on the gate greeted him. 'Good evening, Father, and where are you off to?'

'I am holding mass for one of the captains and his officers on one of the ships,' he said.

This was not an unusual occurrence and so the policeman didn't ask for a pass but let the Frenchman through.

'Say one for me whilst you're at it, will you, sir? I don't go to church much these days.'

'I will, my son,' muttered Jean-Paul as he walked purposefully towards the piers.

Meantime, the police were searching for their missing prisoner. They eventually went inside the church, looking beneath the pews and questioning the one person still sitting at prayer.

'Excuse me, madam,' said the detective quietly, 'but have you seen anyone else in here in the last twenty minutes?'

'No, only an old man who came to pray, that's all. He's just left. He can't have gone far – he was on crutches.'

'And there was no one else?' the officer persisted.

'No, only the priest.'

They made a thorough search, but without success.

'I want the surrounding area covered,' ordered the detective. 'He can't have got very far. I'll get some more coppers out to help.'

Peter Adams was furious that Devereux had slipped the net. He swore that one way or another he would find the bastard. With him it had now become personal!

CHAPTER TWENTY-EIGHT

Once inside the dock gates, Jean-Paul walked towards the water-front, looking at the various vessels tied up there. He perched on a bollard, took a cigarette from his pocket within the depths of his cassock, and lit it. What now? For the moment, he'd escaped the police searching for him, but where was he to go? No doubt the French police would have been notified of his escape and they too would be on the lookout for him. Taking a long drag on his cigarette, he cursed the young reporter. This was his fault. His nosing around had been the catalyst, and now Jean-Paul was in serious trouble.

Despite a prolonged search of the surrounding area, the police were unable to find their prisoner. Jack Hobbs, the chief detective, was livid.

'Where the hell could he be?' he asked his colleague. 'We've searched thoroughly. The docks police couldn't help. Everyone who entered the docks had a pass.' He scratched his head. 'Has every night watchman on every vessel been questioned?'

'Yes, sir. There are only the crew members on board.'

'Right, then we must make sure that all foreign ports are alerted in case he has managed to stow away on one of them.'

'One left for Amsterdam last night. Would he go there, do you think?'

'I think he would go anywhere he could, damn it! We'll circulate his picture. We'll use one of those that Peter Adams took in Paris. There were one or two that showed Devereux very clearly.'

Elsa was opening the shop early the following morning, at seven o'clock; the only people around were the market traders setting up their stalls, so she was delighted to see Peter walking towards her. She flung herself into his arms.

'Peter! What a lovely surprise.'

He swung her round and kissed her thoroughly. 'God, I have missed you,' he said, looking longingly at her.

'Has Jean-Paul been arrested?' she asked.

'No. The blighter got away. I was with the police when they arrested him at his hotel. He *was* surprised to see me, then he made a smart remark and I went to hit him and in the mêlée he got away.'

'Why did you want to hit him, for heaven's sake?'

'He said he had taken care of you during my absence.'

'He what?' Elsa was furious. 'He's lying, you know that, don't you?'

'I didn't stop to think.'

She glared at him. 'You didn't doubt me, I hope?'

'No, it wasn't like that. It was the fact that this man who tried to have me killed would even speak of you. I hated the fact that he had known you at all and it was his smile as he said it. I just wanted to swipe it off his bloody face!'

Putting her arms round his neck, she kissed him. 'Oh, Peter darling. My hero.'

He grinned broadly. 'Well, that was worth everything. Your hero, am I? Does that mean I get some kind of reward?'

Smiling sweetly, Elsa said, 'Of course . . . you can help me put out the vegetables and flowers in front of the shop!'

Pretending to be hurt, he said, 'That wasn't exactly what I had in mind.'

'I know what you had in mind, and I'm a good girl.'

'More's the pity,' he muttered as he followed her into the shop.

Anne Sharpe arrived just then. As she did so, she noticed that there were two police officers talking to Clive Forbes. She stopped and watched to see what they wanted. Elsa and Peter came out with the goods to display and she pointed out the police to them. The three of them stood together filled with curiosity.

'Clive Forbes,' said one of the constables, 'we want you to come to the station with us.'

'What on earth for?' he asked.

'Nothing serious, Mr Forbes. We just want you to help us with our inquiries, that's all.'

'But I've got a business to run,' he protested.

'You'll just be a bit late opening, sir.'

He started arguing vehemently.

'Now look, sir, you can come willingly or in handcuffs, what's it to be?'

Muttering under his breath, Clive closed the doors to his van and locked it. Then, turning, he said, 'Well, all right, let's get this over.'

As he was led away, Anne rushed forward. 'Where are they taking you, Clive?'

'He's just helping with inquiries, miss, that's all. Are you his girlfriend?'

'No she bloody well isn't,' Clive snapped.

'He's the father of my child!' she cried.

Elsa rushed over to her. 'Come away, Anne,' she urged, 'this is nothing to do with you,' and she led the now weeping girl back into the shop.

By now the other market traders had gathered to watch. Ruby turned to Burt and said, 'We all knew he'd have his collar felt at some time. A lot of his stuff was dodgy, I always thought.'

'Yeah. Cocky little bastard he is. It's young Anne I feel sorry for, having a man like that father her child.'

Ruby agreed. 'But she is young and foolish, and you know Clive. He could sweet-talk women; he had the gift of the gab.'

'He ever try it on you, Ruby?' asked Burt with a broad grin.

'You cheeky bugger! I've had my moments, let me tell you.'

'So I heard,' he said as he walked away, laughing loudly.

Inside the shop, Margaret and Elsa were trying to calm Anne down.

'Now you stop this,' said Margaret sternly. 'It isn't good for your baby.'

Elsa handed her a glass of water. 'You drink this,' she said. 'The constable said that Clive was helping them with their inquiries. He wasn't arrested.'

'Isn't that the same?'

'Dear me, no,' said Peter. 'It means he may have some information that may help them with a case, that's all. He'll probably be back later this morning, you'll see.'

This seemed to settle her, but whilst Anne carried on working he said to Elsa, 'It's all to do with Devereux; I'll put money on it. Look, darling, I must go to the office and write up my story. I'll see you tonight.' He kissed her and left.

At his desk in the offices of the *Southern Daily Echo*, Peter sat writing up the story about the smuggling ring that had been broken. The *Echo* would have the scoop and then they could sell it to the national papers, but Peter would get the by-line, which was just what he wanted. He hoped it would gain him enough credibility as a reporter to warrant an offer of employment from one of the nationals.

He liked the headline. LOCAL REPORTER HELPS BREAK INTER-NATIONAL SMUGGLING RING.

*　　　*　　　*

Elsa felt very proud when she saw the early edition and rushed to show her mother how well her fiancé had done.

'Look, Mum, Peter has his name and report on the front page!'

Margaret took the paper from her and read the article. 'Goodness me,' she said, 'this was really dangerous. Is he all right?'

With a joyous laugh, Elsa said, 'He's ten foot tall, but unfortunately Jean-Paul escaped.'

'Yes, it says so here.' With an anxious look at her daughter, she asked, 'You don't think he'll come back here, do you?'

'Why on earth would he risk everything to do that?' But as she said the words, she suddenly knew that Jean-Paul *would* return and a cold chill ran down her back. She tried to shake the thought, but it stayed with her all through the day.

It was afternoon before Clive Forbes returned to his pitch and opened up his van. He'd had a fit when the Old Bill had taken him away. But at the station they had only asked him questions about the Frenchman, Devereux. Clive had been very careful how he'd answered.

'You have been seen talking to Devereux,' said the detective who was questioning him.

'Yes, that's right,' said Clive. 'He came up to me and made himself known.'

'What did he want?'

'He asked me to hold various packages for him to be collected by different people.'

'What was in the packages?'

'I don't know. They were always well wrapped.'

The detective looked at him suspiciously. 'Didn't you wonder?'

'Of course I did, wouldn't you? But he paid me to do it, and I wasn't going to turn down a few quid, so I said yes.'

'Didn't you ever wonder if the packages were dodgy?' the detective probed.

'Why would I think that? Mr Devereux was educated, well dressed, had good manners. I never for one moment thought he might be a villain.'

They questioned him at great length before they let him go, telling him not to leave Southampton.

'Why the hell would I do that? I've done nothing wrong and I've got a living to make. You've cost me a morning's work as it is, and I don't suppose you'll give me any compensation?'

'Don't get cocky, son,' he was told.

Truth to tell, Clive was relieved to be outside the police station. Such places made him nervous. He'd been sailing close to the wind all his working life, and today had shaken his confidence somewhat. But they couldn't pin anything on him apart from holding unknown goods for the Frenchman, and that wasn't an offence unless he knew the stuff was dodgy, and the police would have to prove that.

As soon as he started to set up his stall, Anne Sharpe came rushing over. 'Is everything all right, Clive?' she asked.

'Of course it is. Why shouldn't it be, and what's it to you anyway?'

'I was worried about you, that's all.'

'Listen to me, girl, just get it into your head that nothing I do is any of your business – now or ever! Now bugger off and don't bother me. I've already lost most of the day.'

She turned on her heel and walked away, muttering under her breath, 'Why do I care about that bastard?' But she knew that whatever Clive said to her, however unkind he was to her, he was her first love . . . and probably her last. After all, who would want her with an illegitimate child?

Putting her hand over her stomach, she felt where her baby was growing. At least she would have Clive's baby, someone to love and care for, and whatever hardships came her way she would have something that really belonged to her.

Elsa had seen the exchange between Anne and Clive and saw the hurt the man had caused yet again. When oh when would the girl put the market trader out of her mind?

That evening, Peter took his girl out for a meal. After ordering, he leaned across the table and took her hand. He was lost in thought gazing at her hand in his; then he looked up.

'You know, there was a time when I thought I'd never see you again.'

'Oh, Peter darling, don't say that.'

'It's true. And do you know what really upset me?'

Elsa shook her head; she was too emotional to say anything.

'I was thinking how awful that the last words we had exchanged had been in anger.'

She frowned and looked puzzled.

'It was over the shop and you not discussing it with me. Remember?'

'Yes, I do, but stop thinking about it. After all, you are safe and we are together.' Trying to lift his mood, she said, 'I read your article. It was brilliant.'

He suddenly grinned at her. 'You see, apart from being a hero, I'm a damned good reporter! My God, girl, what a package you will be getting.'

'And I might say, Mr Adams, you won't be doing so badly either!'

The waiter placed their starters before them. As they tucked into the prawn cocktail, Peter asked, 'How is the business going?'

'Really well. And Mum loves being there. It's been really good for her.'

Peter hesitated, then said, 'What will your mother do when we get married?'

'What do you mean?'

'Will she mind living on her own?' At the look of consterna-

255

tion on Elsa's face he said, 'After all, we will need a place, won't we?'

'Yes of course, but we won't be getting married just yet. There's plenty of time to sort that out in the future.'

Elsa felt that it was not what Peter wanted to hear, especially as she had said they would marry when the case was over. But, she wanted to build up the business and save a bit of money, and yes, she did want a place of her own, but she wanted to make sure that her mother was happy and wouldn't mind living alone, and there was Anne to worry about . . . all these thoughts flooded her brain. Much as she wanted to marry Peter, there were other things to consider too. Life was not as simple as he seemed to think.

George Carter was very surprised to receive a letter from the council in the morning post. Even more surprising was that his ex-boss asked him to go and see him as soon as possible.

After shaving, he put on a clean shirt, grateful he'd not used all the clean ones from the laundry, and polished his shoes. He didn't want them to think he'd gone downhill since his departure. But his legs were shaking as he walked up the steps of the Civic Centre and knocked on the door of the inner sanctum, as he'd always called his boss's office.

'Mr Carter – George – please come in.'

The warm greeting made George even more nervous. 'You wanted to see me, Mr Edmonds?

'Sit down, please.' Percy Edmonds smiled and said, 'I owe you an apology.'

George nearly choked on his surprise. 'You do?'

'We've had the auditors in and it would seem that Jenkins has misappropriated some of our money.'

His confidence growing, George said, 'Has he indeed?'

Looking a little flustered, Edmonds said, 'Yes, I'm afraid so.

It would seem I misjudged him as I misjudged you – but for different reasons, you understand,' he hastened to add.

'I did tell you that he wasn't to be trusted.'

'You did, you did.'

'And you asked me here just to tell me that?' George was really enjoying the situation now. He'd been right about the little bastard after all.

'Well, not just that. In the circumstances we wondered if you would consider returning?'

'As office manager?' He met the other man's gaze and raised his eyebrows, waiting for an answer.

'Yes . . . but only on the understanding that you will never be seen to have been drinking. After all, that would not be fitting in that position . . . or any other. I'm sure you understand I must make that clear?'

'As long as you understand that on that particular day I had been driven to it by that bastard Jenkins.'

'I'm sure he was most difficult to work with.'

'What happened to him?'

'He was arrested.'

George leaned back in the chair and smiled across the desk at his superior sitting opposite. 'In which case I'll be happy to accept your apology, and the position of office manager.'

As he left the building, he felt like a man again. There was just one thing more he now needed to do to make his world complete.

CHAPTER TWENTY-NINE

George Carter stepped into Carter and Sharpe, wearing a smile. He walked up to the counter and spoke to his wife.

'Hello, Margaret, my dear. Lovely day, isn't it?'

And indeed it was. The sun was shining from a blue sky, with a few clouds moving slowly as there was but a slight breeze. Only the window blind outside the shop kept the rays of the sun from spoiling the colourful display inside.

Margaret looked at her husband with suspicion. 'Good morning,' she said quietly, 'and what has pleased you so much? I can't remember the last time I saw you so cock-a-hoop.'

He preened as he said, 'I was right all along about that bastard Jenkins. He got caught with his fingers in the till, and this morning I have been reinstated . . . and I have been given the position of office manager!'

'Oh, George, I am so pleased for you. You deserve the post after all these years.'

'You are absolutely right. I wondered if you would care to come out with me this evening and celebrate?'

Margaret froze. She gazed at the man before her, knowing full well the reason behind the invitation. As she studied him she realised that she felt absolutely nothing for him. He was like a stranger to her.

'I am really happy for you, George, but no thank you, I'll pass on the invitation.'

He was nonplussed. He had been sure that now things were

back to normal in his working life, his wife would be only too happy to resume normal relations with him and return to the house. Such was his arrogance; he couldn't believe she didn't want the same thing.

'Why are you behaving like this?' he demanded.

The one or two customers in the shop lingered to hear what she had to say. Elsa who was standing nearby was also waiting, ready to step in if she thought it necessary.

Very quietly and deliberately Margaret said, 'George Carter, I spent over twenty years living with you, in which time you treated me as your chattel, not as your wife, not even as a human being. Why on earth would I want to return to that existence? Give me one good reason!'

There was a sound of polite applause from the watching women.

Only then was George aware of the other people. He looked round and saw them all standing watching, waiting. His cheeks flushed with anger.

'You took your wedding vows, same as me,' he protested.

'Yes I did. To love, honour and obey, as I recall. I obeyed you, but from you there was no love and certainly no honour. No, George, I don't want to live with you again. As a matter of fact, I don't love you, and what's more I don't even like you, so go away and leave me in peace. I am happier now than I have ever been.'

She turned on her heel and walked into the back of the shop amid the cheers of the watching women.

Elsa walked round the counter and, taking her father's arm, led him outside. 'Look, Dad,' she said, 'we are both pleased about your job, but you have to accept that Mum is never coming home.'

He turned on her, eyes flashing with anger. 'It's all your bloody fault! You with your big ideas. If you hadn't started this business, she would still be with me.'

She cast a stony glare at him. 'There you are wrong. I would never have let my mother endure any more beatings from you. We would have left anyway after the last time. Or have you forgotten what happened?'

He glared at her, and stomped away.

One or two of the women were leaving the shop. One stopped Elsa. 'God! I do admire your mum,' she said. 'Many a time I've wanted to say the same to my old man, but I didn't dare.'

'Just remember Mrs Pankhurst,' said Elsa. 'She fought for women's rights. We do have them, you know.' And she walked inside in search of her mother.

Margaret was sitting on a sack of potatoes in the stock room. 'Would you believe the cheek of your father?' she said. 'I could hardly believe what I was hearing. He's forgotten that he raped me, and all the beatings I've taken over the years.'

Putting an arm round her mother, Elsa said, 'I was so proud of you. You told him with such dignity.'

'If I lived with him again, I wouldn't have any bloody dignity!'

'But you live here, and you have, so let's have a cup of tea and celebrate women's rightful place in the world.'

Margaret laughed. 'You and I, Elsa, would have made a fine couple of suffragettes!' And it wouldn't just have been the vote we were fighting for, but equal rights in all things – especially marriage!'

Henry Travers had certainly suffered a loss of dignity when he was arrested and charged with receiving stolen goods. There was no denying it as the police had confiscated the paintings he had bought from Jean-Paul Devereux. When they took them down carefully from the walls of his private art collection, it hurt as he looked at the empty spaces. This large and elegant room had given him hours of pleasure. There were still those paintings left that he had bought legitimately, but the stolen ones had that edge. The knowledge that he really had no right to them had only added to their lustre.

His expensive lawyer had managed to get the aristocrat released on bail, but he had to hand over his passport and promise not to leave the country.

When Virginia read about the case in the paper, she had smiled with triumph. 'What price the family honour now, darling?' she said quietly. After all, it had been his main excuse when he told her to leave. Infidelity seemed such a minor crime in comparison. But as she read on, she was very unsettled when she saw in the report that Jean-Paul had escaped arrest and was now wanted by the police. She was glad that she was living in a place with such security, because she knew that her ex-lover would be wondering where the information about Henry came from. It wouldn't be too difficult to put together the facts. She automatically put her hands to her face in panic. She would go abroad . . . but where? Certainly not France!

Devereux was not that far away. He guessed that the police would assume that he would make a dash to cross the English Channel and would probably have all the sea ports covered; the last place they would look for him would be locally. Still in the clothes of the clergy, which he found was an excellent disguise, he had begged a lift from a van driver who was going to Hamble, a small yachting village on the outskirts of Southampton. There, he had hired a small yacht and sailed up the river to Beaulieu, where he had purchased some suitable clothes and food to give him time to make plans.

He sat in the cockpit of the boat with a cup of coffee and read the papers. He was shocked to read that Henry had been arrested and immediately guessed that the information had come from his errant wife. It had been a mistake to let her go. He obviously had not scared her enough.

Then there was the young reporter who had put him in this position. His eyes narrowed and his mouth set in a tight line. He certainly would be made to realise just who he was dealing with. He lit a cigarette and pondered on the problem. Peter Adams would surely pay for this. And then he thought of Elsa. Everyone had an Achilles heel, and she was clearly Adams's.

Looking in the chart drawer, he searched through them until he found the one showing the Isle of Wight and another for the Channel Islands. He studied them closely, thankful that he had learned to sail at an early age and had owned a yacht for several years, so was quite at home in this environment.

At the moment, money was not a problem, as he always carried plenty with him and the police hadn't searched him when they arrested him. If he could eventually make it to Switzerland, he had money in a Swiss bank account, and there he would be safe . . . but first there was something he had to do.

A week had passed since Peter's story had hit the local paper and then the nationals, and today he was off to London for an interview with the editor of the *Daily Mirror*.

Elsa was thrilled for him when he told her. 'It's what you have worked for,' she said as she hugged him. 'I'll keep my fingers crossed for you.'

Cupping her face with his hands he stared into her eyes and said, 'Whichever way it goes, I want us to make plans to get married, soon – if you still want to, of course.'

Seeing the uncertainty in his eyes, she assured him, 'Of course I do, you goose. Why would you doubt it?'

'Just a feeling I had when we talked about your mother a while ago.'

'Well, I've thought about that,' she told him. 'If she doesn't want to live over the shop on her own, perhaps Anne would like to share with her. After she's had the baby it would be much more convenient to live over the shop.'

This solution had come to Elsa when she'd considered the problem of Margaret's living arrangements whenever she and Peter did marry. Margaret had been more than happy with the idea.

'I'd love it,' she had said. 'Anne will need some help with caring for the baby, she's so young. But I wouldn't say anything to her about this until you and Peter have set a date.' Taking Elsa's hands in hers, she said softly, 'He's a good man, love. He'll make you happy and I couldn't want a better man for a son-in-law.'

After the interview, Peter Adams made his way to Waterloo Station where he put through a call to Elsa at the shop.

'I'm waiting for a train,' he told her. 'I'll go home and have a wash and change before I come and collect you. We are going out for the evening.'

'How did it go?' she asked anxiously.

'I'll tell you when I see you,' he teased.

'Peter! Don't be so cruel.'

Laughing, he said, 'Put on your best bib and tucker, darling, we are off to celebrate . . . and that's all I'm saying.'

'Well?' Both Anne and Margaret were waiting for the news.

'He won't tell me, the little beggar, but he says we are going out to celebrate, so it must be good.'

They both cheered and hugged her. The three of them danced round in circles until someone walked into the shop and wondered what was going on.

Peter and Elsa dined in fine style at the Tivoli restaurant. He described the time spent with the editor and the tour of the presses.

'They are huge!' he said. 'And the noise! But oh, darling, the buzz of excitement in the place.'

'When do you start?'

'Next month. I'll have to catch an early train each morning, and I will probably be late home sometimes, because I'll have to go on whatever assignments they give me.' His eyes shone with excitement. 'You are looking at a junior crime reporter!'

Her heart sank for a moment, thinking of the danger he had already faced in pursuit of a story, but she couldn't spoil his triumph, so she just smiled.

'That's wonderful,' she said. 'I am so proud of you.'

It was a fine summer evening, so they walked home through the park, holding hands, talking about the future.

'I'll be getting a better salary even with the train fares,' Peter said, 'so we'll be able to find a decent place to rent. It'll have to be furnished to start with, but who knows, in time perhaps we will be able to buy a small house.'

'That would be lovely,' Elsa said, 'and with the money I make from the shop as well, we would be able to save between us for the deposit.'

He stopped, and taking her into his arms said joyfully, 'We are on our way, my darling, and nothing can spoil it for us.' And he kissed her with such longing, it made her breathless. 'I can't wait for us to get married,' he said, his voice husky with passion, his hand caressing her breast.

Gently easing him away, she said, 'Well, I'm afraid you will have to. Come on, Peter darling, before we get arrested.'

He chuckled softly. 'Elsa Carter, you are no fun!'

'I will be when I'm Elsa Adams, I promise. Come on, it's late.'

When they eventually arrived at Kingsland Square, Peter waited to see Elsa unlock the door before he hailed a passing taxi to take him home.

Moments later there was an urgent knocking on the shop door.

Elsa, halfway up the stairs, stopped. Peter must have forgotten something, she thought, and went back to unlock the door. She was surprised to see that the figure silhouetted against the very low light of the street lamp was not that of her fiancé, but of a priest.

CHAPTER THIRTY

'*Bonsoir, chérie.*' The priest caught her by the arm and walked into the shop.

'Jean-Paul!' Elsa was so shocked to hear the familiar voice, she thought she was going to faint. Her legs no longer seemed to hold her and she would have staggered but Devereux held on to her, keeping her on her feet.

'Steady now,' he said softly. 'There is no need to be frightened. I am not going to hurt you.'

Pulling herself together, she said, 'Hurt me? Why on earth would you do that?'

'Exactly.'

'What the devil are you doing here? You are wanted by the police.' As she spoke to him she was panicking inside. I must keep calm, she thought.

'Alas, *chérie*, that is true. I had a perfectly good business until your young man interfered with it!'

The coldness in his tone made her heart race. 'Faking antiques and selling stolen artefacts? You call that a business?'

'There are many ways of making money, Elsa. Few people are totally honest.'

She was remembering how he had treated Peter and her anger began to build. She fought to keep in control. 'And others are gullible. You cheated them . . . and you cheated me.'

He sounded puzzled at her outburst. 'Cheated you, *chérie*? How did I do that?'

'I believed you to be a gentleman. I liked you – admired you even. What a fool I was!'

'When I was with you, Elsa my dear, I was a gentleman.'

'No, Jean-Paul, you are a criminal, a wolf in sheep's clothing.'

She heard the chuckle as he said, 'You English and your quaint phrases.'

'How dare you laugh!' She was outraged by this man, standing before her so calmly when he could have been responsible for Peter's death, had her fiancé not been lucky enough to escape.

'You are no gentleman, Jean-Paul. You are a common criminal and I want you to leave. Now!'

'That's exactly what I intend to do, but you are coming with me.'

She was confused. 'What on earth do you mean?'

'I have to get away and I know the police are looking for me. You will be my insurance, *chérie*.'

She was terrified. Suddenly she saw the Frenchman for what he really was. Calculating, sinister – and very dangerous.

'I am going nowhere!' She started to struggle. 'Let me go or I'll scream the place down!'

Devereux bunched his hand into a fist and punched her on the chin, knocking her unconscious.

'I am so sorry, *chérie*, but I had no choice,' he murmured. Then, picking her limp body up, he put her over his shoulder and took her outside, quietly closing the shop door, and placed her gently in the front seat of a car which was parked near by.

When Elsa eventually recovered consciousness, she was completely disorientated. Looking around, she wondered where she was. Nothing looked familiar. She sat up and discovered that she was lying on a bunk, on what seemed to be a boat. She got to her feet and staggered. The boat was moving!

The hatch to the upper deck was open, and as she made her

way to the few steep steps she could see above her a star-filled sky. She climbed gingerly up the steps and saw Jean-Paul at the helm.

'Where are we?' she asked.

'Elsa! How are you feeling?'

'My chin hurts . . . you hit me!' she said, suddenly remembering.

'I am very sorry, *chérie*, but I couldn't have you making a noise and spoiling my plans.'

She looked about her. In the far distance there were lights. It was obvious that they were some way from the coast. It was dark and quiet.

'Where are you taking me?'

'You don't need to know, Elsa my dear. All you need to do is behave. There is no way of escape, so just enjoy the voyage. At least this way we can spend time together.'

'You have no right to do this!'

He laughed. 'Right has nothing to do with it. I need you as a bargaining chip.'

'In other words I am your hostage?'

'*Ma chère*, that is not the word I would use, but if you insist. Now, would you please make us some coffee? You will find everything you need in the galley.'

What choice do I have? she asked herself. She was cold and thirsty, and there was absolutely nothing she could do for now. They must eventually land somewhere, then she would try to get away. She couldn't sail a yacht so she couldn't try to knock the Frenchman out. It would put her in even more danger.

She filled the kettle, lit the burner on the small stove and looked for something warm to wear. Finding a woollen sweater, she put that on over her dress. It was too big for her but at least she was warmer.

Having made the coffee, she filled two mugs and took them

above. She handed one to her captor, then sat down opposite him.

He pushed a rug over to her and said, 'Here, put this round your legs. It will keep out the damp air.'

Elsa tried to reason with him. 'This is a crazy thing to do, Jean-Paul. You are already in so much trouble. Don't you see, taking me with you will only make matters worse?'

'It will buy me time, Elsa. You won't come to any harm, I promise. When I can, I will set you free.'

She wanted to believe him, but how could she? He was a desperate man, fleeing from the law. She might buy him time in some way, but after that . . . ?

As she sat drinking her coffee, Elsa was trying to think. Her mother wouldn't realise she wasn't at home until she woke up. She tried to see the time on her wristwatch by the deck lights. It was two o'clock in the morning. Would her mother get in touch with Peter? She probably would, as she would be worried. Then what would happen? Even when they realised she was actually missing, where would they search? They would not even think of her on a boat in the middle of the Channel somewhere. She was filled with despair. She didn't even know where they were headed. Probably not France, she decided. If not there, where? She was despondent.

'Why don't you go below and try to sleep?' Jean-Paul suggested.

And Elsa did. She was really tired and she thought she might as well try to get some rest to build up her strength for whatever was to follow. She made her way back to the bunk, and snuggled down beneath some blankets she'd found.

When Jean-Paul looked into the cabin a little later, he saw that she was sound asleep.

Margaret Carter rose from her bed at seven o'clock in the morning, washed and dressed, and put the kettle on to boil as she prepared the breakfast. Pouring a mug of tea, she took it up to Elsa's room, as was her habit. When she knocked, then opened the door and found that the bed hadn't been slept in, she knew that something was wrong. Elsa always rang her if she was going to be late and she certainly would have done so had she been planning to spend the night in someone else's house.

Rushing downstairs, she rang the office of the *Southern Daily Echo* where she left a message for Peter Adams. 'Please tell him to ring me on this number,' she told the man on the other end of the phone, 'and please tell him it is urgent.'

She paced up and down until she thought, If I don't do something I'll go mad, so she opened the shop and started to put the goods outside. When the phone did ring, she ran to pick it up.

'Peter?'

'Whatever is the matter, Margaret?'

'Elsa's bed hasn't been slept in. Is she with you?'

'No. I took her home about eleven o'clock last night. I saw her open the door and go in before I left in a taxi.'

'Then where is she? Peter, I am so afraid that something bad has happened to her.'

'I'll call the police and then I'll come straight over,' he said and hung up.

By then Anne Sharpe had arrived. When she was told the news, she rang her brother Jed, who hurried round.

Peter rang the police station and spoke to Jack Hobbs, the detective who was in charge of the smuggling case.

'I am certain this has something to do with that bastard Devereux,' Peter said.

'But I would have thought he would have been long gone by now,' said Hobbs.

'He's a clever bugger; let's face it, the last thing we would expect is for him to remain in the district.'

'But how did he slip the net that night? I still can't figure it out.'

'Think back,' Peter urged. 'What did that woman in the church say when you questioned her?'

'She said that there was a man on crutches, that was all – except for the priest, of course.'

'Then that's got to be it! Who takes any notice of a priest in a church?'

'You could be right,' said the detective. 'We have her address. I'll send someone round there to get some more details.'

'But if he walked out of the church he would have to get away somehow.'

'We questioned all the taxi drivers. I'll check to see if they gave a priest a lift, and I'll check with the public transport too.'

'I've got to go over to Mrs Carter,' Peter told him. 'The poor woman is frantic.'

'I'll see you there. I need a statement from her.'

Kingsland market was buzzing with the news of Elsa's disappearance. Jed was fielding all the questions as Margaret was beside herself with worry. He managed to get the stallholders out of the shop and back to work when Peter arrived, shortly followed by the police, who got a description of the clothes that Elsa was wearing the previous night. They also made house-to-house calls to the buildings opposite the square. One woman said she heard a car door slam around midnight when she was up with one of her children.

'Would that have been you leaving?' Peter was asked.

'No. I left shortly after eleven o'clock. Devereux wouldn't use a taxi to take Elsa in, so he must have hired a car.'

'I'll get on to all the garages immediately,' Hobbs said.

Putting his arm round Margaret's shoulder, Peter said, 'Try not to worry too much, love. Elsa is a spirited young woman. She'll be fine.'

271

'You think that Frenchman has her, don't you?'

There was no point in lying. 'I think so,' he said. 'But he would never hurt her, of that I'm certain.'

'I wish I could be so sure,' said Margaret.

'The best thing you can do is keep busy. I have some things to do, but I'll be back later, all right?'

She nodded.

Peter took Jed aside. 'You'll stay here with her, won't you?'

'Of course. I'm as worried about Elsa as anyone else.'

Peter made his way to Holy Rood church where he retraced the steps taken by the Frenchman, trying to guess what Jean-Paul had done the night he escaped. He walked along the back of the buildings where Jean-Paul would have gone after climbing the wall in the Dolphin Hotel. He walked along the back of Holy Rood church and he too found the door to the vestry open, and saw the cassocks hanging there. How simple it would have been, he thought, to don one of those garments and walk through the church to the street. He walked through the church, then once outside he paused. The building was on a corner. As he stood there a tram slowed to take the bend. It would have been easy for the Frenchman to get on one, he thought. Convinced, he went to the main tram depot and asked for the names of all the tram drivers who were on duty that night at the relevant time. He then asked if any were on duty now.

Armed with his list he systematically went through those who were working, waiting for each one to return to the depot. But his questioning was fruitless. He called at the addresses of those who were at home. Again nothing. Returning to the depot, he asked if all the names were down on his list. This time another man looked at it.

'Ted Greene's name is missing,' he said. 'He fell and broke his ankle yesterday. He's in the South Hants Hospital.'

*   *   *

Ted Greene was sitting up in bed reading the paper when Peter walked up to his bedside.

'Ted Greene?'

'Yes. Who's asking?'

Peter explained why he was there.

'Yes, I remember him,' said Greene, 'he took a flying leap on the tram just as I was speeding up. I told him he'd get to heaven a bit quicker if he did that often!'

'Do you remember where he got off?'

'Yeah. The dock gates. I saw him go in and talk to the policeman on duty.'

Shaking the man's hand he said, 'Thank you so much. You've been a great help.'

Once outside, Peter rang the police station and passed on the news. 'I'm off now to the dock gates,' he said and put the phone down.

After talking to several of the docks police, Peter discovered the one who had spoken to the Frenchman. 'Did you see him leave later?'

'No, sir. I went off duty shortly after, but I'll give you the name of the officer who took over from me.'

But he hadn't seen the priest at all.

Had they known this at the time, Peter thought, everyone would have assumed that Devereux would have boarded one of the ships and sailed away, but he hadn't.

When Peter returned to the shop it was to be told that the car that Devereux had hired had been reported parked near the marina in Hamble, and they had discovered that a Frenchman had chartered a yacht for several weeks. He'd stayed on board in Hamble for a while, but now the berth was empty.

Peter's heart sank. Elsa could be anywhere.

*   *   *

CHAPTER THIRTY-ONE

It was to the smell of bacon cooking that Elsa awoke. Jean-Paul was standing at the stove.

'*Bon matin chérie*. Did you sleep well?'

Rubbing her eyes, Elsa said, 'Strangely enough I did.'

Handing her a towel, some soap, a toothbrush and toothpaste, he said, 'Here you are, the heads are there. Have a wash – you'll feel better.'

Looking at the new toothbrush in a wrapper, she said, 'You are certainly well equipped for all occasions.'

'It's called organisation, Elsa. You have to hurry. Breakfast will soon be ready.'

'Who's driving?' she asked.

Laughing, he said, 'We are on automatic pilot. Now run along.'

In the small cubicle she washed and cleaned her teeth. Looking out of the small porthole, she saw land in the distance, but where were they?

When she returned to the main stateroom, Jean-Paul had pulled out a leaf of the small table where toast, coffee, bacon and eggs were waiting.

Elsa realised that she was ravenous. As she ate, she thought what a ridiculous situation this was. In normal circumstances, it would have been quite an adventure. She glanced across at the Frenchman, who had shaved and was looking his usual handsome self, and knew that she was in grave danger.

After the meal, they cleared the dishes and put the table back to normal, making the small cabin a little roomier. After washing up and stowing away the dishes, Elsa, now wearing the life-jacket she'd been given, followed Jean-Paul back to the deck. Looking round she saw that there was land on either side of them. This time there were other vessels about. Cargo ships; a ferry in the far distance; yachts too. The sea was choppy, sending their yacht at a steep angle. Elsa clung tightly to the rail. Pointing to the left at the mass of land, she asked, 'Where is that?'

'France,' he replied.

And looking to the right she asked, 'And that?'

'England. That's the coast of Devon.'

Devon! she thought. My God, where the hell was he taking her? They had travelled miles during the night. The French coast was nearer, she noted, but surely he wouldn't go there?

'Where *are* we heading? Surely it won't hurt to tell me now? After all, there's nothing I can do about it!'

He gazed at her for a moment and said, 'We are going to the Channel Islands.'

The Channel Islands, she thought. They were miles away! And what would happen when they got there?

'And when we arrive?' she asked.

He ignored her question. 'Sit there. It will help distribute the weight,' she was told.

Sitting in the cockpit, she watched Jean-Paul at the helm and marvelled at his dexterity with the sails. It was obvious to her that he was experienced and she guessed that he had been sailing for a long time. He probably had his own vessel, she thought. Here was a man who was educated, had a genuine business, style, and charisma, and yet he had become involved in criminal activities. It seemed such a shame, she thought; he had so much already. But for some, it wasn't enough.

* * *

Back in Southampton, Peter Adams and Jack Hobbs were poring over sea charts trying to decide just where Devereux was heading.

'Cherbourg is the nearest port. Surely he wouldn't chance it in France?' said the detective.

'Belgium or Holland?' suggested Peter.

Shaking his head, Hobbs said, 'Damned if I know.' He returned to the map. 'What if he went in the other direction?' He traced the map with his finger.

'Other than the French coast, the nearest destination is the Channel Islands.'

'Why would he go there?'

'Why would he go anywhere in particular?' said Peter. 'This is all speculation on our part.' He scratched his head. 'You know, I think we are going about this the wrong way.'

'What do you mean?' Jack Hobbs asked.

'We should ask ourselves, where would he feel safe? France, Belgium and Holland are dodgy. He will need money to help him hide. If he continued on across the Bay of Biscay, he could go to Spain.'

'But he would have to draw from his bank in France, and we would be able to trace him,' Jack Hobbs remarked.

'What about Switzerland?' Peter said. 'I bet he's got money safely stashed away in a Swiss bank. If he went to one of the Channel Islands he could charter a private plane to fly him there. Who would ask why?'

'He could do that anywhere,' said Hobbs.

'Yes, but an island has to have other means than a yacht or a ferry to get to the mainland. There are lots of privately owned aircraft on Jersey or Guernsey. It would be easier there than in Spain. There, he may have to travel further to find such facilities. To me the Channel Islands make more sense.'

'But why take your girl?'

'As insurance in case he was caught.' A frown furrowed his brow. 'He's using her as a hostage, just in case.'

'I came to the same conclusion,' Hobbs confessed. 'But I didn't like to put my thoughts into words. We'll get in touch with the lighthouses along the Channel; they keep a log of passing yachts. Maybe one of them picked up the . . . let me see, I've got the name somewhere.' He fiddled among his many papers. 'Yes. Here it is. *Sea Nymph*. That's the name. We'll ask the coast-guards to contact any shipping in the area to see if anyone has spotted it. It may take some time, and I know how anxious you must be.'

'I have to get back to my desk,' said Peter. 'Let me know if you have any news, will you?'

'I'll give you a shout if we find anything,' said Hobbs.

When he returned to his office, Peter told his editor what was happening.

'It's too late to put this in the early edition of the paper, but if you hurry we can make the late one,' the editor said.

With a frown, Peter asked, 'What are you talking about?'

'This is news and it is a continuation of the smuggling case. The readers will want to know what's going on. Surely I don't have to tell you this will send our circulation up.' Seeing the reluctance on his young reporter's face he said, 'The fact that it is personal to you makes no difference. We are here to report the news. And think about it – someone out there who reads about it may be able to give you some vital information. Now go and work on it . . . and hurry!'

When he had submitted his report, Peter rang Margaret Carter to warn her about its being in the late edition.

'I'm sorry, Mrs Carter, but my boss insisted.'

'That's all right, Peter, I understand. Have you heard anything?'

Not wanting to worry her about the possibility of Elsa's being at sea with the Frenchman, he said, 'Not yet, but the police are pulling out all the stops. We'll find her, I promise.'

'I do hope so,' she said, and hung up.

Elsa and her captor sailed on through another night. She wondered when the Frenchman ever slept. She supposed it was in the cockpit, but that would be dangerous, sailing through waters where there were merchant ships. What if Jean-Paul was asleep and they collided with one? She gave an involuntary shiver at the thought. She wasn't a strong swimmer: she could easily drown. She kept her lifejacket beside her, just in case, then curled up under the blankets to sleep, because tomorrow they surely must anchor somewhere, and Lord knows what was before her then.

As Elsa slept, Jean-Paul was sitting at the helm, drinking strong black coffee to keep awake. He was very tired and kept swilling his face with cold water to keep from falling asleep. They would arrive in Guernsey in the morning, and he would have to charter a private plane to get him off the island. Would it be wiser to take Elsa with him, or leave her there? He thought long and hard about it . . . it would be wiser to keep her with him until he was safely in Switzerland, he decided. And then what?

Lighting a cigarette, he couldn't help but smile. Elsa was an amazing girl. Other women would have probably panicked when they woke and found themselves afloat but she had been almost stoic about it, realising there wasn't anything she could do. He admired her spirit. In different circumstances, it could have been delightful having her so close to him, but what really worried him was what she might do when they landed. He might be forced to deal with her in a way he would regret, but he knew that he would do what was necessary for his own survival.

*　　　*　　　*

Early the following morning, Peter Adams walked into the police station to see Jack Hobbs.

'Any news?' he asked the detective.

'I was just about to give you a call,' he said. 'The yacht has been seen by a few vessels, heading for the Channel Islands. You were correct in your assumption.'

'What are you doing about it?'

'We have police at St Peter Port at Guernsey and other likely places around the coast, keeping a watch. And in Jersey too in case he goes there. They have been told to keep their distance and not alarm the man, but if he goes to the airport they have to step in, stop him getting away and arrest him. The coastguards are keeping watch too.'

'Do they know that Elsa is with him? I don't want any harm to come to her.'

'Don't worry,' said Hobbs. 'They are fully in the picture.'

'I want to go there,' Peter declared.

'Where? You might go to one island and he's on the other. We have to be patient. When we know where he is, then we'll make arrangements.'

'If I could get my hands on the bastard I'd kill him!'

'And then we would have to arrest you. You are not to do anything foolish, understand?'

Looking somewhat downcast, Peter agreed.

'Look,' said Jack, 'I know how you must feel, and if I were in your shoes I'd probably react the same way. But we have to keep within the law or he could outsmart us. I want the bugger as much as you do.' Putting his hand on Peter's shoulder, he said, 'We'll bring your girl home safely, I promise.'

Just after daybreak, Jean-Paul steered the yacht towards the harbour of St Peter Port, then went below to wake Elsa.

'It's time to get up,' he told her. 'When we dock, I'll be taking

279

you ashore, but you will not cry for help or do anything foolish, understand?'

'You are taking a chance on my behaving, aren't you?' she said bravely.

From behind his back, where it had been tucked into the waist of his trousers, he produced a small revolver and showed it to her.

'*Ma chère*, it would indeed be a sad day if I were forced to use this on you, but I want you to know that, if necessary, I certainly will do.' The coldness in his gaze convinced her that he meant every word.

'And if I do behave, what then? Aren't you going to kill me anyway?'

Pulling her to her feet, he said, 'No, *chérie*, that is not my intention, but it will be up to you.' He pulled her into his arms and kissed her with passion. When he eventually released her he said, 'What a great pity we didn't have the time to get to know each other better. Now get yourself ready.'

Elsa sat on the bunk, in turmoil. Jean-Paul's kiss had taken her by surprise. Even more of a surprise was that she had returned it! This man, who had threatened to kill her if necessary, was keeping her prisoner . . . and she'd kissed him back! She must be losing her mind. But there had always been a chemistry between them and it was still there, despite the circumstances.

She quickly washed and tidied herself, then went up on deck, wearing the large sweater, as the early morning mist was damp. As she waited for the yacht to enter the harbour, she racked her brains. Didn't any boat or ship have to report to the customs when they docked? Would he do that? Surely not! If he did then he would be putting himself at risk. Yet if the customs watched him arrive, would they come down to the jetty to see him? She would have to be very careful during these next moments; after all, she didn't want to die.

Jean-Paul furled the sails and took the yacht into the harbour on the engine. Moving slowly along the line of crafts already tied up, he waited until he saw an empty space and deftly manoeuvred the *Sea Nymph* into position. He cut the engine, put out the fenders, jumped ashore and tied up with the ropes he'd made Elsa throw to him, all the time keeping his eye on her.

With the yacht secure, he picked up a briefcase. Putting on a jacket, he placed the revolver in his pocket and said, 'Come on, and please don't be foolish.' He took a firm grip of her hand and led her up the jetty towards the town centre.

CHAPTER THIRTY-TWO

When the story of Elsa's abduction hit the late edition of the *Southern Daily Echo*, Ruby and several of the other stallholders called at the shop to see Margaret and offer her their help and sympathy.

'Anything any of us can do, duck,' said Ruby, 'you just let us know.'

Margaret was overcome by their kindness and said so to Jed, who had been in the shop all day.

'Elsa is well loved,' he said. 'We all care about her.'

At that moment, George Carter rushed into the shop, waving the paper. Jed tried to stop him, but Margaret caught him by the arm.

'It's all right, he's not here to cause trouble. After all, Elsa is his daughter.'

George looked upset as he asked, 'What has happened?'

'I know only as much as you have read in the paper,' she said, then, asking Jed to look after the shop, she took her husband upstairs to make a cup of tea and try to calm him.

Carter gazed round the living room, which by now looked cosy with the second-hand furniture that had been bought. He sat in an old armchair and lit a cigarette.

'I was shocked when I read the paper,' he said. 'I couldn't believe it.'

'You can imagine how I felt when I discovered she was missing, then,' Margaret said as she put the kettle on to boil.

He sat shaking his head. 'You read about such things,' he said, 'but you never ever think it could happen to one of your own.'

She let him sit lost in his thoughts as she made the tea. 'Here.' She handed him a mug and sat with him. 'I don't dare think of the consequences,' she said, tears wetting her cheeks.

'Now then,' George said, 'you know our girl. She has plenty of spirit. She'll be all right.' He patted his wife's hand awkwardly. 'We just have to wait.'

'That's the worst part,' she said.

'Waiting is the worst part,' Peter Adams said to Jack Hobbs as they sat in the police station, waiting for news. 'If I drink any more tea, I'll drown!'

The phone on the detective's desk rang. Picking it up, he listened intently. 'Right, let me know what happens,' he said and put down the receiver. 'They have just landed in St Peter Port. The police saw them arrive and they are being followed.'

'Elsa's all right?'

'It would seem so.'

Getting to his feet, Peter said, 'I want to go there.'

'Sit down, lad,' urged Jack. 'Let the police do their work. That's what they're trained to do.'

Peter sat, wringing his hands with worry.

Hobbs pushed a packet of cigarettes towards him. 'Here, it'll give you something to do.'

Still holding on to Elsa, Devereux walked along the pavement in St Peter Port, looking for a telephone box. It was early and the shops were not yet open, but the population of office workers and shop assistants were all making their way to start the day, passing the Frenchman and his prisoner, unaware of what was happening. Elsa tried to catch the eye of a passer-by, but they all had other things to think about and ignored her and her companion. After all, Guernsey folk were used to seeing yachtsmen walking around.

Spotting a telephone box, Jean-Paul hustled Elsa into the small space and picked up the telephone directory, flicking through the pages until he found what he was looking for. Putting his coins in the box, he dialled a number, waited and then spoke rapidly in French.

Elsa couldn't understand what was going on, but she saw him smile and replace the receiver.

'Come along,' he said and opened the door.

'You spoke in French,' she said with some surprise.

'*Oui*. French – or a patois – is spoken on the island as much as English.'

'Have you been here before?'

'Yes, several times, but not of late.' He caught her hand again and walked purposefully along the coast road until he saw a taxi rank. He leaned in the window of the first cab and said something to the driver, then opened the car door and pushed Elsa inside.

As she gazed at the back of the head of the driver, wondering if this was her opportunity, Devereux put his hand in his pocket and rammed the revolver into her ribs.

She looked at him and he shook his head at her.

'It would be most unwise, *chérie*,' he said.

Deflated, she sat back, watching the scenery as they drove on.

When the car eventually stopped, Elsa saw that they were outside an Aero Club. Beyond the building, several small aircraft were sitting on the hard surface. She saw a runway and a small plane coming in to land. She watched in horror as it taxied in. Where was the Frenchman taking her? Wherever it was, she didn't want to go. There was no way he would get her on a plane; she would just have to take her chances.

Dragging his reluctant companion behind him, Jean-Paul

walked into the office of the club, where it was evident that he was expected. The man at the reception desk spoke in French and after a short conversation he indicated the seats in the waiting room and walked out of the door behind him.

Pushing Elsa into a seat, the Frenchman glared at her.

'Do not be foolish,' he warned. 'If you try anything stupid at this stage I will not be happy, and believe me, Elsa, you do not want to see me when I'm angry!'

She didn't answer.

The man returned. He and Jean-Paul spoke for a moment before the man left them once again.

'What's he doing?' Elsa demanded angrily.

'I have hired a plane and the pilot is filling out the flight plan, which you have to do when flying anywhere.'

'I am *not* flying anywhere with you!' she exclaimed.

'If you refuse, Elsa, you will never see your young man or your family again. Is that what you want?'

She was in despair.

The office door opened and the man gave Devereux directions. Hauling Elsa to her feet, the Frenchman left by the main entrance and walked round the building, and then on towards the waiting aircraft.

The pilot stood beside the plane, a sheaf of papers in his hand, and another man was checking the exterior of the aircraft.

'Just doing the usual checks,' the pilot explained. 'If you don't mind waiting a few minutes.' Turning to Elsa he said, 'Nice morning for a trip, miss.'

As he did so, the other man walked round and said, 'Everything is just fine.'

'Right,' said the pilot. 'Now, miss, you get in first,' and he took Elsa's arm, pushing her forcefully on to the plane before she could do or say anything.

Suddenly behind her she heard a scuffle. Turning, she saw that

both the men had grabbed hold of Jean-Paul, and were struggling with him until eventually they manoeuvred him to the
ground.

'Look out, he's armed,' she cried. 'He has a gun in his pocket!'

One of the men held the Frenchman's arms as the other searched
the jacket until he found the weapon, after which he handcuffed
Devereux, then dragged him to his feet.

'There, my son. You won't get away this time!'

Elsa climbed down from the aircraft and asked, 'Who the hell
are you?'

'Police, miss. We were warned of your arrival. You can stop
worrying – you're safe now.'

Looking at Jean-Paul, dishevelled after his struggle with the
law, she said, 'For a man who had so much, you are a fool!'

He gave a wry smile and, shrugging his shoulders, said, 'It was
always a gamble, *chérie*, that was half of the fun of it, knowing
the chances of being caught were against you. But you will never
understand the thrill of the chase.'

She slapped him hard in the face. 'The thrill of the chase! You
would have had your man kill my Peter. Did that give you a thrill
too?'

'Come along, miss,' the detective said as he intervened. 'I don't
want to take my prisoner in covered in bruises.'

They were led to the front of the building where two police
cars were waiting. Devereux was led to one and Elsa to the other.

'We need a statement from you, miss,' she was told, 'and then
we can think of getting you home.'

'Will you let my family know that I'm safe, please?'

'I'll radio the message through now, miss. You try to relax.'

When the telephone rang in the office at Southampton's police
station, Peter got to his feet as Jack Hobbs picked up the receiver.
The detective listened carefully to what was being told, and then,

placing the receiver back in its cradle, he beamed at Peter Adams.

'They've arrested Devereux and Elsa is fine.'

'Thank God!' Peter sank into a nearby chair and covered his eyes with his hand, trying to hide his emotion.

Jack opened a drawer in his desk and took out a half bottle of Scotch. He poured a small amount into two glasses and handed one to Peter. 'Here, drink this. I keep it on hand for emergencies.'

Peter downed it in a gulp. 'I really needed that,' he said. 'I don't know what I would have done if anything had happened to Elsa.'

'Now listen,' said Jack, 'don't fall into the trap of thinking what might have happened or you'll end up a basket case. She's safe and sound, that's what you must focus on.'

'When is she coming home?'

'The police are booking her on an overnight ferry. They've got her a cabin so she can sleep. It docks at nine o'clock tomorrow morning. I assume you will be there to meet her?'

'Try to keep me away!' Peter grinned broadly. 'I'll go and break the good news to her mother.' Shaking Hobbs by the hand, he said, 'Thanks for everything.'

'Just doing my job, son, that's all. Invite me to the wedding,' he added with a smile.

'Definitely!' said Peter, and he hurried from the room.

The staff at Carter and Sharpe were taking in the outside display in preparation for closing when Peter arrived. He put his arms round Margaret.

'Elsa is safe!' he cried. 'She'll be home in the morning.'

She burst into tears. Anne rushed to comfort her. 'Now then,' she said, 'Everything is fine. Elsa's coming home.'

'I know,' said Margaret, smiling through her tears. 'I was just so worried. So was her father.'

'He was here?' Peter asked.

'He read it in the paper.' Seeing his worried frown, she said, 'It's all right, he was no trouble. I gave him a cup of tea and sent him home. I said we would let him know if we had any news.'

'Tell you what,' said Peter, 'whilst you shut up shop, I'll go and let him know Elsa is safe and I'll get some fish and chips for all of us on the way back. What do you say?'

'I think it's a splendid idea,' said Jed. 'None of us have been able to eat a thing all day.'

Peter didn't stay long with George Carter. He had no time for the man, but he had to admit he did seem really concerned about the welfare of his daughter, so he had at least one redeeming feature, Peter thought.

Stopping at the chip shop, he bought four suppers and took them back to the shop.

Margaret had plates ready but Peter insisted they eat with their fingers, with plenty of salt and vinegar on the food.

'It tastes so much better out of the paper,' he declared.

They all sat round, tucking into their fish and chips. The mood was happy and filled with anticipation of Elsa's return.

'I'll meet the ferry and bring her straight home,' Peter promised.

When eventually he left them, he was absolutely exhausted. The strain of the past days had taken its toll. He climbed into his bed and slept soundly.

The following morning, Peter stood at the quayside with a photographer from the *Echo*, waiting impatiently for the ferry to dock. It seemed to take an age and he hopped from one foot to another. Eventually the gangplank was lowered and he watched as the passengers disembarked.

'There she is!' the photographer cried, and lifted the camera, snapping rapidly as Elsa left the ferry.

At the bottom of the gangway, Peter took her into his arms and held her tightly. 'Don't you ever do anything like that to me again!' he said, and then he kissed her soundly.

Elsa clung to him. 'Oh, darling, I was so frightened. I didn't know where he was taking me.'

'Did he hurt you?'

Shaking her head, she said, 'No, he didn't. He promised to let me go if I behaved, but deep down I didn't believe him.' She gazed into Peter's eyes. 'I really needed you there.'

Holding her close, he nuzzled her neck. 'I was going crazy wondering if you were safe. You have no idea just how much I love you.'

'Absence makes the heart grow fonder, they say,' she teased.

He stared at her intently. 'There was nothing funny about it, Elsa, I can assure you.'

'I know, I know,' she said, 'but if I don't make light of it, I won't be able to cope.' But suddenly her composure finally deserted her and she clung to him, sobbing quietly.

Peter took her to a workmen's café nearby where they sat and had a cup of coffee, allowing Elsa to gather herself together before going home. They just sat quietly until she felt ready to leave.

When eventually the taxi they hailed drove into the market it was to see all the stalls festooned with balloons. The traders all wanted to show their joy at her safe return.

Margaret, Jed and Anne stood outside the shop waving wildly as the taxi drew to a stop in front of the parade.

Elsa got out of the taxi to be enveloped in the arms of her mother, then Anne, and then Jed. The stallholders gathered round her, smiling, muttering their greetings and messages. She was overwhelmed by their kindness.

When she was free of the well-wishers, she went inside the

shop and said, 'What I really need is a hot bath and a change of clothes. I feel really grubby.'

'You go ahead,' said Peter. 'I have to go to the office. I'll be back this evening and we'll go out and celebrate.'

Catching hold of his arm, Elsa said, 'Do you mind very much if we stay at home, quietly? I just need a bit of time to settle down.'

'Of course not. How stupid of me,' said Peter. 'It's just that I am so happy to have you back in one piece.' Kissing her cheek, he left her alone with her mother.

As he walked through the park back to his office, Peter was in as much of a turmoil as Elsa. He was relieved and delighted that she was safe, but he boiled inside with anger against the Frenchman who had caused so much trouble in their lives. Well, he hoped that the police would throw the book at the bastard. Peter would have to go to court eventually to give evidence against him, so he would be able to pay him back in that way, but right now he wanted to beat the hell out of the man. He felt his fists close at the thought. Thrusting his hands inside his trouser pockets in an effort to control his rage, he started to construct the story that he would write about Elsa's kidnapping and safe return, to take his mind off the Frenchman.

By the time he sat at his desk and put a sheet of paper in his typewriter, he was composed and ready to do his job.

CHAPTER THIRTY-THREE

Jack Hobbs and another detective escorted Jean-Paul Devereux back to Southampton where he was charged on counts of fraud, theft and abduction.

'You will be going away for a long time,' Jack Hobbs told him.

Devereux just shrugged his shoulders. 'What is it you English say, "Some you win, some you lose?" I have had a good run for my money.'

'Your assets will be frozen for the time being.'

'If I am going to prison, I won't want any money, will I?' he remarked with a smile.

'For your information, Lord Travers has been charged with buying stolen goods. We have recovered all the paintings, and,' Hobbs continued, 'your Dutch associate has been arrested too. We caught him trying to smuggle diamonds past the customs.'

There was no comment from the prisoner.

'And if you are wondering whether your German mate has got away with everything, he hasn't. The two men in the warehouse have fingered him. So he is in custody in his own country.' Jack Hobbs leaned back in his chair and with a broad grin he said, 'That's what we Brits call a clean sweep! I call it a bloody good day's work.' Leaning forward again, he said, 'Criminals always get greedy. That's when they slip up, and that's when we catch men who think they are so clever they are beyond the law.'

Later that day, Devereux spent a short time in court where he was told he would be held without bail until his case came before the court in three months' time. He was bundled into a Black Maria and driven to Winchester prison to await trial.

Peter and Elsa sat together reading the account of Devereux's arrest in the evening paper.

'I can't believe a man of his calibre would be so foolish,' Elsa remarked.

'Who knows what goes on in the mind of a criminal?' said Peter.

'He told me it was the thrill of it. Can you imagine that?'

Putting his arm round her, Peter changed the subject. 'Never mind him, what about us? I want to set a date for the wedding. Making you my wife is a thrill enough for me.'

'You say the sweetest things,' she teased. 'You just want to have your wicked way with me.'

Nuzzling her neck, he said, 'And what's wrong with that? When you love somebody, you want to be close to them in every sense, and I do love you, Elsa.'

'I know, and I love you too, but this case comes up in January. Can't we wait until it's all over? I dread going into court and giving evidence. It will take the shine off everything else. Besides, it will give us longer to save for a really nice flat. The shop is doing well and you will be on a better salary from the *Daily Mirror*. Then we could have a wedding without worrying about other things.'

With a look of disappointment, he asked, 'When are you thinking of?'

'A spring wedding would be nice. By then Anne will have had her baby and Mum will be busy helping her to look after it, so she won't miss me living with her so much.'

'All right, spring it is. Although I will be a basket case by then, having to wait so long.'

'Take some bromide in your tea!'

'You cheeky monkey!' He drew her closer and tipped up her chin so she was looking into his eyes. 'Elsa Carter, I would wait a lifetime for you if I had to.'

Seeing the honesty shining in his expression, she kissed him. 'We are going to have a good life together,' she whispered. 'Not like my poor mother.'

'At least she's happy now,' Peter said, 'and we will take good care of her between us. Now come here.' And he kissed her.

As the following weeks passed, things returned to normal in Kingsland Square. The shop was doing well; Elsa and Margaret were kept busy, helped by Anne Sharpe who was now hugely pregnant. Under the watchful eyes of Elsa and her mother, she was never allowed to do too much and was told not to lift anything at all.

Things were looking somewhat brighter for the girl, as the young man who delivered the goods from Oakley and Watling had been paying attention to her. When he had first invited her out, she had refused.

'As you can see, I'm pregnant and not married, so why would you want to take me out?'

He smiled at her and said, 'I know all about you, I made a few enquiries in the market when I saw you weren't wearing a wedding ring.'

She didn't know whether to be flattered or annoyed. Encouraged to go by the other women, who liked the young man, she finally accepted. Although she also liked Frank, Anne was uncertain about their friendship, and one evening when she and Margaret were together listening to the Home Service on the wireless, she voiced her worries.

'I really like him, Mrs Carter, but I find it strange that although I'm pregnant with another man's child, he still wants to see me.'

'He sees beyond the baby,' Margaret said. 'He likes *you* as a person so much that it would seem the fact that you are pregnant doesn't matter.'

'But what happens after the baby is born? I don't want to get used to him and then have him leave me. I don't think I could bear it.'

'Then I think you need to ask him what his intentions are. Then you'll know, won't you?'

Peter Adams had started his new job with the *Daily Mirror*, and took the train every morning to Fleet Street where he assisted the chief crime reporter. He was in his element and whenever he saw Elsa he regaled her with the details of his work.

Clive Forbes still had his stall on the market, but was a little quieter these days. He still flattered the lady punters, but he'd stopped being so arrogant since the Frenchman had been arrested, knowing how lucky he was that he'd not been involved. The police couldn't prove that he knew he was holding stolen goods, so he was free to carry on. But he still looked at Elsa with lustful eyes, at the same time ignoring Anne, who was carrying his child.

Elsa poured contempt upon him whenever she had the opportunity. After the Frenchman was arrested she marched over to Clive and confronted him.

'You should be in prison too,' she told him. 'You were mixed up with the stolen goods. I used to see Jean-Paul leaving things with you.'

He shrugged his shoulders. 'How was I to know what I was holding for him? I never opened the packets.' He leered at her. 'I hear you have set a date for your wedding. That Peter Adams will never be man enough for you.' Knowing her weakness for the Frenchman, he added, 'Devereux might have been, but sadly he's out of the picture now.'

'I hardly knew the man,' she protested.

His eyes narrowed and he said, 'But you would have liked to. I often wonder what went on when he had you alone on that yacht.'

'Nothing went on. I was his prisoner!'

'That's what you say. And now you have the reporter laddie.'

'He has more character in his little finger than you have in the whole of your body!' she retorted.

'Ah, but will his character alone be enough to please you in bed?'

'You are despicable! You try to come anywhere near me again and I swear I'll castrate you!' She stormed away as he laughed loudly at her outrage.

But it was Elsa who had the last laugh when, later that day, Clive Forbes was arrested and taken away for questioning. The police had not been fooled by his protestations of innocence, and under questioning Jean-Paul had admitted that Clive had been under no illusions about the goods he had held for him. They had also searched his lock-up garage and found stolen goods housed there. They had charged him with being in possession of stolen goods and aiding and abetting the Frenchman.

Perhaps the only person who did feel sorry for him was Anne, but she could see how she had, in fact, had a lucky escape. Clive, sitting in his cell waiting for his case to come before the court, cursed the day the foreigner had walked into his life. All his plans for the future now lay in ribbons and he was a bitter man.

The month of November arrived with cold east winds blowing across the market. The stallholders were smothered in layers of clothing and the customers all in a rush to get back to the warmth of their homes. Elsa and the staff in the shop were all relieved that they were inside out of the cold. Ruby used to pop in for a cup of tea when things were quiet. Rubbing her hands and holding them near the electric fire, she complained bitterly. 'I'm getting too bloody old for this caper,' she said.

Elsa grinned at her. 'You've been saying that as long as I've known you.'

'I know, but each year I grow older. It's my sciatica what gives me the hump these days, and that cold wind is a devil.' She cupped the mug of tea in her hands and said, 'You'll soon be going to court, I suppose?'

Elsa's expression changed. 'Not until January,' she said, 'and to be honest with you, Ruby, I'm dreading it.'

'Well, it'll be good to get it over with. All you have to do is tell the truth.'

'I know, but my stomach turns whenever I think about it.'

'Never mind, love. Once it's over all you have to worry about is planning your wedding, and believe me that brings its own problems. Who to invite so as not to upset anyone.'

'I won't have any worries there,' Elsa told her. 'It's going to be a quiet affair, just family and close friends.'

'Best way,' said Ruby. She finished her tea and rose. At the door she paused, 'If you see me frozen and unable to move, you'll have to carry me in here to thaw out!'

'Get along with you,' chided Elsa. 'You are a tough old bird – you can take it.'

'One day it will bloody well take me, mark my words!'

December eventually arrived with the usual run-up to Christmas. The nation was still reeling after the abdication of Edward VIII. The papers were now full of pictures of the former king and Mrs Simpson. Before the broadcast, Fleet Street had seethed with frustration as there had been a 'conspiracy of silence', inspired by Lord Beaverbrook, on what had been a sensational story, while all foreign papers had been free to print articles about the couple as soon as the rumours of their relationship had begun.

Now, of course, all bets were off and the papers were having a field day.

The new king, George VI, addressed his Accession Council nine hours after his brother had gone into exile. Almost everyone who came into Elsa's shop had something to say about it.

'Bet that Mrs Simpson is sick as a dog now,' said one. 'She thought she'd be queen. Now I wonder what will happen to the two of them? Well, she's made her bed . . . bloody woman.'

'Great pity,' said another. 'He was a king for the people.'

'I never liked the look of her,' an elderly lady said. 'Hard-faced bitch she was in my estimation!'

The shop looked quite festive the following week, filled with holly and mistletoe for sale, and Christmas trees standing outside. Walnuts, hazel nuts, Brazils and chestnuts filled baskets inside. Elsa had bought a few pot plants to see how they sold and was delighted when she had to order more.

Jed was thrilled. His business was quiet at this time of year, so he was in the shop most days, helping, allowing his sister to take a break. She would sit in the shop to be with people, saying that being upstairs was too lonely. Many of the stallholders brought in baby clothes for her, their natural generosity helping her to collect a layette. And Frank too would pop into the shop when he could. He had made it clear to Anne that he wasn't going to leave her when the baby was born.

'I come from a large family,' he told her one evening. 'I love kids. Does it really matter who the father is? You are the mother and that's all that is important to me. Next year we'll get married and be a real family. Later we'll have more kids to keep this one company.'

He'd spoken to Jed about his wishes for the future and Jed, seeing that he was a solid chap, was delighted for his sister, especially as he had started seeing a young lady himself.

George Carter called in from time to time. He had accepted that Margaret had her own life now. He took comfort in his position at work, which allowed him to fill his need to control people, and he had a girlfriend whom he saw from time to time.

When Margaret heard about it she was relieved. 'At least he won't come round here bothering me to go back to him,' she said.

'What about you finding a man friend?' asked Elsa.

'No thanks! I've had enough of looking after a man. I like to be able to please myself. I am very happy as I am, thank you.'

The day Elsa was dreading came round eventually. The court case was due to start at nine o'clock in the morning. Margaret insisted she eat some breakfast before she went.

'I'm not hungry, Mum.'

'Never mind that. I've made you some porridge, that'll line your stomach. Goodness knows how long you will have to wait.'

A little while later, Peter collected her in a taxi and they were driven to the police courts in the Civic Centre. They sat in the back of the car, silent, but holding hands. As they were witnesses, both were asked to sit outside the courtroom until they were called. It seemed an interminable time. Peter went to get them some coffee as they waited.

He was the first to be called. He squeezed Elsa's hand and walked into the courtroom, where he was shown to the witness box and sworn in. He looked across at the prisoner seated in the dock. Jean-Paul stared back at him, a grim expression on his face.

The prosecutor than began to question Peter about his investigation, which eventually led him to the warehouse, his incarceration in the cellar and his eventual escape. The defence lawyer cross-examined him and tried hard to discredit his evidence, but being a reporter who dealt with facts Peter was sure of all the times and details, and was unshakeable. He was eventually dismissed and seated within the court.

Then Elsa was called.

She entered the court looking nervous, but she took the oath in a firm voice. Then she looked across at Jean-Paul, who, with a half smile, bowed his head slightly in greeting. The fact that he could be so cool enraged her. Her anger made her feel stronger and she faced the prosecutor and his questions. He led her all through her meetings with Jean-Paul and her eventual kidnapping, the boat trip, the landing in Guernsey and the vital intervention of the police.

But when it came to the defence lawyer, he tried a different tack.

'Would it be true to say, Miss Carter, that you were attracted to Mr Devereux?'

This took her by surprise. She saw Peter watching her, waiting for her answer. What was she to say?

'Well, he was certainly different from the usual customer in the market,' she said.

'Am I right in saying that at the time you met Mr Devereux you were engaged to another man?'

'What has that got to do with anything?' she retorted.

'Just answer the question,' he snapped.

'Yes, I was and I am still engaged.'

'I put it to you that you were enamoured with the prisoner and that you met him for dinner on two occasions, that you found him exciting and went willingly with him on his trip to Guernsey and that you said he had kidnapped you to cover your own deceit.'

'Objection!' called the prosecutor.

'Overruled!' said the judge. Turning to Elsa he said, 'Answer the question please, Miss Carter.'

'That is a lie!' Elsa cried. 'Jean-Paul was dressed as a priest when he called at the shop. He took me quite by surprise. I said that he was a common criminal and told him to leave. Then he punched me and knocked me unconscious. The next thing I knew was when I woke up on the yacht, which was at sea. He had a gun and he threatened me. I had no choice but to do as he said.'

'We have only your word for that.'

Elsa stood tall and said quietly but firmly, 'May I remind you, sir, that I am under oath. I am telling the truth.'

The man tried to trick Elsa with one or two more questions until the judge intervened and told him to move on.

'No further questions, my lord,' he said reluctantly and sat down.

Elsa was dismissed. She went to sit by Peter, who took her trembling hands in his. 'You did just fine,' he whispered.

When the court retired for lunch, he took Elsa to a nearby public house and bought her a sandwich and a brandy.

'Here,' he said, 'drink this. It will help to calm you down.'

'You don't think I was attracted to Jean-Paul, do you?' she asked.

'Not in the way the lawyer was trying to make out.'

'What do you mean by that?'

'Let's face it, darling, he was a smooth character and too damned attractive. You did dine with him, but I know it didn't mean anything. You were trying to pump him for information. At least the second time.'

'Are you implying the first time was different?'

'Look, Elsa love, let's not quarrel about something so unimportant. This man could mess up our lives if we let him. He has done enough damage as it is, and he'll pay the penalty. We have a wedding to look forward to and a life ahead of us. When this case is over we can move on.'

'You're right,' she said. 'He'll be behind bars and that won't suit him at all.'

When they returned to the court it was to be told they wouldn't be needed again. They left the building and walked back through the town.

Outside Parkhouse and Wyatt's, the jewellers, Peter stopped.

'Come on,' he said, 'let's go and choose our wedding rings.'

It was just what they needed to end what had been a traumatic day.

The case of Jean-Paul Devereux took a week to reach its conclusion and the judge gave his final summing up before he sentenced the Frenchman.

'Jean-Paul Devereux, you have been found guilty on all counts. For a man in your position to take to a life of crime is reprehensible. You had no need financially; you did it for the thrill, putting the lives of innocent people at risk, thinking that you were above the law. You will have plenty of time to reflect on this . . . Jean-Paul Devereux, I sentence you to serve ten years in His Majesty's prison.'

There was a sound of expletives in French from the dock and Devereux was taken down to the cells before being transported to Winchester Prison.

CHAPTER THIRTY-FOUR

Almost a month had passed since the court case, but the excitement in Carter and Sharpe continued when Anne went into labour. Elsa rang the midwife when the girl's contractions became more frequent. Anne wanted to have the baby at home and Margaret had agreed to look after her.

'I had Elsa at home,' she said. 'It's so much nicer being in your own room with your own bits and pieces around than in a ward in a hospital.'

Everything was prepared: clean sheets, baby clothes and a small crib that Frank had made himself. He and Jed paced up and down the living room like expectant fathers, as the midwife cared for the new mother-to-be and the other two women boiled endless kettles of water in readiness.

It seemed an age listening to Anne's cries of pain, which the men found hard to cope with . . . until at last there was the welcome cry of a newborn baby. The two men stopped in their tracks, listened and then hugged each other.

'This calls for a drink,' said Jed. He poured out a couple of beers and then shyly handed Frank a cigar. 'It's traditional,' he said.

A while later the men were invited into Anne's bedroom to see the new arrival.

'It's a girl,' said the weary mother. 'I'm going to call her Holly.'

Looking at the small bundle in his sister's arms, Jed said, 'I'm an uncle!'

Frank put out a finger and stroked Holly's cheek. 'She's as beautiful as her mother.' He leaned over and kissed Anne.

'Right you two, out you go,' ordered Margaret, 'this girl needs to rest. You can make yourselves useful and make us all a cup of tea.'

Later in the evening when Peter called round, he too was shown the baby. He and Elsa looked into the crib.

'Isn't nature wonderful,' he said softly. 'Just look at those perfect little fingers.'

'She's lovely,' said Elsa.

'Just wait until we have children too,' Peter said. 'Can anything be more satisfying than having a family of your own?'

'You're just an old softy,' said Elsa.

Looking at her, he said, 'And there's nothing wrong with that, young lady.'

'I was thinking,' she said, 'that when Frank and Anne do get married, they could live here above the shop with Mother. After all, they don't have much money and Mother is looking forward to helping with the baby. What do you think? I was going to suggest it to Jed. It would solve a lot of problems.'

Putting an arm round her he kissed the tip of her nose. 'Not exactly hard-hearted yourself, are you?'

The streets were filled with bunting and the church bells were ringing when, on the twelfth of May, King George VI was crowned. Everyone who could listened to the broadcast of the ceremony on his or her wireless set.

Peter Adams teased his bride-to-be that all the bunting was laid on for them as they were to be wed a few days later.

'You are my queen, Elsa darling,' he told her as he picked her up and twirled her round.

'Put me down, you fool,' she cried. When once again her feet were firmly on the ground, she pointed a finger at her fiancé. 'Now you listen to me. I don't want you getting paralytic on your bachelor do and coming to the church with a hangover!'

'I've already thought of that,' he said, grinning broadly. 'I'm having it tonight. That will give me three days to get over it, which should be just about long enough.'

On the following Saturday morning, Elsa was wakened by her mother bringing her breakfast on a tray.

'Good heavens!' she exclaimed. 'What's this all about?'

'It's a bride's privilege,' said Margaret, 'and there's a method in my madness. Whilst you eat, I'll go and have a bath and get changed, then the bathroom will be free for you. Jed and Frank are running the shop today so you have nothing to worry about. They will come to the reception later. Jed is bringing his girl with him.' Leaning over her daughter, she kissed her cheek. 'Happy the bride the sun shines on,' she said and went to open the curtains. The sun beamed through the windows. 'I ordered it especially,' she said.

Elsa sat up in bed and poured herself a cup of tea. As she sipped it she gazed at her bridal gown hanging in front of the wardrobe. Soon she would be a married woman. 'Elsa Adams,' she said quietly, and smiled.

She was standing in the kitchen, waiting for her mother to finish in the bathroom, when Jed came up the stairs carrying a bouquet of flowers.

'These have just come for you,' he said. 'Can't stop, we're busy in the shop.'

Looking at the magnificent blooms, Elsa removed the small card from the envelope and read, *Good luck, chérie*. It was unsigned. She looked for the address but all it said was that the bouquet was sent by Interflora. How on earth could this be? Jean-Paul was in prison, and how on earth would he know that today was her wedding day? She tore the card into tiny pieces and threw them into the waste basket. This she would keep to herself. He was not going to spoil her special day.

The next two hours sped by. When she had taken her bath, the hairdresser arrived to do her hair; then she put on her new under-wear and stockings, carefully applied her make-up and, with the help of her mother, put on her wedding dress. Her headdress was a small diamanté tiara with a flowing veil.

Margaret stood back to look at her and with tear-filled eyes said, 'You look stunning.'

'Do I really?'

'Really.'

'You look pretty glamorous yourself, Mum.'

Margaret was wearing a pale lilac dress and matching coat. Her straw hat was of a deeper shade with a feather across the brim.

'Well, it's a special day – and I am the mother of the bride, after all!'

A few moments later, George Carter knocked on the door and walked in. He'd been thrilled when Elsa had asked him to give her away. He'd not expected it after all that had happened. But as Elsa had said to her mother, 'He is my father after all, and it wouldn't have felt right to ask anyone else.'

He stood silent as he looked at the vision standing before him. 'Is this really our daughter?' he asked Margaret at last.

'I know what you mean,' she said.

George kissed Elsa and said, 'You have made me a very happy and proud man this morning, I want you to know that, and I wish you and Peter all the happiness in the world.'

'Thanks, Dad.'

Turning to Margaret, he said, 'I don't know when I have seen you look so lovely.'

At that moment, Anne, who was to be maid of honour, came into the room dressed in a pale pink dress, carrying Holly who was also in a pink frilly dress and bonnet. 'The flowers have just arrived,' she said. 'Jed is bringing them up.'

Elsa's bouquet was filled with spring flowers: pale lemon narcissi, white tulips and cream roses. Anne was to carry a posy of pale pink rose buds to match her dress. There were special buttonholes for Margaret and George, and white carnations for a few friends and family.

'The first car is here!' called Jed.

'Come on, Anne, that's us,' said Margaret. Giving Elsa a quick peck on the cheek, she said, 'Good luck, darling.'

Left alone with her father, Elsa didn't know what to say, so much had happened between them, but it was George who spoke.

'I want you to know that I deeply regret what has happened in the past and I know it was all my fault. I have lost the two most precious things in my life and that is my punishment. But you, Elsa my dear, have a good man and I know you'll be happy. All I ask is that you and Peter visit me from time to time.'

She was overwhelmed by his speech. It was so unlike the man she knew, and she recognised how hard it must have been to put his feelings into words. Leaning forward, she kissed his cheek.

'Thanks, Dad. I promise that we will.'

'Car's here!' called Jed.

As Elsa walked carefully through the shop, she saw that a small crowd had gathered outside. All the stallholders were standing waiting for her. They had made an arch for her to walk through, made of all the goods they sold. There were yard brushes, kettles, saucepans, closed umbrellas and all manner of odd articles.

Elsa started to laugh. 'How wonderful!' she said, and proceeded to walk under this extraordinary display, then climbed into the waiting limousine, aided by her father.

'Good luck, darling. Save me a piece of wedding cake,' called Ruby.

'You look lovely, girl!' yelled Burt.

They drove away to St Michael's church, amid loud cheers and the sound of saucepans and kettles being rattled.

Peter Adams was sitting waiting for his bride in the front pew, with his best man, Gerry, who was trying to calm the groom. Peter was a bundle of nerves, wiping his forehead constantly.

For the umpteenth time he turned to his friend. 'You've got the rings, haven't you?'

Patting his pocket, Gerry chuckled and said, 'They are where they were the last three times of asking. For goodness' sake, calm down!'

The organist started to play Mendelssohn's Wedding March and the groom and his man rose from their seats.

Elsa walked slowly down the aisle on her father's arm, smiling at friends and family as she made her way towards the altar.

Peter stepped forward and looked at his smiling bride. 'You look beautiful,' he said.

As she listened to her daughter taking her vows, Margaret felt her eyes fill with tears of happiness. George, she noticed, was blowing his nose quietly. They smiled at each other with parental pride.

At last the ceremony was over, the marriage certificate signed, and now the bride and groom were standing outside the church having their photographs taken before going to the church hall where the small reception was being held.

Mingling with the guests, Elsa saw Jack Hobbs the detective, talking to the best man. She walked over to him.

'Can I have a word?'

Gerry diplomatically left them alone.

'Congratulations,' said Jack. 'May I say you look absolutely lovely.'

'Thank you,' she said, 'and thanks for coming.'

'I made Peter promise to invite me,' he said. 'He did such a good job during the Devereux case; he's a sharp lad. What did you want to see me about?'

'This morning I received a bouquet from Jean-Paul.'

'Ah, I see. I had to go to Winchester Prison to question Devereux. He asked after you and I told him I was attending your wedding today. He must have arranged to send the flowers.'

'Can you do that in prison?'

'There are many things that get done in prison, one way or another,' he said wryly.

'How is he?'

'Organised! He is a smart man; he's got everything taped in there. Don't waste time worrying about him, my dear. Put it all down to experience.'

At that moment, Peter came over and putting his arm round his bride he said to Jack, 'Don't you think I am a lucky man?'

'I do indeed. I can recommend married life; my wife and I have thirty years behind us. Where is the honeymoon to be spent, or is it a secret?'

'We're off to Bournemouth,' Peter told him, 'and we have a new flat in Harborough Road to go home to when we return. Fortunately this woman can cook, otherwise I wouldn't have married her.'

With a chuckle, Elsa said, 'There's romance for you!'

Taking both their hands in his, Jack Hobbs said, 'Romance is one thing, but when somebody really loves you, that is far more important. It will take you through the good and the bad days ahead. And there will be both. That's life.'

*   *   *

Later, as they sat in a taxi taking them to the train station, Peter took Elsa into his arms. 'Hello, Mrs Adams. I love the sound of that,' he said as he kissed her. 'My wife . . . I like that even better.'

'I wonder if you'll feel the same in thirty years' time?'

'By then I plan to swap you for a younger model,' he teased.

'You horror! What a thing to say on your wedding day.'

'You know I'm only joking,' he said, smiling at her. 'Till death us do part, we said in church, and I aim to be around for a long time. Oh, Elsa darling, we are going to have such a grand life together.'

She sat contented within his arms, knowing that she was with a man she loved, that, unlike her mother, she would have a husband who would care for her and make her laugh. Peter had fulfilled his dream of working in Fleet Street and she had a business that was prospering. They had so much already . . . and each other. Who could ask for more? Certainly not Mrs Peter Adams.